The Late Emancipation
of Jerry Stover

Also in this series

The Late Emancipation of Jerry Stover

Andrew Salkey

Longman

Longman Group Limited
Longman House,
Burnt Mill, Harlow, Essex, UK

First published by Hutchinson and Co (Publishers) Ltd 1968
First published in Longman Drumbeat 1982

ISBN 0 582 78559 6

Printed in Great Britain by
Richard Clay (The Chaucer Press) Ltd,
Bungay, Suffolk

Contents

To the memory of My Mother
and to Pat, Eliot, Jason
and My Father

Ideally, no man should ever be enslaved; therefore the moment a slave is set free, that very first moment of freedom becomes a 'late emancipation'
From a letter by Roger Mais, the Jamaican novelist

. . . substitute

For Slavery's lash the freeman's will . . . .
Derek Walcott, *Lines in New England*

Prologue

It was a long time after the New Constitution of 1944.

It was the time of public anguish for parents whose sons and daughters were not selected by the Civil Service Appointments' Board for employment in one of the approved offices of the Island Treasury and the Colonial Secretariat (the status of the other departments was always a matter of doubt).

It was also the time of the coming élite of the Ministries.

Indeed, it was the time when to be a civil servant, however *unestablished* the post, however *temporary* the clerkship, was clearly to be on the winning side (not to be a civil servant was to be considered an acknowledged failure: a limp, damp thing inevitably headed for the sinister depths of commerce and industry in some back room along Barry Street, or even deeper still, along Port Royal Street).

It was the time when nobody bothered to discuss the challenge of private enterprise, when nobody cared to work in it, except, of course, the immigrant Chinese, the Syrians and the Jews; it was the time when almost everybody was busy sneering at farming and large-scale agriculture, except the East Indians and the British expatriates.

It was, in fact, altogether a splendid time for the desk, and a rotten time for the land.

It was the heyday of overseas scholarships (public and private sponsorship to distant, ancient and not so ancient universities and other establishments of higher education) ensuring hopefully a flood of returning graduates, glossy and impatient doctors, dentists, barristers, historians, geographers and the English literature brigade, returning curiously enervated and with doubtful assets; it was also the time when there was a mere trickle of returning teachers, economists, sociologists, agriculturists, agronomists, engineers, architects (geologists, mineralogists, botanists, tropical marine biologists were always borrowed experts).

It was the time of the Kirby-Rybik Kingdom, the unique duo of opposing politicians who opposed each other's theories but served common Whitehall ends.

It was the growing-up period of young men like Jerry Stover who drank *Black Seal* because it was cheap, because it was called 'bad rum' by the 'whisky-aspiring' *bourgeoisie*, and because it gave the drinker a hopelessly bad name.

It was the time when a bad name could easily be an asset, when hard drinkers could be mistaken for frustrated young men of tingling sensitivity, or for disillusioned middle-aged men of dwindling sensibility.

It was the time of easy credit and predatory creditors.

It was the time of the NEXUS literary review, of the tourist bonanza, and of Back-to-Africa movements.

It was the time of the juvenility of the Termites: a group of very junior civil servants, commercial workers and unpublished writers: and their aimless rebellion against the colonial *status quo* and the Kirby-Rybik Kingdom.

It was the time of the Island's growing pains.

It was a halcyon time.

Book One

The Termites
Drinking round the 8 in the afternoon
P.D., Paula and Jenny
Carmen

After the jump-up, *jou'vert bambulai*,
He was a slave again.

Edward Brathwaite   *Jou'vert*

Chapter One

The boys had had a bitch of a night.

The Half Way Tree parish clock had just struck the half-hour: six-thirty. It was Thursday morning and Civil Service pay day throughout the Island.

Hundreds of civil servants had been celebrating as they usually did on the night before pay day, taking everything on credit, signing fantastic wine cards, borrowing extravagantly. They did this simply because they knew that during the next day between mid-day and four o'clock in the afternoon they would be disappearing from their offices before their eagle-eyed creditors, the past month's money-lenders, bill-collectors, food-vendors, merchant tailors, travelling salesmen, car dealers, night club waiters, barmen, barmaids, estranged wives, divorcées, cast-off sweethearts, the usual assortment of dependents and near-relatives, touts and trusting prostitutes had time to catch up with them and humiliate them by asking for what was owed, promised or otherwise coming to them.

Six-thirty. At that hour of the morning the Constant Spring Road looked desolate and much wider than it really was. Jerry Stover walked up the long drive-way of his mother's house and tried to avoid crunching down noisily on the marl stones. He stole quietly past her bedroom window and took a deep breath. He stretched out his left hand to balance himself over the gutter which ran from under the house to the side of the fence. He was doing well, and he knew it. He took another deep breath and held it, for luck.

At that moment, his mother called out, 'And where are you coming from, may I ask?'

Jerry stood perfectly still. He disliked being surprised, being caught out. Feeling suddenly angry and rebellious, he replied, 'Australia!'

His mother pushed up the window above the gutter, hung her head outside and smiled. Jerry, disarmed, smiled too.

'Let me see you before you go to work,' she said. She smiled again and closed the window.

Jerry went to the back of the house and tried the back door. It was locked. He fumbled with the door handle and finally slapped the centre panel with the flat of his hand.

The noise had awakened Miriam. She was blinking and craning her head awkwardly round her bedroom door in the maids'-quarters. 'Is wha' wrong now, Missa Jerry?' she called out sleepily.

He looked at her and smiled weakly. 'Sorry, Miriam. Locked out again.'

She closed her door, and he heard her say, 'I soon come wid the key. Jus' make me put on some clothes. Time I get up anyway.'

He walked across to the maids'-quarters and stood in front of Miriam's door. He heard faint rustling sounds. He listened for a moment and then pushed the door open very slowly.

Miriam was moving about in the darkness. Jerry called her name. She was not surprised, but, out of habit, she protested, 'Wha' you doin' in 'ere, Missa Jerry? You well know it not a right an' proper t'ing you doin'.'

Jerry admired her pretence. He depended on it. It always provided a good bolster for his advances which were inevit-

6

ably well received and rewarded.

He sat on her bed and began to undo his shoe laces. He dragged off his shoes, slipped off his jacket, his shirt, and fumbled with the zipper of his trousers.

Miriam sat beside him. 'Can't understan' why you mus' usual come to me when you' block up in you' Black Seal?'

He didn't reply. He was now completely undressed. He felt cool and relaxed and tired. He tried to find Miriam's face but his eyes hadn't yet got accustomed to the darkness of the room. He wriggled his toes, twisted and turned his body, and yawned.

'You don't 'ave to answer the question I jus' ask' you, an' you know why?' She went on. 'Because you don't 'ave answer for it.'

He sighed, sprawled backwards on the bed and ignored her. But Miriam was insistent. 'I goin' tell you why you can only take me when you' block up in you' Jeyes. It because you can't muster courage to take me when you' sober an' in you' right class o' mind. An' you know why? Because you t'ink I not good enough to sit table wid all o' you in the house, black as we all together. That's why. Me's dirt, nothing but a servant gal. Well I goin' tell you something. From now on, this piece o' flesh bar to you!' She slapped her thighs emphatically.

Always the same, Jerry thought. Her own private ritual before the big give.

He looked in her direction and jibed silently: Class jumper like everybody else in this striking country. Nothing unique about using what you're using to make the jump either.

'Wha' you say to that?' Miriam persisted.

'To what?'

'To the piece o' law I jus' lay down.'

'Oh, that.' He paused. 'Nothing. Nothing at all.'

She sniggered and waited for his next move. They had played the game before, and the result was always the same, but this time Jerry was going under sooner than he ever had previously, and Miriam was gaining ground fast. Her pretence was developing into self-righteousness; she was beginning to believe her own plea for decency. He felt that, if he once allowed himself to make the slightest slip, she would begin her dream of attaining what lay beyond the maids'-quarters, beyond the suffocating darkness of her small room.

Unable to achieve his customary aplomb to play the game with enthusiasm and guile, he decided to pretend to be asleep. It was up to Miriam now.

She finished her dressing quietly. She tip-toed to the door, pulled it towards her and listened like a thief. It was all part of the game, even with Jerry apparently asleep. Satisfied that nobody was about, she took the hoop of keys off its rusty hook, crept outside and left Jerry behind her in the room. She walked on tip-toe through the back hall into the dining-room and then into the kitchen. After a while, she felt calm and assured enough to start her early morning duties. She had begun to sweep the kitchen floor when she heard Jerry cry out. He cried out a second time and she ran through the kitchen, out of the house, and back into her own room. She left the door open so as not to have to turn on the light. As soon as she reached the edge of the bed, Jerry caught her round the neck-flap of her uniform and threw her down beside him.

She was utterly confused and terrified of being discovered by Thelma, the cook, whose room was next to hers, or by Jerry's mother who would soon be up and walking about the house. She tried to struggle. She tried to say something in sharp protest, something sincerely reasonable, but Jerry was working energetically. She managed to remind him that the door was open, but he was incapable of giving the matter his attention.

It was an uneven contest. Miriam allowed herself to be beaten. Jerry noticed her generous lack of fight and was grateful. He felt her relax perceptibly. Then he heard her gasp very nearly soundlessly. He was pleased and followed shortly afterwards.

Feeling calm and satisfied, he dressed quickly and stole into the house. He went straight to the bathroom and had a tepid bath and then a cold one. He dried himself vigorously and ran out with the large rough bath towel wrapped securely round his middle. It was eight twenty-five. His mother and his brother had been waiting breakfast for him for several minutes. Thelma stood by nervously. Her hands were folded under her starched apron. The blue of her uniform shone brilliantly.

Jerry appeared dressed for work. He looked exceptionally elegant in his recently dry-cleaned navy blue Sunbridge tropical suit, his cream Arrow shirt, sky-blue silk tie, and his black leather shoes. There was merely the slightest trace of rum on his breath. It was Jerry's turn to say the grace at breakfast. His mother insisted on it, every morning of the week.

He realised quite suddenly that he had forgotten the opening sequence of words of the recitation. He stared in front of him, through the space between his mother's furled linen napkin and the heaped plate of buttered toast, and hoped. It seemed an age. Thelma shifted uneasily.

'Well!' his mother said.

'Of course, I could be wrong, but I think he's forgotten it,' Jerry's brother, Les, suggested.

Jerry squirmed in his chair. The residue of the Black Seal rum rumbled deep down in his stomach and his lips stuck together in spite of his sly attempts at moistening them. His knees were beginning to ache.

'Black Seal blockage?' Les further suggested.

Jerry ignored him.

'Well!' his mother said again.

Les stared at him firmly in support of his mother's reminder.

'Do we have to?' Jerry pleaded.

'Yes, Jerry,' his mother commanded. 'And what's more, *you* are going to say it.'

This sort of thing's always happening to me, Jerry consoled

himself, and there's only one way out of it: try harder; concentrate.

'All right, Mother, I'm ready,' he said slowly, and closed his eyes. He clasped his hands tightly and concentrated.

At last, his mind, his murky Wednesday night memories of past delights, secrets, violence and indelicacies began to clear. Then, gradually and easily the grace came back to him. It came sincerely, word after word, every emphasis correctly placed, the entire recitation ordered and felt. It slipped piece by piece into a pattern of near-song. Jerry was surprised. At the end of it, his pause came naturally and well-punctuated.

His mother smiled. Thelma smiled. Les looked uncomfortable; he had never heard the grace spoken so beautifully before.

They ate quietly, and Jerry and Les asked for second helpings. Thelma was happy.

I tell you! The day begin on a correc' footin' a'right! she thought.

After breakfast, Mrs Stover said that she would be late home from school but that when she did get in she wanted to have a talk with Les and Jerry. She reminded Jerry, however, that she would talk to him alone in her bedroom as soon as he had finished his breakfast and was ready for work.

Les raised his left eyebrow and whistled softly when he was certain that his mother was out of earshot. Jerry glared at him, took another slice of toast and bit into it savagely. He scooped up a spoonful of *ackee*, dusted it with fine black pepper and shovelled it into his mouth. His jaws bulged and tiny streams of coconut oil trickled over his lower lip. Thelma was overjoyed.

Les watched Jerry and thought of what their mother had said about Jerry's coming to talk to her after he had eaten.

We're nothing but unmanageable children as far as Mother and Thelma are concerned, he reflected self-pityingly. Then he recalled the violent struggle which Jerry had been engaged in through the years, and he smiled to himself. He thought of the little irksome reminders that he himself had had to put up with for his mother's sake. And he also thought of Jerry's rebelliousness and of his own curious restraint and evasiveness.

Jerry left the table. He tried to face up to the ordeal of brushing his teeth, but the smell of the creamy toothpaste made him sick. He went back to the breakfast table, got a fistful of table-salt and returned to the bathroom. He dipped his toothbrush into it and tried to brush the upper and lower front teeth, then his tongue; and finally after steeling himself, he took in the full range of teeth, in both upper and lower jaws. He shuddered and washed out his mouth, rinsed his hands, dried them, and headed for his mother's bedroom.

She was fully dressed for school and waiting. She pointed to her bedside chair, and he sat down.

They said nothing to each other for a few seconds. Jerry fidgeted. His mother watched him and smiled coldly.

'Well, you've started it, again, I see,' she said. She smiled again. Jerry looked away. The taste of the salt in his mouth was sharp.

He had to say something, so he said, 'What?'

'Your carousing.'

'That?'

'Precisely.'

Jerry remained silent.

'It's getting late, Jerry,' she continued. 'Before we go off, I think it would be best if we came to the point.' She stared straight into his eyes, and he blinked rapidly. She smiled. He steeled himself. 'You're drinking. You'll have to stop.'

He resented that. Suddenly he felt sure of himself. What could she know? She's always safely tucked away in bed when I'm out.

'What have I got to stop, Mother?'

She didn't hesitate. 'Sleeping with Miriam. At seven-thirty in the morning.' She smiled and added, 'Or at any other time.'

She straightened the bulky bun at the back of her head, patted it twice gently, and waited for his reply. He said nothing. She picked up her parasol, tested the clasp on her brief case and moved towards her bedroom door which led to the front veranda. 'Well, Jerry, I've got to go now, but remember, I want to see you tonight to discuss a matter of importance.' She turned and inclined her left cheek towards him.

He kissed her, and she walked through the door, closing it behind her and giving the impression of having closed off a part of the morning which was, for her, a minor irritation, something casually swatted and forgotten.

Les was waiting to kiss her goodbye at the foot of the veranda steps.

Jerry had a few minutes to spare before he caught the bus to the office. He went back to his bedroom and sat on the edge of the bed and brooded.

Chapter Two

At twenty-three, Les Stover was considered an impressively serious young man by everybody but Jerry. Jerry was reasonably aware of his brother's personality, but he found him straightforward and unremarkable: his music degree seemed an anachronism; his poise and sense of restraint, an affectation; his talent, a doubtful asset.

Mrs Stover had no time for a favourite son at home, or for that matter, a favourite pupil at school. Yet Jerry thought Les was his mother's favourite, and Les thought the same about Jerry.

Les had worked diligently and had been sent to America to the Julliard School of Music. He had also worked very hard there and had graduated with distinction. After his graduation, he had stayed on in America for an extra academic year, playing the piano at concerts and lecturing at the School. He had returned to the Island with certain personal hopes and even higher expectations for the Island's musical future.

His plans and efforts had been met with apathy and ignorance. Where they had been met with enthusiasm and intelligence, Les knew, from experience, that they and his other original ideas would be modified and ultimately wrested from him either by some official body or by some influential person. In the end, he had settled for the modest security of private teaching and thinking about the Island Symphony he hoped to write.

Jerry knew that many of Les's plans had been frustrated but he was unable to make the first move to sympathise or even to talk things over with him. Les, in turn, was also aware of Jerry's attempts to escape the Island's extreme colonial stranglehold, but he, too, was unable to make the first move to show his understanding of the situation. Yet, there were certain secret concessions which they granted each other. Jerry's devotion to revolt and escape and his efforts to encourage his friends to break out of their prolonged depression made Les think of his brother with respect and admiration. Jerry respected Les's love of music and Les's ability to live with his unrealised dream and carry on in spite of his blighted future.

Chapter Three

Jerry Stover was early. With three minutes to spare, he was leisurely climbing the winding stairs at the back of the Resident Magistrate's Courts at Half Way Tree, when he ran into the Clerk of the Courts, R. A. D. Randax-Lee, affectionately called Randy. A Negro Chinese, fifty-three, balding and a zealous civil servant, he was Jerry's only work problem. Unnoticed, socially unimportant, and entirely predictable, Randy had been the Clerk of the Courts at Half Way Tree for seventeen years. He had never been thanked, praised, liked, and for seventeen years had never been promoted. Randy knew his job but he was qualified for nothing more than the position he held. Barristers came, went, and became Resident Magistrates, but Randy remained the Clerk of the Courts and served them faithfully, and in some instances, openly resentfully. He was highly sensitive about his Chinese ancestry and deeply regretted his Negro blood; altogether he disliked the way he looked.

He bullied Jerry because he could do so to no one else in the office; everybody had long ago learned to resist Randy's attacks.

Jerry and Randy passed each other, Jerry going up the stairs, Randy coming down, both silent, both watchful, until Randy said, 'I know about your exploits last night, Stover agitator. Lucky you weren't arrested, boy. Had the VPP meeting taken place in Jones Town instead of Rollington Town, you would've been up before me this morning. On the other side of the railings, I mean, Stover.'

Jerry smiled unconcernedly, innocently, while staring at Randy's large bald spot. 'Good morning, sir,' he said respectfully. 'I hadn't heard of your promotion. Congratulations.'

Randy felt assaulted. His nerves were electrified. Coolly, he asked, 'And what does that mean, Stover boy?'

'Your promotion, sir.'

'*My* promotion, Stover.'

'That's right, sir.'

'Being personal, Stover?'

'Hardly, sir.' Jerry was adamantly respectful.

Randy stepped up two steps to be level with Jerry; but even then, Jerry was about seven or eight inches above him. Randy quickly made up the difference by climbing another step which made him just about level with Jerry's forehead. Quite casually, he climbed yet another step.

'What exactly are you inferring, Stover?'

'*Inferring,* sir?'

'Yes. Inferring!'

'The prisoner appears before a Magistrate, not the Clerk of the Courts: before the Judge and not his Clerk, sir.'

Randy trembled.

Jerry turned away and continued up the stairs. When he got to the top, he heard Randy say, 'As soon as the morning session is over, I want to see you in my office, Stover!'

'Sir,' was all Jerry said. He pushed the office door and slipped in, signed the register and sat down at his desk.

They were all there and they had already been informed of Jerry's VPP escapade. Van Farson, the Acting Deputy Clerk of the Courts, was the only one who acknowledged Jerry's entrance; he winked. Van was thirty, a burly half East Indian, half Negro, who was proud of his East Indian half. He was Jerry's close friend. He strolled over to Jerry and sat on his desk.

They looked at each other and Jerry knew what to expect.

'You just made it, Jerry.'

'Yes,' Jerry said impatiently. Then he added, 'Look, Van, who told everybody?'

'You were seen.' He smiled.

'By whom?'

'Randy, the big bad man.'

'Randy? You serious?'

'Told us everything before you came in. Gloated over it, in fact.'

'Is he VPP?'

'Suppose so. Hardly shows. Thought he voted the other way. Never imagined an opportunist like W. C. Kirby would've impressed our Randy.'

'Kirby's the civil servant's lily black hope, Van. What's so strange about Randy supporting him?'

Van Farson didn't reply. Jerry knew why and didn't press the matter. He was going to ask him about Randy's office report of the VPP incident when Van eased himself off the top of the desk and strolled back to his own across the room.

Blissful, stoical Hindu, Jerry thought affectionately.

The office was busy and impersonal, and Jerry felt the usual disgust and contempt which overcame him from time to time when the office was quiet and everybody was slavishly at work, filling in forms, putting the finishing touches to criminal records, examining ancient bundles of Informations tied with dusty pink ribbons, and being wholeheartedly *civil* and *serving*.

As soon as Van had settled down to a batch of Informations, checking them carefully and making sure that they were in order as they were the first lot to be taken into Court later on, Jerry decided he'd telephone Silba Lane; but before he did that, he wanted to complete the conversation with Van.

He went across to Van's desk and leant over him. 'Have I offended you, *Coolie Babu*?'

Van looked up slowly, and they both laughed quietly.

Van said, 'Point taken, Jerry.'

'Not calling me "black boy"?' Jerry asked.

'Obvious enough.'

'Point again,' Jerry said, conceding it with a nod.

'Seriously, Jerry,' Van said, 'a man like Kirby is no good to a man like me, and you know it. I'm more Indian than anything else.'

Jerry looked furtively round the office, grinned and said, 'You're a civil servant, Van. You're an established, paid-up member of the Island Civil Service, man!' He stopped and they both chuckled at the imitation of W. C. Kirby's platform oratory.

But Van wanted to clinch his own point. He interrupted Jerry's self-congratulatory chuckles. 'I'm an Indian, nothing but a *coolie babu* to your W. C. Kirby, the glorified leader of the Voice of the People's Party, who's arrogant enough to tell me and my kind to vote for the other side.'

'Nothing's wrong with the other side, with Dr C. W. Rybik; he's an upstanding Syrian,' Jerry said, pretending seriousness but really trying to provoke the situation.

Van folded his arms, slid back into his creaky swivel chair, and said, 'In this *rass hole* country of ours, there are only two political parties: the VPP which is supported by civil servants and middle class people, and the Just Proletarian Destineers which is the party for the working class and poor *Quashie*. As an Indian, which am I to choose? Kirby or Rybik?'

'Three parties, Van,' Jerry said. 'The Rastafarian Brethren is a budding third. Anyway, you're wrong about something else. You're not an Indian. And we don't vote by race.'

'Not yet,' Van said.

'Something else: the JPD is packed with all the races and disgraces, as Kirby said last night. His own mob, the VPP, has them too; so has the budding third. Make your choice. Indian or no Indian, Van. Thieves on all three sides, opportunists on two, and everybody *rassing* around and aspiring to middle class status.'

Van was embarrassed by Jerry's overstatement. He showed it.

Jerry didn't care. 'What did Randy say about last night?'

'Told us about you and the fight.'

Randy entered the office and walked down to Van's desk. He unzipped his brief case, rested it on the desk, stood with his arms akimbo and glared at the two men. He cleared his throat and asked Van for the first session's Informations. He snatched them from Van's hand, stuffed them into his brief case and went back to his office.

'Hope we get paid early today,' Jerry whispered. 'As soon as I collect, the door.'

He went back to his desk. Van went into Randy's office.

Jerry remembered the telephone call he wanted to make. He walked leisurely across the room, making sure he wasn't noticed, and asked Lily, the messenger, to get the Administrator General's Office. She grinned knowingly and dialled the number.

'Who you wan' talk to, Missa Stover?' she asked.

He liked her and had tried half-heartedly to make her at the last Christmas party. She'll keep for next Christmas, he consoled himself.

'Ask for Silba Lane. Accounts.'

She did so, using her special accent, handed him the receiver and walked stylishly away.

He took in her wiggle. She knew he would.

Silba Lane's voice was husky and tired.

'You sound like twelve o'clock last night,' Jerry said.

Silba was glad to hear from Jerry. They planned to meet either at the Administrator General's Office or at the Niagara, as soon as they had been paid. Jerry asked about the outcome of the lovers'-row between Paula Watt and Albert Ley. Silba said that he was sure that everything would be all right. Jerry reminded him that there would be other scenes, possibly more serious, if Paula didn't stop playing Albert for a fool.

Silba's voice betrayed signs of stress. His naturally light tone thickened and became hesitant. 'Paula fancies me, Jerry. But Albert's a buddy. Can't *jacket* a friend, can I? Besides, what's going to happen is a big nil, if she decides to go back to England and leave us both stranded. Got to pluck it cool.'

Jerry asked him if the news of last night's VPP incident had been circulated round his office. Silba assured him it hadn't. They reminded each other of their appointment and hung up.

Jerry felt a little more confident. At least the VPP affair hadn't spread to the Kingston Civil Service offices yet. Nevertheless, a telephone call from anybody in his own office at Half Way Tree could easily do so.

He returned to his desk and fidgeted with his ruler and indelible pencil. He put them on the counter to his right. Then he prepared the necessary piles of blank Information forms on his left and waited for Lily to open the folding doors to the public.

Randy came into the room. 'Before you attend to the public, Stover, I want to talk to you in my office. Won't have any time later on as I thought.'

Randy's office was drab, brownish and depressing. Stacks of Informations, law books, green and blue files and back copies of the *Law Report* fringed the window sills, and a thin triangular-shaped film of dust covered the floor in all four corners.

'Sit down, Stover.'

Jerry remained standing.

'I said sit down, Stover!'

Jerry smiled politely and sat down. Randy stood a little way off. Jerry folded his arms.

'You're still in a temporary position in the Service, in spite of your Higher School Certificate. The Appointments Board

20

may very well ask my opinion of your conduct in the office, and possibly of your conduct outside.'

Jerry beamed respectfully. But Randy wasn't fooled. Jerry shifted slightly. He realised that he had been caught out. Randy sat down. He was at ease. He was in *'im power an' glory,* as Lily might have observed had she been present, Jerry thought.

Randy extended the forefinger of his clenched right hand and shook it towards Jerry. 'I will not put up with insubordination, Stover.' He spoke emphatically, syllabically.

Jerry counted the syllables. He had arrived at a total when Randy perversely added four more.

'I'm warning you!'

Lily was opening the folding doors, and Jerry could hear the roar of scrambling noises as the public rushed to the counter.

'May I go, now?' he asked.

'Yes,' Randy hissed, 'and don't forget what I've just said, Stover. I will not put up with insubordination!'

Jerry was glad to get away. He liked welcoming the public with their heart-breaking stories of Bastardy, Assault and Battery, Abusive Language and Maintenance. He always listened to their complaints and grievances as if it had been the first time he had heard them. He filled up forms, chatted, gave routine advice, teased, flirted and made a date with a pretty Syrian girl who had wanted to sue her mother's lover for Slander. Jerry dutifully persuaded her to think the matter over again and expressed calculated sympathy throughout the interview. He made her promise to stay away from her mother's lover until he was able to give her further advice, and he told her that he would give her this when they met in the foyer of the Carib Theatre on Saturday afternoon at four o'clock. 'Two days' time,' he reminded, 'and we'll know what to do.'

As she was going through the centre door, she turned and smiled gratefully at him. He winked masterfully.

He worked hard and expertly until twelve o'clock. At five past twelve he was handed his pay envelope, and at seven minutes past twelve, without notifying anybody, not even Van Farson, he left the Courts' Office and hopped on a Molynes bus heading for Kingston

Randy had already ceased to exist.

Chapter Four

The bus stopped and started, bumped and jerked down Max-field Avenue. Jerry remembered Van's insistence on thinking of himself as an East Indian.

He's wrong about that, Jerry reminded himself. He's an Islander, not merely half East Indian or half Negro. And what's the VPP doing about it? Or for that matter, the JPD? Kirby and Rybik, the VPP and the JPD. Jerry thought of nothing else as the bus jangled down Brentford Road and into Slipen Road. Quickly, he reviewed them: W. C. Kirby, forty-five, Negro, lisps attractively, spokesman of the middle class and Leader of the VPP, the Opposition party; Dr C. W. Rybik, fifty, Syrian Islander, physician, champion of the working class and Leader of the JPD, the Majority party.

Silba Lane was waiting for Jerry in front of the Administrator General's Office on King Street. He was dressed impressively in a light blue Sunbridge tropical suit, a white shirt, royal blue shantung silk tie, and black leather shoes. Silba was black, about twenty-six, a Second Class Clerk, and unmarried.

He was attractive to women, particularly to English and American tourists. He had served in the Royal Air Force a year before the end of the War. He wrote poetry during office hours and read the best of his short poems to his current girl friend, and Jerry. He had prepared his first slim volume and was curious about finding a sympathetic English publisher. Paula Watt had promised to help him, but her boy friend, Albert Ley, didn't approve, hence their interminable scenes of jealousy. Silba liked Paula but he was trying his best to be loyal to Albert. Silba was like that, occasionally.

'Anybody caught up with you, yet?' Jerry asked him.

'Not much owing,' Silba said. 'Almost a free man this month.'

King Street was dusty, crowded and hot. Zig-zagging lines of heat haze bobbed up and down between the white frontages of the public buildings on both sides of the street. Jerry eased his tie and pulled the collar button of his shirt. He shoved his hands into his pockets and remembered that he hadn't yet had lunch. 'Patties and Red Stripe?' he asked.

'All right by me. Owe a lot at the Niagara?'

'A few bob.'

'That all?'

'Think so. Twenty-five shillings maybe.' He noticed Paula Watt and Albert Ley walking down King Street, arm in arm, in a stale-drunk Black Seal haze, and in love, presumably.

Paula Watt was English and on permanent loan to the Island. She had become an actress and a freelance journalist on the *Springboard* as soon as she had settled in. The boys believed that she could be almost anything she wanted to be, if she applied herself to it. She was a Londoner, blonde and about twenty-nine. She was brash, Socialist, an indefatigable supporter of what she referred to as the 'emergent Islands' Nation', a reader of contemporary American fiction in preference to anything else, and an excellent Black Seal drinker. She was in love with Albert Ley, openly and very nearly challengingly.

Albert Ley was twenty-seven, Negro and bad tempered. He worked as a radio engineer at Omatt's on Harbour Street, an electrical appliances store, owned by an integrated and indulgent Island Jew. Albert was the youngest of five sons, and the outsider in a respectable Lower Saint Andrew family. His four brothers were all graduates and professional men. Albert was a Black Seal devotee who began as an enthusiastic Sunday drinker and was soon helped along the way to proficiency by Jerry and the others.

Albert grinned broadly and saluted. 'Going down to the Niagara?' he greeted them in his sing-song accent which sounded high-pitched and strident.

They nodded, in ritual, and the four of them walked down King Street. It was one-thirty. The sun was extremely hot. They turned into the Niagara and ordered four cold Red Stripes. They paid their wine cards, and Paula breathed a sigh of relief; they all assumed the right of ownership of the bar's untapped stock for the forthcoming month. Lola, the barmaid in charge, liked prompt payment from all her Civil Service regulars, and particularly on pay day.

Lola was a whore made good. Everybody liked and respected her. She was twenty-three, Portuguese Negro and voluptuous. She was very fond of Jerry, and he, too, of her. But they were wise; they never met. Jerry feared it would spoil his chances of making Vie, Lola's assistant. As soon as he had had her, Lola would be next, he promised himself. In the meantime, he teased his luck along.

Vie disliked Jerry intensely. Once he had made an unfavourable remark about her Indian hair and she had never forgiven him. She was twenty-one, short, plump, half East Indian and half Chinese. She claimed her Chinese half but hadn't the eyes to back it up. She wasn't giving anything away, and least of all to Jerry. But he knew that he'd have her, perhaps when she wasn't looking.

'What do we do this afternoon?' Paula asked the boys; and not waiting for an answer because she had plans of her own, she added, 'I'd like to go to the Institute, in a few minutes, to hear the lecture by that visiting American sociologist. Anybody up to it?'

Albert smiled appreciatively. Silba and Jerry looked at each other and shrugged. This meant that they could be influenced one way or the other. Neither was willing to admit how daunting the sociology of the aftermath of slavery and early colonialism might prove.

'Well?' Paula demanded. 'Do we grab ourselves some culture in the afternoon?' Hemingway's *Death in the Afternoon* inspired highly personal variations for Paula's conversations. The mere title was enough.

Six months before that afternoon in the Niagara, while Jerry, Silba, Albert and Paula were discussing the doubtful merits of the Kirby-Rybik Kingdom, NEXUS, Prudence Kirby's literary review, and class and caste in the Island, it occurred to Jerry that all they were really doing was trying to bore away at the *status quo* over cheap rum and water, and he said so quite strongly.

'If that's the case,' Paula suggested, 'why not let's think of ourselves as termites, threatening the system in the afternoon?'

'Right!' Albert said. 'We're Termites from now on, *to rass*!'

They accepted his obscene comment.

'*Rass* to the Kirby-Rybik Kingdom in the afternoon!' was Paula's contribution.

But Jerry wasn't happy about being called a Termite. 'After we've helped destroy the Kingdom, what do we put in its place?' he asked.

'Any *rass* thing'll do,' Albert shouted.

Ignoring him, Silba asked, 'What d'you think, Jerry? Worth it?'

'The way I see it is this: the Termites ought to . . .' Jerry was immediately interrupted by Paula.

'There you go!' she said. 'We're Termites now. Don't you

26

see?' She clapped her hands, delighted to have caught Jerry out.

They left the Institute and walked back to the Niagara. The others had arrived: Sally Dawes, Berto Sabyo, Mason and Jenny Jones, Wyn Stone and Van Farson.

The ten Termites were gathering for their pay day binge. They were looking to Jerry for the first move, for the signal, as Paula said, to pitch a bitch in the late afternoon. 'Well, do we or don't we?' She spun round and faced him. He winked. They extended and palmed their right hands American Negro style, hunching their backs and doing a soft-shoe shuffle, their hands barely touching, and marked their decision to begin the pay day binge.

The others were busy placing two large round tables together, forming a huge 8.

They all sat down.

Paula and Albert sat facing each other at the two indented spaces in the 8. Van and Silba sat at opposite ends round the arcs. Jerry sat on Van's right. Sally Dawes, a part-time hairdresser, poet and short story writer, sat beside Paula, on her right.

Sally liked Jerry and had once, under Black Seal, believed that she was in love with him and had told him so. Jerry liked her and often praised her poetry. It was Silba's pet theory that Sally had Carib blood. Nobody believed him or thought it important. She was light brown with pleasantly *straightened* hair, and a Semitic nose. She flaunted it constantly. In a fit of drunken confidence, Jerry had mentioned that he suspected that Sally's lone Jewish vestige was the only thing that gave her any aplomb in a society as shade- and feature-conscious as the Island's. Paula had accepted Jerry's confidence but could not quite equate aplomb with Jewishness. After thinking about it, she attributed her inability to make the connection to her not being an Islander. As far as Paula could observe, most Islanders were almost wholly unaware of the European's

27

ritualistic mythology of the Jew, and she was grateful to the people of the Island for being so unmindful.

At twenty-two, Sally's one serious objection in life was quite simple: she disliked anybody who 'behaved like a nigger'. Being Negro herself, the term nigger had a very special meaning for her; it had ceased to be a specific racial term of contempt, and in its refined form, it had become an abstraction, a curious state of Sally's own mind. Anybody black, white, brown or yellow had what she defined as *nigger moods, nigger ways, nigger attitudes, nigger sentiments, nigger animus.*

Sally was a born poet.

Berto Sabyo, the photographer-in-chief on the *Springboard*, sat between Jerry and Paula. His expensive high-speed German camera was on the floor in its usual place beside his chair. He was distinguished-looking and almost blue-black. He was well aware of the former. Any awareness of the latter he hadn't time for, either in himself or in anybody else. At twenty-four, he was the youngest top-professional in photo-journalism. His pictures in the *Springboard* were sinisterly original and eagerly awaited daily by the paper's readers.

Mason Donne-Jones, a near-white Islander, and Jenny Donne-Jones, an English blonde, husband and wife, sat beside each other at the top half of the 8 facing Jerry and Berto. They had unofficially dropped the Donne from their name.

Jenny was about twenty-eight but looked forty-five because of Black Seal. She worked, according to Paula, in an executive capacity at Thanan's in the afternoon. Thanan's was an English firm on King Street. Jenny liked referring to Thanan's as the Selfridge's of the Caribbean, but did so only when Mason wasn't listening.

Mason was thirty, an Oxford graduate, and unemployed. Again, when he wasn't listening, Jenny would confide, 'Frankly, old Mason's unemployable. Nearly all Arts graduates are. Mason has tried everything. The only thing left is teaching and that would be too much for any child to bear.' Both she and he were remarkably able drinkers, and they drank their

Black Seal, like the rest of the Termites, with only two or three drops of water.

Wyn Stone sat at the bottom half of the 8, beside Sally. He was ex-RAF, a civil servant and twenty-seven. He was tall, shy and pure East Indian. He was an Acting First Class Clerk in the Treasury, and he wrote poems, short stories and political essays which he showed to Silba and Jerry. He was the Termites' only pacifist.

The Termites always sat at two round tables, in the same position and in the same order, on Civil Service pay days.

Lola brought them three quart bottles of Black Seal, a large cut-glass goblet of water and a basin of cracked ice. She was smiling. Jerry stretched across the top half of the 8 and took the tray from her. They both began to unload it. The others waited for Vie to come in with the glasses. When she did, Silba winked at her. She strolled towards the bottom half of the 8 where he was sitting. She returned his wink and together they distributed the glasses. They were passed left and right of Silba and soon everybody had one. In the meantime, Berto and Van had been opening the bottles. Jerry passed the first bottle to his right, and Van the second to his left. The others helped themselves, and the bottles met at the bottom half of the 8 in front of Silba. Ice and water were handed round and the Termites were ready for the toast. Everybody looked at Jerry and waited.

'To an early death!' he said, and everybody drank. In a matter of seconds, all the glasses were empty. The binge had got off to its usual ritualistic start.

After the last of the three quarts was drained, Van, Silba and Sally struck matches and dropped them into the bottles and quickly placed their palms over them and created a strong suction which caused them to stick securely. Then they dangled the three 'dead men'.

Chapter Five

Jerry remembered that he had to see his mother. He thought it would be to his advantage not to go to her drunk, and consequently he decided to ease off. He did so as cunningly as he could, without drawing any attention to the fact. He drank slowly and concealed the level of his drink, and he avoided most of the routine refilling round the 8. He secretly planned to leave the Termites at about five o'clock and go straight home. He could always get back to the Niagara in time for the evening session. He didn't want to miss it. Yet he didn't want to break up the 8. It usually stayed together until far into the next day after pay day. Quite often it lasted for two or three days.

He turned to Van. 'Anything I ought to know?'

'Like what?' Van asked.

'Randy.'

'Nothing.' Van grimaced and drank up. So did Jerry, coolly covering the empty glass with his clenched fists.

He left the Niagara at about four-thirty after promising faithfully that he would be back by six-thirty. The others understood and wished him luck.

When he got home, his mother was sitting on the front veranda and waiting for him. Les was sitting beside her. He was holding a tall glass of brown sugar lemonade in one hand and a copy of the *Concertgoer* in the other.

Jerry greeted them with calculated politeness and drew up a chair. He crossed his legs, rested back in the chair confidently and waited.

Mrs Stover tugged at her rimless glasses and prepared to read a letter she had received from her husband. She read slowly and emphatically.

'Well, boys, how do you both feel?' she asked after she had read the postscript to the letter.

Neither replied. Les drained his glass of lemonade.

'Do you think he's wise in doing what he says in his letter?'

Still no reply.

'He wants to know how we feel.'

No reaction.

'Of course, it's too late. But your father has always been like that. He acts first and asks for criticism afterwards.'

Nothing.

Les was embarrassed. Jerry was annoyed.

Les was concerned with his father's situation. Could it be as desperate as his letter sounds? he thought. He's had much more difficult problems and he's solved them. Why the dependence now? The sudden humility?

Jerry was annoyed because of his mother's insistence on making a family issue of a seemingly simple matter. He was also upset that his father had waited so long before mentioning anything about his plan. 'It's quite simple, Mother,' he said. 'He wants to come home after eighteen years in Cuba, so he sells his houses, his business, and takes a plane back to the Island. Can't see an insoluble problem there.'

Les circled his empty glass between his thumb and forefinger and thought of something intelligent to say to counter Jerry's glib suggestion. He cleared his throat and rested the glass on the broad arm of the chair. 'What about his reception in the Island? What'll he do here if he's squeezed out? He's no longer an Islander for people he'll meet in business.'

Jerry dragged his body to the edge of his chair, pointed at his brother and said, 'A man's been away eighteen years. In that time he's had the guts to raise a family and support it. He's had the added guts to set up a business in a strange country and make a packet, from which we've benefited handsomely. So, he's well over fifty, and he wants to return home and set up shop. What's so wrong with that? And how do we know he has to anyway?'

Mrs Stover listened patiently. When she was certain that Jerry had come to the end of his speech, she said, 'You don't understand. Your father's a bankrupt.'

Jerry slipped back in his chair. Les stared helplessly at his mother and then down at the book-jacket of the *Concertgoer*.

Mrs Stover continued: 'He's coming home penniless. True, he owns this and another house in town, and a few acres of land in the country, but the point remains he's lost everything in Cuba. Now, do you understand, both of you?'

'The letter didn't say that,' Jerry said.

'I know. The others did but I kept the truth from you. I was hoping things would have worked out for him.'

Jerry fumbled in his trousers pocket with his packet of Four Aces cigarettes, opened it, took out two crushed butts, put them aside and lit a whole cigarette. Almost immediately after that, he stubbed it out and threw it in the front garden. Les noticed Jerry's uneasiness and he secretly admired him for it.

'Well, there we are, Les and Jerry. What's it going to be? Do we congratulate him?'

Neither replied.

Mrs Stover took off her glasses and rested them in her lap.

Inside, Thelma was laying the supper table, and to Jerry, her tiny rustling noises seemed like another world, another time. He pinched the two cigarette butts between his fingers and flicked them into the nearest garden bed. Les excused himself and went into the house.

Mrs Stover turned to Jerry. 'You two boys aren't exactly, what any parent would call, family credits, are you?'

Jerry smiled. 'Never have thought of myself in that way, Mother. Still, the old man and I might find something to talk about. Black Seal is a great leveller.' He smiled again.

His mother sighed. 'Flippancy is a child's way out.' She paused and looked away. 'What are we going to do?'

Jerry shrugged and said nothing.

The Stovers had met at a Roman Catholic garden party on Christmas Day, 1922. They saw each other twice after that. And on the 31st of December Mr Stover proposed. They were married in June, 1923. And in August of the same year they emigrated to Cuba and to the adventure of a new beginning in a strange country.

Les was born on the 19th of June, 1927, and Jerry on the 5th of August, 1929.

Four months after Jerry was born, the Stovers returned to the Island. Then three years after that, Mr Stover went back to Cuba and to better prospects. Mrs Stover remained in the Island because she wanted Les and Jerry to go to school there, to be English-speaking and to secure their British nationality, as she had put it then to her husband, in defence.

In a matter of two months after Mr Stover had settled down in Cuba, he won two first prizes in ending numbers on the national lottery, about four thousand dollars. And also within two months, he had invested three-quarters of his winnings and had lost it almost immediately; had invested the remaining thousand and had lost that too. He wrote his wife about his misfortune and she sympathised, but did not offer her advice. After he had been away for six months, she realised that he had decided not to return to the Island, so they both came to an agreement and kept to it for eighteen years. Of course, he threatened many times to return, and each time Mrs Stover had smiled stoically, knowing that her husband would indeed come home one day, after he had proved himself in his new country.

Les returned with a half-filled glass of lemonade. He sat down and sipped it noisily, much to his mother's annoyance. Jerry ignored him. He lit another cigarette. He thought of his father. He also thought of his own private images of his father and his life in Cuba, his grand sense of responsiblity, his sense of urgent ambition, and his unrepentant selfishness. But Jerry did not blame his father. He thought of his mother, her schoolteaching, her matriarchal role, her nobility, her intellect, her faithfulness, her beauty. He respected her. He loved her.

'When does he arrive?' he asked her.

'In two weeks' time.'

'The letter didn't say so.'

'No. But the one before did.'

Les drained his glass. The sucking noises had come to an end. His mother was relieved. Jerry was pensive. Too pensive, Les thought. 'What great imponderable is it this time, Jerry?' he asked.

Jerry frowned and didn't reply.

'Shall we go in to supper?' Mrs Stover asked.

They rose and walked quietly into the house. Mrs Stover led the way, followed by Les, and Jerry who hung back intentionally and gazed at his mother's stooping shoulders. Supper was slow and pleasant. Thelma moved about expertly, assuming her duties like a self-created ritual. Jerry ate very little and his mother noticed it but said nothing. She knew that her conference and the supper had interrupted his drinking. She was well aware that he had come to the supper table because he felt that she had expected him to and that he had forced himself to take a cup of country chocolate and a spoonful of sweet corn to avoid Thelma's censure. After supper, Mrs Stover went out to the vegetable garden at the back of the house. Jerry followed her. They walked together through the central beds of garden eggs and *ponderoso* tomatoes.

'How old is Father?' Jerry asked.

'In his fifties.'

'Late fifties?'

'Yes.' She paused. Then she turned and cupped his face in her hands. Jerry nodded. His concern puzzled her. She hadn't before realised how much he cared for his father. He hadn't hinted and she hadn't probed.

It was different with Les. He admired and respected his father, and had shown it in many familiar ways throughout the years.

Jerry usually appeared not to have the time to care about his father, his mother, his brother, or any other member of his family. He was self-centred, egotistical, arrogant and impatient.

It was getting late and the Termites were waiting. Jerry kissed his mother and told her that he had to meet the boys at the Niagara.

She squeezed his arm. 'Work tomorrow, eh.'

He grunted and left her. She continued her walk through the upper part of the vegetable garden, thinking of him and his father.

The Constant Spring Road bus crawled. Jerry was preoccupied. What do I say that'll sound like a son talking to his father? Eighteen years aren't all that long, I suppose. Might even like him as a person. He, me. Might be critical of the whole show. Might hate his guts. He, mine.

The bus crawled over Sandy Gully bridge. Jerry broke away from his reverie to gaze at the cluster of Public Works lanterns dotted about the basin of the gully. They'll never finish that thing, and what's more, they know it.

The lights at Cross Roads were spiky, bright and vulgar. The J. Wray & Nephew illuminated sign, with its moving picture of hundreds of small coloured bulbs, attracted Jerry for a few seconds, just long enough for him to notice that nothing was pouring out of the bottle of rum into the shot glass below it.

Parade and King Street were dimly lit, and in some places, not at all. Temple Lane was totally dark, except for the raw flood of urine-coloured light which splashed through the windows and half swing-doors of the Niagara.

The Termites were well away. They greeted Jerry vociferously. Sally ran to him and threw herself headlong into his arms.

Van made a V sign with his elbows touching and his forearms splayed.

Jerry knew how to take the impermanence of Sally's advances. He knew she would cool off and regret it as soon as she had sobered up after the binge. He hugged her and led her back to her chair round the 8. He filled her glass for her and raised it to her lips. She drank slowly and held on to his wrist. After she had drained her glass, he filled it again and put it down in front of her.

'Pure wickedness, man!' Berto said. 'Sweet *rass*!'

Sally lit a cigarette. Jerry left her and sat at his position round the 8.

Vie came in smiling. Jerry was surprised. He pulled her down to him, gazed at the smooth brown flesh of her massive breasts, then suddenly pretended innocence and whispered, 'Anything I should know?'

'Like what?' She ignored his brief scrutiny.

'Like murders.'

She grinned. He winked.

'How much have they had in all?'

'Not sure.'

'Must be a basinful by the look and smell of things.' He winked again and looked round the 8.

At that point, Lola came in with a bowl of ice and a goblet of water. She showed immediately how happy she was to see Jerry. He understood and smiled. Then, as if by second nature,

36

he looked at her breasts, compared them with Vie's and found both sets equally splendidly over-developed and impressive.

Mason and Berto started a discussion about whisky-drinking in the tropics, and Jenny listened long enough to sneer. Jerry was staring at Sally. She and Wyn were trying to concentrate on what Mason was saying. Silba was helping himself to ice and water and earnestly pretending not to be interested in the topic. Berto was nodding mandarin fashion to Van and agreeing how extremely complicated life must be for those who neither drink Black Seal nor whisky, nor anything else. Berto distracted Jerry once or twice and was promptly told to have another drink. He obeyed willingly, much to Jerry's relief.

Ten-thirty. The Termites were about to leave the Niagara. Lola was pleased and had given them each a large rum for the road; she knew it was expected of her.

'Might see you later at the Jam Pot,' were her parting words to Jerry.

'None better,' he said boastfully. 'None more deserving.'

She raised her eyebrows. 'Later, if you still can stand up,' she whispered.

Chapter Six

The Termites left the Niagara and walked up Water Lane to the Writers' Nook, the inescapable first stop, before the Jam Pot.

Berto was convinced that it was Saturday night. Mabel, the secretary of the Writers' Nook, braced herself against possible attack, staggered over to the Termites' table with a calendar to prove Berto wrong, but he told her that he had no confidence in calendars and promptly led her away in the direction of the men's toilet.

'Taking Mabel's picture so soon, Berto?' Sally asked.

The Termites knew that Berto liked Mabel. In fact, they had, in their own wilfully insensitive way, encouraged him to take her seriously. Paula and Sally had tried laying ineffectual traps for both of them. Jenny had coaxed the friendship along, with firm, seemingly objective hints of the mutual benefits for them both, but Berto continued to work at his own pace. He was resolute. He liked taking his time. 'You get the best pictures unplanned,' he reminded Jenny. He called his technique the Sabyo method, not caring too much and always being around when things happen.

'Remember the camera!' Sally called out.

Before Berto ducked out of sight, the others heard him say, 'Doesn't matter a *rass* what day it is, Mabel, you come and let's find ourselves.'

Mabel was away for a long time. Jerry was certain that she knew how to protect herself. Paula pretended to wince; so did Jenny and Sally.

'Tough,' Silba said and lit his pay day cigar and pulled hard on it.

They were all drunk, but being Termites, they looked as though they were merely playing at it. Everybody else in the room knew this. The more serious-minded members of the Writers' Nook disliked the Termites. Most of the older members of the club disapproved of them strongly; they had gone so far as to lobby to get them barred for life. The officers-elect consented to treat them as spoiled children whose nuisance value was strictly equal to the money they spent at the bar. The senior working newspapermen considered themselves the élite of the Island's writers, and acted the part sternly whenever the Termites were around.

Once, after Sally had been told precisely who a journalist was by Josiah Blake, one of the founder-members of the Writers' Nook and the editor of the *Scythe,* the Island's leading daily paper, she said, 'So, you're a journalist, Josiah? All right. I write short stories and poems. That's all right, too. Who'll be remembered? A journalist without a by-line? Or a writer with one?' Josiah showed he was hurt. He said, 'You won't be forgotten, not with that nose you carry around with you. It's bound to be the only Negro hook in the literary business.' Sally was proud of the shape of her nose and considered it an asset in an otherwise Negro 'setting', as Berto had remarked. Because of her pride in her peculiar escape from her Negro setting and because she had been humiliated, together with the fact that she was obviously more Negro than anything else, she looked her tormentor up and down and hissed venomously, 'Nigger!' And all that Josiah could find to say was: 'Imagine a nigger calling a nigger a nigger!' They laughed raucously at each other for a long time afterwards. The atmosphere in the Writers' Nook was like that.

It had also earned a reputation for its lavish Celebrity evenings, when its members entertained visiting American journalists, Fleet Street castaways and disused blondes who had managed to marry ageing newspaper magnates from Denver, Pasadena or Minneapolis; the president had once secured Paul Robeson for those members who had been growing tired of the usual parade of Pulitzer Prize winners *manqué*, *Time* rejects and Canadian women reporters on the loose. Robeson was the finest thing the president had ever done and he drank out on it for months afterwards. He even acquired the nickname, Saint Paul. From then on Saint Paul's real name, Burns Hector, was hardly ever used; in fact, it became fashionable to call him Paul for short.

It was Paul who caught Berto and Mabel wrestling and scuffling about at the entrance to the men's toilet. He was appropriately shocked. 'Sabyo, what are you supposed to be doing with the club secretary?'

'Supposing nothing with your secretary, Saul of Tarsus, baby,' Berto managed to get out, while fighting off Mabel and trying to keep his balance.

'Sabyo!' Paul ordered.

'Why don't you take a running jump, Mr Saint?' Berto suggested. His trousers were concertina-ed round his ankles.

'Mabel!' Paul ordered again. 'What's this lunatic doing to you?'

Mabel was drunk and carelessly happy; and besides, she was being interrupted. She took close aim, lunged at Berto's middle, grabbed, missed and landed on the floor. Paul jumped back in pained consternation and stared at her exposed thighs. She got up, lunged recklessly at Berto's underpants, grabbed, missed again, clasped his right leg instead and slid down gently on it.

Paul wrenched them apart and told Berto to pull up his

trousers. Berto looked at Paul and said, 'You're a hell of a man. Can't you see you're spoiling Mabel's fun?'

Paul spun round and held her under her chin. She was crying. 'It's nothing, Paul,' she said, sobbing quietly. 'Just a tease. Trying to out-bluff Berto. That's all.'

Paul shook his head slowly and muttered, 'You've never done that with me.' He walked into one of the unoccupied booths.

Berto and Mabel went back to the club bar. When Mabel got to the counter, she said, 'I'm glad it happened. Always wanted to show Paul. Too black, for one thing.' She laughed and wiped away a stream of mascara tears from her cheek with Berto's damp handkerchief.

The other Termites were sitting at a large table to the left of the counter and downing their Black Seal, almost twice as expensive as they had paid for it at the Niagara.

It was long after midnight when the ten Termites together with Mabel and Paul stumbled and banged their way down the front stairs of the Writers' Nook and on to the pavement in Water Lane. Jerry was the first to raise the cry: 'Do we go on?'

'Yes!' was the unanimous response, Paul included.

'Where to, then?' Jerry yelled.

'The Jam Pot!' they all shouted back.

They roared down the Lane and bundled into Mason's spacious American station wagon which he had left parked outside the Niagara.

The Jam Pot was an expensive night club in Upper Saint Andrew which remained open sometimes until seven o'clock in the morning. The proprietor, Major Derek Carshalton, believed implicitly in kicking his customers where their pound notes are thinnest, as Silba announced at the top of his voice during a pause in the floor show at the club's first Christmas Eve ball. The Major was flattered. After the floor show, he congratulated Silba on what he called a well-timed offensive.

'Very English, that,' the Major said almost too jubilantly, too openly, 'desperately English, in fact. Does the Pot the world of good to have chaps like you around. Magnificent job of heckling.' And that was precisely the way Silba found out how best to get around the Major. And of course, when the Major discovered that Silba had served in the RAF, naturally Silba's 'Englishness' became even more manifest; he was the first Termite to be given a wine card, and right after that, Wyn, the only other ex-RAF Termite. Within a week, Silba and Wyn had, somehow, managed to have the other Termites put on the books. The Major, however, had to think twice about honouring Paula and Jenny, but Silba again was courageous and adroit. 'They're English, too, Major, but their hearts are in the right place, deep in their Barclay's DCO cheque books, and just as inky black as yours and mine.' Then they shared a broad mutually admiring smile. The Major was flattered again. He had also been particularly attracted by the dramatic use of the word black, which he took as a sign that he had been fully accepted as an Islander, and that, at long last, his Englishness had become of no importance, at least, to the Termites.

But in spite of all that, the Major's prices were among the steepest and most scandalous in the Island. In his own defence he would say, 'If I don't charge a damn' good lick, somebody else will.' And if he were pressed still harder, he would laugh hoarsely, swish both sides of his cream serge double-breasted dinner jacket round to the small of his back and say, 'The steeper the prices, the bigger the mystique. High prices and class-aspiration are fellow travellers. The Pot will live; don't you worry about that.'

As the Termites drove in to the forecourt, part of the chorus and the last verse of a *mento* boomed out to meet them:

> Solderin'!
> Is wha' de young gal want,
> Solderin'!
> Gal, from I know you,

You never make me lay down
'Pon top o' you' belly
An' bruck water give you.
Solderin'!

Three o'clock. The band was playing *Cuernavaca Mambo*. Paula and Jerry were dancing closely. 'I don't honestly think Albert would approve,' Paula teased and then slammed her body hard against Jerry's thighs and middle even more closely.

'It won't kill him,' Jerry said and absorbed the broad impact of her frame.

They were jostled to the centre of the floor where the concealed spotlight was positioned for the late cabaret : part of the Major's plan of action for entertaining his patrons, part of his habit of tactical planning. The music stopped abruptly; the spotlight swung into action; and Paula and Jerry were caught kissing. The compère's announcement further complicated the situation. 'A'right, a'rightie!' he warned in his hoarse warmed-over American accent. 'We've caught you where it's sweetest. Ladies and gentlemen, we present our first act : the spotlight lovers!' The band rattled and snarled an excursion, half classical, half improvised *mento*. 'Our spotlight lovers will dance . . .' and then he paused, turned to the band and said, 'What's it goin' to be, boys?' The boys, fully rehearsed, unanimously suggested *Mambo No. 5*.

But before the compère could turn round again, Albert had dashed on to the floor. He tore Paula away from Jerry, slapped her face twice and punched Jerry on the nose and kicked him in the ribs. Jerry scrambled to his feet, knocked him down and went after Paula.

In a desperate effort to get at Jerry, Albert grabbed a chair and threw it at him. Jerry ducked in time and the chair landed in a party of civil servants. One of the women in the party immediately hurled it back at Albert and missed him. The chair crashed into yet another party of civil servants, and two members of each offended party leapt up, knocking over everything in sight in their attempt to get at one another. As soon as they met in the centre of the floor, other interested groups rushed in, some in sympathy and prepared to take sides, some out of sheer curiosity and not.

Pandemonium. Tables were overturned. Glasses and bottles were flung and smashed. Columns and walls were splashed with drink. Fists flashed and battered bodies helter-skelter. There were volleys of screams, obscenities, and blood. The Major grabbed the microphone and announced, 'We're all free men! Freedom and discipline, eh!' A bottle caught him at the back of the head and sent him reeling towards the bar. Shortly afterwards, he was beaten up at the cash register, a distance of nearly sixty feet away from the hub of the outbreak. He raised the key of the register, dangled it and shouted, 'Law and order.' Somebody snatched the key from his hand and dropped it into the cistern of washing-up water.

The members of the band had retreated to the back of the bandstand and the compressed cardboard star-and-sky canopy and its wire scantling had fallen in on them, pinning them down securely. Berto had climbed on to the lattice-work at the side of the bandstand, positioned himself expertly, and was taking pictures of the brawl.

The fighting spread to the club entrance, and male and female bodies were being heaved and propelled into the car park. Jerry found himself propped up against a 1939 Buick.

'Slip in beside us, Jerry,' someone said.

A little dazed, Jerry stumbled to the side of the Buick and came face to face with Lola and her escort, a fellow civil servant from the Colonial Secetariat. Suddenly, the top of a table came crashing into the windshield of the Buick, and Lola's escort, who had been half-hidden in the shadow of the steering wheel up until then, his body sunk deep into the driver's-seat, leapt out of the car angrily and chased after a man whom he thought had thrown the table-top. Lola opened her door and pulled Jerry down towards her. He plopped heavily on to her large cushiony breasts and sank easily into

44

the soft parts of her broad stomach and thighs. She hugged him and kissed his lips and neck. 'Not to worry,' she consoled him, 'he ain't nothing to me, and besides, he ain't getting any rudeness.' She unzipped the side of her skirt. 'He ain't coming back in a hurry, by the looks o' t'ings to me.' She shifted her position on the seat and made herself attractively accommodating. Jerry uttered a mild protest, something about going back inside to see if the girls were all right, but Lola had begun to encourage him passionately. They remained locked together for several minutes while the fighting outside became more brutal and boisterous.

Jerry felt surprisingly sober. He gave Lola a parting kiss and ran back into the club. He was knocked down twice while bulldozing his way to the corner of the room where he had left the girls. When he got there he found Paula, Sally, Jenny and Mabel neatly wedged behind a pile of broken chairs and tables. He led them into the bar, through the back door of the kitchen, round the side yard, and into the car park. He had difficulty in finding Mason's station wagon but as soon as he had, he bundled the girls inside and ran back to the club. This time he made sure that he dealt the blows first which he aimed as wildly and as offensively as he could. He glimpsed Mason, Van, Berto and Silba scrapping and defending themselves as a group at the entrance to the women's toilet. He grabbed Berto. 'Anybody missing? Where's Albert? And Wyn?'

'Dunno, boy,' Berto said, ducking stylishly out of the way of a flying bottle which crashed against the wall next to Silba.

'Where's Paul?' Jerry asked.

'Search me,' Berto said, clutching his camera to his chest.

'We've got to find them and get out before the police arrive. Sure the Major's seen to that already.' A sliver of windshield glass slipped off the elbow of his jacket and splintered on the floor. He looked down at it and smiled.

In the meanwhile, Mason, Van and Silba were throwing punches and ducking and looking over their shoulders to see if anybody was creeping up on them from behind. Someone shouted, 'Police!' and there was a hectic rush for all the doors and windows in the club. Jerry, Mason, Van, Berto and Silba kept closely together and ran Indian file into the women's toilet and out through a small window above a paper-towel rack. When they got to the station wagon, they found Paul, Wyn and Albert waiting for them. 'How's the old pacifist?' Jerry smiled at Wyn. Wyn grinned, licking blood from the corner of his mouth.

Mason reversed the wagon about thirty yards up the car park and drove through the Major's private drive gate. He headed the wagon towards Stony Hill but nobody questioned his obvious misdirection. 'We're going to the country,' he called out when the wagon rounded Red Gal Ring. 'No work today, so what's the odds.'

'I know a little man in Dallas,' Jerry said, suddenly inspired. 'He's up at the Courts nearly every other week. If it isn't Assault, it's Indecent Language or something else. Always on to me to come up and see him. Always promising free rum and food. He's got some kind of grocery and rum bar. What about it?'

'Dallas?' Mason asked. 'The other side, isn't it?'

'Yes,' Jerry said hopefully. 'Might as well.'

'Fine by me, Jerry. We've got to keep scarce for a few hours, anyway.' He turned the station wagon round at a convenient spot in the narrow lane and hoped he would find the right road for Dallas. The others in the back seats had dozed off. Berto had his head in Mabel's lap and his camera stuck between his legs. Jerry took it from him and passed it up front to Jenny who slipped it into one of the spacious dashboard cabinets. Mason checked the lock on the cabinet, depressed it a couple of times and slammed the metal flap shut.

Chapter Seven

It was long after seven o'clock on Friday morning when the station wagon jerked to a stop on the marl road leading into the small village of Dallas.

'Where to, now?' Mason asked Jerry.

'Don't ask me.' Jerry chuckled insecurely.

'What's your man's name?'

'Don't ask me that, either.'

'Don't you know?'

'Coming back slowly,' Jerry promised, tapping his fingers on his knees and chuckling nervously. 'Don't rush me. Coming up.'

Mason drove into the village. Three little boys came out to meet the wagon. Mason braked just in front of them.

'Know a man with a rum shop round here, sonny?' Jerry asked the boy nearest him.

'Missa P.D.?' all three said.

'Always going to Court House at Half Way Tree,' Jerry explained.

'Is 'im same one,' the boy farthest away said.

'What's the P.D. for?' Mason asked the boys.

'Name,' one said simply.

'What name?'

'Percy Dixon, sah,' another boy said and tittered confidently.

Mason told them to sit on the front fenders and show him the way to the rum shop. They liked the idea and Mason drove slowly, partly to avoid any possible accident and partly to prolong the drive for the boys. After about a half-mile, the boys hopped off the fenders and disappeared into a clump of wild aurelia at the side of a narrow track.

'You don't think they want us to follow them?' Mason asked Jerry.

Jerry got out of the wagon and walked to the wild aurelia and parted the branches. He saw the three boys climbing a wall which separated the track from a dry river bed. 'We've been ditched!' he called back to Mason, and he explained what had happened. They both laughed, and Jenny sat up. When they told her what had happened, she nodded her approval.

'I hope I shan't hear any more nonsense about the peasant children being simple, innocent, under-privileged colonials,' she said, clapping her hands and ridiculing them both.

'Can we turn round?' Jerry asked.

'Hardly,' Mason told him.

'Let's see what's ahead for a bit, eh?'

Mason drove much faster and found a spot wide enough to reverse the wagon. Just as he was about to do so, a voice called out from behind a breadfruit tree.

'Bless eyesight if it isn't Missa Stover 'imself from Court House! Wha' you doin' in me back yard?'

Jerry recognised Percy Dixon as he came running towards the station wagon. Jerry and Mason were glad to be rescued. The others were still sleeping soundly. Jenny didn't know quite what to think. She was fairly sure of one thing: she liked P.D.

He sat on the right fender and directed Mason to the centre of the village. When they arrived, he opened the driver's-door and helped Mason and Jenny out. Jerry got out on the other side and ran round to shake his hand. 'Look, Mr Dixon, we're on the loose for a few hours.'

P.D. was delighted. 'Got a good store o' Black Seal,' he told him, 'the real ol'-time bottles wid 'nough dus' an' cob-web.'

As they were entering the shop from the back, three little boys ran into the yard and circled P.D. They were the same boys who had deserted Mason earlier on. They mumbled some-thing to P.D. and he shook his head. 'Mine,' he told Jerry. 'You see, when police come wid summons, a man got to know how to dodge or else 'im live in Court House all year roun'. Special trade o' mine, dodgin' summons-server.'

He led Jenny, Mason and Jerry into the back room of the shop. It was spacious and spotlessly clean. The long low table was scrubbed foam white, and the air was light and scented with country jasmine which grew outside the shop. He pointed to his outhouse washroom and pit toilet. 'Better fresh' up while I get the Missis to fix the food. You can find soap, an' the boys will fetch water as you want.'

Jenny and Mason were very impressed. Jerry was won-dering how much it would cost, even with going Russian doubly. P.D.'s clever charm might be very expensive in the long run, he thought.

As if he had read Jerry's thoughts, P.D. pointed at him accusingly. 'Business is only for people who can't afford to thank God for the good t'ings in life, Jerry.' He paused. 'The entire car load can't eat an' drink me out. Never! An' you been doin' me plenty favours down at Court House, so now the table turn an' my time come.' He rubbed his hands together. He left the back room and entered the shop.

After they had washed, they followed him in. Spread along the length of the counter was a floral oil-cloth. On it P.D. had placed five vintage quart bottles of Black Seal, about two dozen shot glasses, packets of Four Aces and Royal Blend cigarettes, hard dough bread, butter, about two dozen enamel mugs, plates, knives, forks and spoons. 'I sorry 'bout no ice, but I suppose you can do widout for the time being',' he apologised.

Jerry pointed to one of the vintage quarts, rubbed his hands appreciatively and smacked his lips.

'Man, you sure can belt it on empty stomach,' P.D. said with great admiration.

'They've been practising for years, my dear P.D.,' Jenny said, curling her lips in pretended nausea. 'These two could drink Lysol without batting an eyelid.'

P.D. winced at the mention of Lysol. 'That word cause me a lot o' worries in the distric', you know. Now an' then, somebody drink the t'ing an' get 'way from payin' me me rent. Wicked drink that, mos' wicked.'

All four had a pre-breakfast drink and discussed its smoothness and potency. P.D.'s wife and two small girls came in with trays laden with *ackee* and salt fish, tinned salmon and boiled eggs, avocado pears, *ponderoso* tomatoes, salted cucumber, Scotch bonnet peppers, Johnny cakes, boiled rice and steaming hot country chocolate. P.D. introduced his wife and two daughters and promised that there would be more of his children to introduce when they all got back from their early morning digging and planting. 'Chil'ren pure blessing, people say,' he said doubtfully. 'They should know how much it cos' to feed the blessing.' He excused himself graciously and went out to call the others in from the station wagon.

The breakfast was taken in the country-style, long and leisurely, everybody having second or third helpings. Most of the Termites ignored the country chocolate. P.D. noticed it and complimented them on their good sense in leaving it alone. 'Pure woman drink that,' he said. 'Rot the guts sure as fate.'

After breakfast, Paul announced that he had to go back to town. The others teased him, but he was adamant. He said that he had to do some work at the office and one or two things had to be seen to at the club. Berto sympathised and asked him to take his rolls of film in to the *Springboard*. Paula asked him to take in her report, which she dictated to Mabel in a few minutes.

'Institute lecture and pictures of the Pot about to be delivered,' Paul said and asked Mason to drive him to the main road.

'Coming, Mabes?' Mason asked.

She smiled. 'No such luck.'

Paul frowned and then quickly shrugged his shoulders. He was hurt, and Mabel knew it and revelled in her new attachment to Berto. He, however, was unmoved, stale drunk, and on the way to becoming even more drunk. He raised his glass to Paul and winked.

The drive out to the main road seemed shorter to Mason. Paul nodded and said something about the early-morning heat. Mason grunted his agreement.

'What's bothering you?' he asked Paul, and when it was obvious that he wasn't going to get a reply, he added, 'Mabes?'

'Look, Mason, you're an intelligent man. I want to get to the bottom of this business between Mabel and Berto. She's nearly off her head with this Termite idiocy.'

'Mabel's old enough.'

'So're you, Mason.'

'My business, Paul.'

'Oxford, man!'

'What's that got to do with the price of rum?'

'It means you're educated. You can think like an adult. The Termites are all small boys, *rassed* up by the Island and floundering like bitch, man.'

'Oxford meant a list of books to read, lectures to go to, essays to write, tutorials, and imitation.'

'What're you trying to say?'

'Got a degree out of it, Paul; that's about all.'

'That's more than most people ever get out of a whole life-time anywhere. Couldn't you lead the others to something real and profitable? Make them settle down to something reasonable?'

'Like getting Berto to hand back Mabes?'

Paul shrugged.

Mason continued, 'What d'you think the university is anyway, Paul? A moral influence?'

'It ought to be.'

'What you really want are loads of reformers, teachers, philosophers and moralists, opening shop all over the Island. I'm only one of the returned grey blobs, and one without a vocation.'

Paul was silent. Mason began to hum a *mento*. They got to the main road, and Mason waited with Paul until his bus arrived.

On his way back to P.D.'s rum shop, Mason thought about Paul and his peculiar anxiety about Mabel, about his Victorian reverence for the university graduate, and indeed, of his own carelessness, his own rootlessness.

Mason had been sent up to Oxford because his father before him had been. He read English because his father had done so. And he tried to get a 'First' because this is also what his father had got. He came down with a good 'Second', and had returned in time for his father's funeral.

He parked the station wagon and walked into the rum shop. The Termites were talking loudly and gesticulating. He thought again of Paul and wondered just what he had meant. This was his slice of Island life. This was what was happening to him and it all had a meaning far beyond its everyday, meaningless appearance, far beyond its apparent exhibitionism and escape. He joined in wholeheartedly by pouring himself a half-glass of rum and gulping it down. He poured another in a shot glass and did the same. The impact was the same, though the measures were different. He lit a cigarette and went in search of Jerry. He found him in a corner of the room sitting by himself. He sat beside him and said nothing.

Jerry turned and winked.

'I suppose my old man's money shows through,' he said to Jerry. 'Does it make me look terribly different from you and the others?'

'Black Seal levels,' Jerry said.

Mason told him what Paul had said on the way to the bus stop.

'Mabel's Paul's problem,' Jerry said, 'And Berto's the hog in Paul's cocoa. Life.'

P.D. stood behind the counter and stared at his young visitors. Each was a guest of honour; for P.D., all civil servants were guests of honour, charming, complex and privileged. Indeed, for many others, the Civil Service was Island society at its most enviably concrete, its most fruitfully realised, the very essence of an emancipated and progressive élite. The service was always a good target to aim at, to aim one's children at, successive generations breaking out of the mould of one kind of mediocrity and hurling themselves headlong into another: from domestic servant to Courts Office messenger; from plantation time-keeper, assistant tally-man, or book-keeper to accounts clerk in the G.P.O.; from pupil teacher to temporary clerk in the Education Department; from elementary school headmaster to sub-Inspector of schools; from small farmer to Agricultural Inspector or Travelling Officer in the Lands Department; from solicitor's clerk *via* Gray's Inn to the Solicitor General's Office; from freelance journalist and occasional short story writer to G.P.R.O.; from newspaper sub-editor to Head of News in radio; in no special sequence of ascendancy, with ever-increasing frequency, year after year.

Mason left Jerry and leant against the counter and watched P.D.'s face. He wasn't at all sure of what he was supposed to be watching for or why, or indeed, just what he was hoping to find, but he kept staring; he felt he should and he did so. P.D. smiled and offered him a vintage bottle.

Silba and Paula were sitting comfortably wedged between two large codfish crates in a far corner. He had his right hand tucked into the top of her blouse, and she was drinking from his glass which was tilting precariously in his left. Her legs were crossed and clenched tightly up to her upper thighs.

Mabel was sitting on Berto's knees and humming snatches from *Brown skin gal, stay home an' min' baby* in a tired, doleful minor key while he listlessly massaged her bottom.

Albert and Wyn were maligning Kirby-Rybik politics. Jenny, Van and Sally were recounting what they called the Jam Pot siege.

By mid-day everybody was irresponsibly alive and affectionate. Outside, small groups of villagers were passing the usual remarks about the visitors and telling stories they knew would flatter the strange, liberated young people from Kingston. For the villagers, all good civil servants and their friends came from Kingston.

Imperceptibly, and just as P.D. had planned it, the Termites had been joined by the hard-drinking representatives of the village. It was the kind of bottle conference that he had hoped for and had every intention of sustaining now that it had actually come to Dallas.

Paula slipped away from Silba's grasp and ran over to Albert. 'D'you know what the Pot crowd are calling me? White trash! Because of last night and because of you. Proud?' She sounded brazenly aggressive.

Albert backed away.

'We're through, Albert,' she said, inching towards him.

'Right,' Albert said.

'I want Silba and I've got him. *Right?*'

Albert didn't answer. The others were absolutely quiet. Jerry moved towards Paula.

'I could've had you, if I wanted,' she said to him and laughed.

Jerry backed away. Silba got up and started towards Paula. Albert jumped him and knocked him down. Silba got up, slightly dazed and staggered to a chair; he was fighting to get back his breath. Albert sprang at him and collared him with both hands and squeezed his neck. Then he rushed to the nearest wall and banged Silba's head on it. P.D. dashed towards them and held them apart. Albert got loose and pushed P.D. away. P.D. fell and chuckled to himself, while remaining where he had fallen on the shop floor beside a huge crocus bag of brown sugar. Silba grabbed Albert and struck him behind his neck a couple of times and brought up his knee under his crotch. Albert sagged and collapsed beside P.D. P.D. got up, lifted him into the back room and laid him out on the table in the centre of the room. Silba followed him inside. P.D. had Albert's head cradled in his arms.

'You mus' be learn the knee tactics in some bad town fightin', nuh?' he asked Silba who didn't reply.

P.D.'s wife came in with a bottle of Bay Rum and bathed Albert's face with it. He came round slowly. The pain in his groin grew less, and he rubbed the back of his neck and spat little blobs of blood into his shirt.

'You won't always win,' he said to Silba who was sitting at the bottom of the table.

Silba hung his head.

Jerry felt tired. He had been going since Thursday lunch time. He knew that he had to ease up, if only for an hour or so. He noticed Paula waving to him and he waved back. She beckoned him slyly. He hesitated. She stood up. He ignored her and sat down. She walked over to him. 'Too sober to talk to me?' she asked.

'You drunk enough?'

She moaned impatiently. 'Let's sit in the station wagon,' she said.

He followed her. They sat in the row behind the driver's-seat. He lit a cigarette and placed his legs over the top of the flaking upholstery. He imagined the next scene of jealousy and the fight with his good friend. He crossed his legs. Paula slid round and rested her head in the crease between his chest and his stomach. They were resuming their nervous game.

Jerry held her round her waist awkwardly and mumbled the appropriate words of false endearment which made him feel useless and guilty.

She's one of us, he thought. Stupidly one of us. Hopelessly drifting, confused, dependent, like all of us. What do I do now? He held himself in check. The pressure of her body impressed itself directly on his, but he fought to control himself.

'You're tense, Jerry,' she said tenderly.

'I know.'

'Why are you fighting it?'

'Don't know.'

'Do you want to?'

'No.'

'A farewell before Silba?'

'No.'

From where Jerry was sitting, he could see P.D.'s wife and the two girls carrying the food to the table in the back yard. He could also see P.D., dancing attendance on his guests, and the musicians, arriving from the outskirts of the village.

'Food!' P.D. shouted. 'We goin' eat firs' t'ing, then we goin' jump up later.' He danced a ragged *shey-shey*.

'Changed your mind?'

'No.'

'I could rape you.' She laughed quietly.

'Like hell.'

She nestled her head slowly, gradually, with increasing pressure, into his midde. Then she raised her left shoulder and drove it sharply into his groin. She got up and said, 'They'll notice we're not there, I suppose. We'd better go back.'

'You O.K.?' he asked with cool irony.

'Fine. You?'

They walked slowly from the station wagon and headed towards the table. They tried to give no hint of what had transpired between them. Paula assumed a casual, light-hearted, faintly careless air. Jerry was wishing away the pain in his groin and refusing to rub the spot. Silba met them, smiled drunkenly at Jerry, and led Paula to her position at lunch.

P.D. had prepared a feast. There were huge tureens of white rice, curried goat and 'jerk' pork; P.D.'s wife was unloading a tray of firm fried plantains, sliced avocado pears, sweet potatoes and three large jars of pickled peppers. Everybody ate ravenously and P.D. was pleased.

It was six-thirty. Dusk had fallen quickly. The musicians had taken up their positions on the sturdiest of the milk crates in the yard. P.D. stood before them and waved an imaginary baton. 'Jump-up for those who can stan' up straight!' he ordered. He guffawed and gesticulated, pointing to his protruding belly and patting it lightly.

Jerry looked around the back yard, and for the first time, he saw the young women of Dallas, attractively dressed, barefooted and shy. They had obviously been waiting for P.D.'s invitation ever since they had heard he was entertaining his friends from Kingston.

The music began. The Termites, Mabel and the others took off their shoes and jostled their way among the dancing couples.

'Country style, drop you' drawers!' Van exclaimed and waved frantically to no one in particular.

'Bruckin's!' Wyn shouted back.

Mabel was dancing with Berto and holding him up expertly. 'Support me, sweet girl,' he said, 'nice and low, tight and slow.'

'You lie down and take a rest after this one, eh?' she advised cautiously.

'Never,' he boasted. 'Die first!'

'You can go alone when the time comes,' she replied and guided him gently towards the nearest doorway, coaxing him along and giving him the full spread of her body and pushing and heaving into him, as she went.

Mason and Jenny had been exchanging partners so rapidly

that they had again met before the music had had time to stop. They were both breathless and sweating.

Sally was dancing with Van and putting on an exhibition of improvised *shey-shey*, spiced with free form *adagio*. Paula and Silba were standing near the musicians and beating time to the *mento* lilt with their feet. Albert and Wyn were dancing with local girls.

Jerry stood behind the table and held a tall drink. He spotted Mason and Jenny and waved with his glass. He admired them. In all the chaos of Termite life, Mason and Jenny had managed to remain faithful to each other. The Termites took their mutual fidelity for granted.

Jerry sat at the table with his back turned to the dancers. He finished his drink and poured another, chased with a drop of fresh lime and water. Will he really return? he wondered. Then he thought of his mother. He chuckled quietly and gulped down his drink. He forgot the matter and put his head down on the table.

'Let's dance!' He looked up and saw Sally clutching his arm and making 'stamp-and-go' movements with her hips and legs.

They were swept up in the mass of swirling, bouncing bodies in the centre of the yard. Sally clung to him and forced his head downwards and kissed him. He was drunk enough not to care. They clung to each other, kissing and being bounced along from one end of the yard to the other until the music stopped.

'Let's go over to the coffee-walk when it starts up again,' she suggested.

'Why wait?' he asked and squeezed her waist.

'Reckless?' she said, countering his sudden daring.

'Anything to please.' He bowed and stumbled. She straightened him up and placed his right arm over her shoulder.

The music began again, and they were jostled along, as she had hoped. They found themselves on the outside of the circular mass of dancers, and they walked away casually.

'How d'you know about the coffee-walk?' he asked her, playfully twisting her right ear.

'Mabel and Berto,' she said, slipping away from him and imitating his drunken stride.

They passed the station wagon. A voice called out.

'That you, Berto?' Sally asked and turned round.

Jerry tried to stop her but she began to run towards the wagon before he could call her back or get hold of her arm. As soon as she got up to the door, she turned away suddenly, put her hand to her mouth and ran back to Jerry. She said nothing. He knew that something was wrong but he decided to wait, realising that he would hear in time, when it suited her to tell him.

They entered the coffee-walk and sat down on a mound of dry leaves. Jerry lit a cigarette and buried the dying match in a loose clump of parched earth. Sally turned to face him.

'I've got to,' she said.

'Not if you don't really want to,' he said, stubbing out his cigarette under the heel of his shoe.

'I want to.'

'Well, why did he call out?'

'That's what I don't understand, Jerry.'

He waited.

'Why?' she asked herself, her voice faltering slightly. 'Why did he bother?'

'Does it matter?'

'Of course, it matters, Jerry. He must've known I'd see her.'

'Mabel?'

'No.'

'Well?'

She hugged herself and hung her head in an attitude of concentration and doubt. 'It's such a shock. I don't know what to think, what to make of it. I don't even know what to say I saw.'

'One of the girls from the village?' Jerry tried to keep her talking.

'I don't know what to believe any more.' She rubbed her eyes and blinked.

'Right. Who did Berto have with him, Sally?' He gripped her shoulders firmly and held her at arm's length.

'No!'

'Come on, now.'

'Don't ask me, please.' She started to cry, and between sobs, she said, 'Jenny.'

It was early Saturday morning. None of the Termites escaped the usual pangs of remorse. Jerry had a good deal of explaining to do at home and at the office. Home was easy; he had the urge to tell the truth; in fact, he told it with relish. The office was a different matter; it was difficult; he had to lie. And so had Van. Randy, however, was not convinced and said so. His warning was authoritative and menacing.

Jerry and Van left work at one o'clock. They were both grateful for the half-day closure. They got to the front entrance of the Administrator General's Office at about the same time. Silba was waiting for them. He was leaning against one of the huge white-washed columns at the Barry Street side of the building. He looked perversely rested and fit, elegantly dressed, and ready to become involved in the first available plan of action.

'Skirt-watch for a bit?' he asked eagerly, hoping it would lead to something positive and rewarding.

'Might as well,' Van said.

'Please yourselves,' Jerry muttered, thinking about Berto and Jenny, and Silba and Paula. He leant against the column next to Silba's, and in his stale-drunk reverie, he asked himself: Why should all this matter? What am I proving to myself by pretending to care?

Silba was exclaiming, sometimes jumping up and down and sometimes calling out to the shop girls and Civil Service secretaries who were passing by and ignoring him with studied pertness. He eyed them all, sizing them up speculatively, imagining, inventing, never censoring, and exhausting himself. 'D'you know something, Van,' he admitted, 'there's nothing to beat the beefy recklessness of a real high-pitched black arse. But nothing!'

Van chuckled. 'You're a poet, and I'm proud of you, Master,' he said mock-respectfully.

Silba laughed and slapped his thighs jazz-style.

Jerry remembered his appointment with the Syrian girl at the Carib Theatre. He still had a few hours to wait. 'Think I'll buy the *Springboard* and take a stroll,' he told Van.

'The Niagara for me,' Van said.

'Meet you there, then, Jerry,' Silba agreed.

'Half an hour.' Jerry moved off.'

They parted at Tower Street and Temple Lane. Jerry continued down Tower Street to the Institute. He bought the *Springboard* on the way, crossed over to East Street and climbed the library steps slowly, counting them under his breath. He walked across the reading-room and sat on the window-ledge. He read Paula's article in the *Springboard*, then he looked at Berto's pictures of the Jam Pot brawl.

He had been there about twenty minutes when he felt somebody tap him on his shoulder. He looked up and his Syrian girl friend smiled. 'Saw you when you came in,' she whispered.

'Miss Cole might descend on us if we keep this up,' he suggested. He took her arm and tip-toed past Pet Cole, the assistant librarian. When they were outside, he turned left and pointed to the reptile garden. They sat on the first bench they came to.

'What's your name?' he asked.

'Carmen Dabdood.'

'Jerry Stover.'

'Carmen,' she completed the courtesy exchange.

'Jerry,' he said and offered her a cigarette, and she accepted. 'You always smoke?'

'Not often. Only when I'm offered one. Incidentally, why don't you get on with Pet?'

'She's a librarian; I'm a mere reader.'

'We went to Saint Hugh's. She's a bit stand-offish. Always was.'

'Some black people are.'

'Like you, maybe?'

'Blacker.' He smiled. 'Where d'you hang out?'

'I don't.'

'Live, then.'

'Retirement Road. 9a.'

'How's "mister man"?'

'Everything's fine, now, thank you.'

'No more Slander?'

'No.'

'How'd you manage?'

'Mother fixed things.'

'We still go to Carib, I hope?'

'Sure.'

Her reply gave him new confidence. 'Glad everything's patched up.'

'Oh?' She was curious.

'Haven't a clue about Slander. Didn't even ask at the Office, to tell the truth.'

'So we meet this afternoon on false pretences perhaps?'

He liked talking to her. She was an attractive change for him, especially after his recent close association with Mabel, Sally, Paula and Jenny. He tried to find something definitive about her Syrianness but he could find nothing he could be sure of, or which would add up to something he might be able to recognise; he tried again but he soon gave up and stopped searching. She was simply a welcome change, for him, after the Termites, an extremely interesting find, a lovely light brown-skinned girl whom he would try desperately hard to make.

'What're you going to do between now and four o'clock?' he asked.

'Go home, I suppose. Why d'you ask?'

'Nothing.' He felt stupid. She was obviously not a Termite. He would not have had to ask that kind of question. He knew he had to change his style. He had to think again. He must not be caught off balance.

'Would you like to meet my mother? It would give us both something to do until Carib. I told her I was meeting you this afternoon.'

He was surprised but tried not to show it. They walked across to Church Street and took a Beechwood Avenue bus. When they got in, Carmen's mother was not at home. She had left a note.

'Mother's gone out,' Carmen said.

'Pity,' was all he said; he delighted in the lie in his remark.

She took him into the sitting-room and offered him a glass of lemonade. He accepted. They sat on the sofa and talked about her imminent departure to America. He finished his lemonade and lit a cigarette; he conveniently forgot to offer her one.

'What're you going to do?' he asked her.

'Music.'

'Where?'

'Julliard.'

'My brother's a graduate.'

'Piano?'

'Hmm.'

Carmen's interest was obvious, yet she didn't follow it through. She deliberately held herself back and Jerry noticed her restraint. 'You seem surprised?' he said directly.

'What does your brother do?'

'Teaches. At home.'

'No concerts?'

He grimaced. Then he asked casually, 'Boy friend?'

'Not now.'

'What happened?'

'Nothing, really.'

'Nothing?'

'More lemonade?'

He was relieved. She told him what she wanted to do in America after she graduated. He listened and nodded. It wasn't his world and he was willing to be informed, guided from one wild hope to the other, each more alien to him than the other.

'You hope to do all that in how many years?'

'Six, maybe seven years. America's a big country, and then there's the Continent and London, of course.'

'A lot of time and money.'

'Mother's always wanted me to study Music and travel while doing it.'

'Where's your father?'

'Dead,' she replied offhandedly.

'And your old lady's in charge?'

'Of what?'

'His business.'

'He didn't leave a thing. It's all Mother's money, actually.'

'Was your father Syrian?'

'Yes, but not Mother. She's a little lighter than you. An Islander. Father came from Syria.'

'Wouldn't have guessed hadn't you told me,' he said; then he realised the idiocy of his reply.

'How could you have guessed, Jerry? Either could have been Syrian. More likely the old man, I suppose. History and race relations and stuff like that.'

He liked her easy charm, her poise, her dignity. He liked her calling him Jerry. 'Sorry about the quiz,' he said, shrugging self-consciously.

'I don't think of myself as coloured or Negro or mixed or anything. Too Syrian-looking for that. And thank goodness, the Americans won't guess. I hope not.'

'Americans don't guess, Carmen. They *know*.'

'I'm safe where that's concerned.'

'They know everything. Even if you have two ounces of Negro blood. They use a thing called a **niggerometer** and they hound out every drop of black blood in your veins and bring it right to the surface with a loud *pop*.'

They leant forward slightly, stared at each other and laughed loudly. They stopped laughing long enough to look at each other a second time, and then they began again. She held on to his right arm and wasn't aware she had done so. He kissed her.

'I had a feeling you were going to do that,' she said affectionately, touching his lips tenderly and smiling. 'I've been waiting.'

'How long?' He held her hand.

'Since Thursday,' she said simply.

They kissed again. Then they got up and walked into the adjoining bedroom.

Book Two

. . . what can we recall of a dead slave or two
except that when we punctuate our Island tale
they swing like sighs across the brutal
sentences, and anger pauses
till they pass away.

Dennis Scott   *Epitaph*

Chapter Eight

Mrs Stover received a cablegram two days before her husband was due to arrive:

PLANS CHANGED. IMPOSSIBLE HAPPENED. LETTER
FOLLOWS.

The letter came on a Saturday afternoon three days later and Mrs Stover called Les and Jerry to her room and read it to them.

'*I've picked up the grand prize on the Lottery, enough to help fix things. I don't think I ought to leave right away. I'll be coming over on holiday, as soon as I can get things working again. It will take a bit of negotiating but I'll manage.*'

For the rest of that afternoon Jerry stayed in his bedroom. He sprawled across his bed and buried his face in his pillow. He thought: Bit of a puzzle. At least he's broken even, more or less. Yet, I wonder why he . . . ? He fell asleep and his dreams came one after the other, terrifying and erratic. He awoke to hear Thelma outside in the dining-room laying the supper table. He flopped back on to the bed and waited for her to call him. He thought about certain images in his dreams, fragments he could recall, one or two faces he seemed to recognise.

Thelma struck the supper gong. He felt tense and irritable. He went to the bathroom, brushed his teeth, washed his face and the back of his neck, sponged his arms and chest, and dried himself vigorously with a rough towel. He tried to convince himself that he ought to be hungry. Thelma was in one of her happy, mumbling moods. She had been preparing herself for Mr Stover's arrival. She was serving and saying, 'Nice to 'ave a real proper man to look after at las'. Mus' get everyt'ing lookin' lovely an' so. Can't wait to see wha' he look like.'

Mrs Stover heard her last few words. 'He isn't coming, Thelma.'

'Why so?'

'Change of plans,' Jerry said. He felt genuinely sorry for her.

She went into the kitchen.

Les sighed and heaped his plate with bread and butter. Mrs Stover said the grace slowly, while Les and Jerry closed their eyes and bowed their heads. When she was finished, she poured herself a cup of country chocolate and sipped it, looking towards the kitchen and silently hoping that Thelma would not ask any more questions.

Les asked Jerry what he thought of the report of the Celebrity lecture in the *Springboard* which he had read two weeks before. 'She one of your friends?'

'Yes.'

'Stupidly provocative.'

'Your opinion.'

'Why do expatriates carry the old native burden so well, as if they're the only ones capable of understanding it?'

'Maybe they do.'

70

Their mother looked from one face to the other, during the exchange, and asked, 'What's this about?'

'Paula Watt's report of the American sociologist's lecture at the Institute,' Jerry said, 'two weeks ago.'

'Expatriates are often highly perceptive about our affairs,' she said, smiling at Les. 'Anyway, the lecturer ought to come and live with us. We could give him enough to lecture about for a lifetime.'

They left the supper table and Thelma came in and cleared it. Jerry went back to his bedroom. Les picked up a sheath of sheet music from the music room and sat on the front veranda. Mrs Stover went out to the back garden.

Thelma wandered into Jerry's room with a letter. 'It came from early mornin' but I didn't 'member to give it to you,' she said. 'Hope it not too late.' She put it on his pillow, looked around the room in her usual proprietorial manner and left quietly.

The letter was from Prudence Kirby.

Dear Jerry,

I'd like you to come to this month's editorial meeting. We have a lot to discuss. I've invited a few people you might like to meet. We ought to have a very good meeting, as I trust we'll find a great deal to disagree about, particularly about the new format for the magazine.

At my house on Sunday, then. Four-thirty.

Sincerely,
Prudence Kirby.

Jerry crushed the letter and threw it on the floor. The meeting was the next day and he had no intention of going. He wondered whom she had invited.

At eight o'clock he went out. He wanted to see Carmen, to talk to her about anything, everything. She was in; so was her mother. Mrs Dabdood was dressed to go out. 'Hello, Jerry,' she said, clapping her hands. 'I'm glad you've come round tonight. You can keep Carmen company. I wanted to take her to the Women's League end-of-term party but she isn't interested.' She left the room breezily.

Carmen kissed Jerry. 'What's wrong?'

'Do I look it?' he said, leading her to the sofa. She jeered sympathetically and touched the tip of his nose.

Her mother passed through, waving them both goodbye. They waved back. For a moment, she reminded Jerry of a middle-aged household fairy, forever on the move, forever in search of a wand she had lost in her early youth. He liked her.

'What about telling me what's wrong?' Carmen asked.

'What about not asking?' he teased, with a straight face.

'Suit yourself.'

He felt safe, confident. The Termites didn't know about her and he wasn't eager to tell them anything. It was his idea of refuge. It was the kind he hadn't bothered to repudiate, one he would defend as necessary, intelligent, convenient. The Termites were beginning to be a problem. He had come to the conclusion that he would soon have to make up his mind about remaining in the group. He was afraid that he would find the answer too easily, too quickly. He wasn't sure what he would put in its place. The substitute for the rebellious Termites would be difficult to find. Carmen? He wasn't sure. She would be going to America. England? He had begun to think about London, as a possible escape.

'Would you like to go to a magazine meeting tomorrow?'

'What sort?'

'A literary review.' He frowned.

'What time?'

'Four-thirty. Pick you up at a quarter to.'

He walked over to the window beside the front door. He stared vacantly into Retirement Road.

'What're you looking at?' she asked.

'Talking to myself about myself, as usual.'

'Didn't hear you.'

'Just as well.' He sat on the sofa tentatively, as if it might give way under his weight, looked at her suspiciously and folded his arms. 'What d'you think of the Civil Service?' he asked. 'For a career, I mean?'

'It's all right, I suppose. At Saint Hugh's we hardly ever gave it a thought. You know what I mean? Most of the girls go away to study or do something. A few go in as typists for a time, then get married, but I've never fancied it myself. Don't think Mother has either.'

'Saint Hugh's?' he interrupted her.

'Well, you know there's nothing special about the school. It's different with girls. Isn't it?'

'Little rich ones?'

She had never seen this side of him before. She wanted an explanation. 'What's wrong with going to a school if your parents can afford it?'

'Sorry.' He suddenly felt like a drink, with the Termites. He had come full circle. He had made a fool of himself and he had been found out. He got up. 'Tomorrow afternoon. A quarter to four?'

'Fine.'

He walked to the door and she followed him. 'Kiss me goodbye?' she asked.

He kissed her and started down the steps.

'Getting tired already, Jerry?' she called out to him.

He waited for her to catch up with him. He kissed her forehead and then her lips. She smiled. She watched him walking up Retirement Road towards Cross Roads, and then she went back inside and sat in the corner of the sofa where he had been sitting and followed him in her mind's-eye all the way up the road.

He walked into the Niagara at about nine o'clock. He found Paula, Silba, Berto, Mabel, Sally and Van at the bar. Lola winked, quickly wiped a glass and put it down in front of him. Sally poured him a drink and Mabel helped him to ice.

Berto bowed and almost slipped off his stool. Mabel moved quickly and caught him round his waist.

'Where's Mason?' Jerry asked.

'Just left with Jenny,' Sally said. 'They'll be back.'

Paula got up from her stool at the far end of the counter and sat beside him. 'Don't you done love us no more, country boy?' she asked.

'Your American accent,' he said, holding his nose, 'deadly.'

'Seriously, why've you stayed away so long? Me?'

'No.'

She left him and went back to her stool. Silba hugged her and whispered in her ear. She pretended to slap his face. They embraced. The others cheered.

Jerry was alone. Lola came up to him. 'You people mash up the poor Major bad two weeks ago the other night, eh,' she said. 'How you manage?'

'All right,' he whispered. 'Thanks to you.'

'Cho! You never even stop an' tell me if it nice you. You bad, eh? You jus' ups an' fly back inside like you hear news.'

'Life.'

'Hope you don't broadcas' it to you' friends?'

'Didn't have time,' he said, chuckling and squeezing her arm. 'Next time, maybe?'

'Ain't goin' be no nex' time, sweet boy.'

He watched her walk away. She seemed, to him, to be stronger and more prepared for all the encounters the Island society could provide, more intelligent than any of the Termites; he was certain of it. He admired her ability to mock respectability and assume her own special variation of it, flexible, individual and self-preserving. She'd survive anywhere, he thought.

Vie passed by and nodded.

'Not talking?' he asked.

'What for?' she said, going through the wicket gate and slamming it shut with the side of her thigh.

Mason and Jenny came in. They spied Jerry and ran straight over to him. Jenny leapt the last two paces and kissed his cheek, and Mason grabbed his shoulder. 'Long time no see, man!' he teased, exaggerating the sing-song of the dialect.

'You know!' Jerry said. He was happy to see him. 'How's the girl?' he asked Jenny.

'She's prepared,' she said wearily.

A quart of Black Seal was placed before them. The Termites cheered unnecessarily and noisily. Jerry felt himself being sucked into the customary, purposeless activity and knew that if he resisted, he would again find himself outside everything. The Termites were standing and shouting improvised toasts all round. Jerry tried to shut out the charade and surrender himself to the bottle of rum, but it was no good. Things have gone stale, he thought. He decided he would go home.

Outside, he walked to Parade, turned right into Upper Church Street, walked up a little way and then turned right again into East Queen Street. He got as far as the Duke Street intersection and stopped. He leant against the parapet of a dentist's surgery and asked himself why he had taken the unnecessary walk away from the bus terminus at Parade. He shrugged and walked on. Straight along East Queen Street. Up South Camp Road. He covered more than half the distance towards Half Way Tree before he had realised it. When he got home, it was long after one o'clock. He went to his bedroom, knowing that he wasn't drunk enough for Miriam. He stripped and flung himself on the bed.

Chapter Nine

One of the first things Jerry deliberately left behind was the folder with his ideas for the new format for NEXUS, which Prudence Kirby was expecting him to submit to the editorial meeting; the others were his tie and jacket. He knew she would be more upset had he turned up improperly dressed than by anything else he might do to annoy her. When he thought about it again, however, his small revolt seemed futile Termite behaviour. After Saturday night's self-criticism and his decision to resign from the group, he was now confused and doubtful about everything that had to do with the Termites; yet he willed himself to be one for the occasion. More confident now he felt like going without his shoes as well.

He and Carmen arrived at Kirby Lodge at four-thirty precisely. He was disappointed about being on time. He thought of hanging around outside for a while, but he realised he could not bolster his revolt without making Carmen suspicious. He did not want her to know about his private struggle against Prudence Kirby.

The house was set far back from the road and surrounded by an expansive lawn-area, terraced gardens and topiary shrubs. There were two rock and concrete fountains, and a central gravel path through an avenue of tall aurelia, from the main gate to the front steps.

'Like it?' Jerry asked.

'Marvellous!' Carmen said. Her voice sounded discreetly low.

He held her hand and they walked slowly up the avenue of aurelia, he indifferently, she with wild, inquisitive eyes, staring at the well-swept path, the opulent greenery on both sides and the spaciousness beyond. Her hand was sweating in his and her fingers were fidgeting. He wondered about her being so surprised and delighted by the surroundings. He tried to figure out just what she had expected. Surely, not a weekend shack in Gordon Town?

Prudence Kirby and her group were sitting on the fern-laden front veranda. They all looked awkward and reverential, except Prudence. She smiled charmingly and made a mental note of the way Jerry was dressed. She had her own method of dealing with recalcitrance. After Carmen had been introduced right round the group, the meeting was called to order. Prudence talked animatedly about production costs; she had the group's undivided attention. Jerry was the only one who remembered that she had given the same speech at the last meeting three months before. He began cynically reviewing her biographical details: about forty, very attractive, a lukewarm poet, dictatorial, near-white but also near-black because of her stubborn tripartite nose, liver lips and doubtful hair, Oxford Arts graduate, editor of NEXUS and second wife of W. C. Kirby, Leader of the Opposition.

Somebody asked a question. Prudence dealt with it robustly, and she continued, 'And now to contributions. I really don't know what we're going to do about our short stories; really I don't. Do you?' She paused rhetorically. Anxiety spread among the waiting faces. She savoured the pause and moved on. 'We have more poems than we can handle. Far too many.' She paused again, briefly. 'Why don't *you* try your hand at a short story, Leonard?' She pointed to a Chinese boy still in the sixth form at Island College.

'Me?' he said stupidly.

'Yes, Leonard, *you*,' she said brutally emphatically. 'Why not try something to do with school life? Scholarship heartbreak, staff-room intrigue, master-pupil relations, anything!'

'I suppose I could find something, Mrs Kirby. It might take a little time, though.'

'Of course, Leonard,' she said indulgently. 'Look, write your story and give it to me by Wednesday. That gives you three clear days. What about "My Last Days at School" for a title?'

Leonard agreed.

'Good. That's fixed.'

After Leonard, Prudence encouraged everybody, except Carmen and Jerry, and obtained five short stories, bringing the total to nine, all of which she had provided with titles. She then handed out vague technical advice, together with hints on plot and characterisation. She attempted to dictate her private theory about style, but withdrew it graciously, saying that *that* would emerge out of the necessary earth of the content, and flourish accordingly.

The meeting continued smoothly. She explained the history of NEXUS to the new contributors. Even Jerry had to admit to himself that she did it superbly well; he listened without once straying off into one of his reveries. Finally, she asked for the ideas for the new format. The proposals were nearly all dull and unenterprising. Jerry said that he had not thought of anything suitable. She knew instinctively that he had lied. She hid her annoyance, and approved her own design and composition.

The meeting ended abruptly and she announced refreshments. Turning to Jerry, she said, 'A walk in the garden? Shan't keep you long.' They sat on the edge of the fountain in the terraced garden to the left of the house, right away from the group on the veranda. 'Why did you leave your format idea behind?' she asked.

'Because I wanted to.'

She frowned. 'Gained anything?'

'Not really. You?'

They left the fountain and walked slowly back to the house. Jerry ran up the steps, ahead of Prudence, and went in search of Carmen. He found her sitting in a corner. 'Let's disappear,' he said, cupping her chin in his hands.

'So soon?'

'Yes.'

'Why?'

'I'll explain later.' When they were outside and walking away from the house, he took her hand in his and squeezed it. 'I'm sorry.'

'About what?' she asked innocently.

'Spoiling it for you.'

'We might've said goodbye to Prudence.'

'Won't ruin her complexion.'

'What's up between you and her?'

He had to think twice before he could decide eventually what he would tell her. Most of what he hurriedly thought up seemed implausible. Much of the burden of proof rested on him. He knew that Carmen would wonder about the one-sidedness of his complaints about Prudence. 'Complicated,' was all he said, after arguing the matter closely with himself.

Carmen tried again. 'She's mad about writing and that sort of thing, and she's trying to encourage you people to get started.'

'I agree,' he said and kissed her forehead. 'I'm sorry.'

She closed her eyes and smiled. 'You're funny sometimes.'

'Mother at home?' he asked.

'Mightn't be. She's always out these days.' She was pleased. She wanted him.

When they got back, Mrs Dabdood was sitting on the veranda. Carmen was disappointed, but Jerry was secretly relieved.

Chapter Ten

Monday morning. Jerry had been beaten by the clock by exactly ten minutes. Randy caught him signing the register and admonished and discharged him all within two minutes, in public view, and loud enough for everybody to hear. Lily, who had been listening, waited until Randy had shut his inner office door; then she crept over to Jerry's desk, and, as if talking to the ceiling, she gazed upwards, placed her arms akimbo and said, 'I'm nobody, only a messenger, but I wouldn't like anybody, not even Jesus Chris' Himself, to talk to me so rough an' shamin', an' 'specially in front o' everybody.' She left Jerry's desk at a trot and went back to her table by the wall telephone.

Jerry admired her kindness, her considerate attention, and winked at her as soon as she sat down and looked his way.

Van passed by and whispered, 'Come the Revolution and the new deal, boy!'

'Farson!' Randy shouted from his office.

'Call, if you need help,' Jerry said, smiling and adjusting his tie. Van adjusted his, too.

The Deputy Clerk at the other end of the room crossed his fingers and held them up. Van ignored him.

'I've called you twice, Stover!' Randy called out. 'Last night's rum? Come here at once.'

Jerry followed Van into the office. Van turned and winked. Randy sat down and folded his arms.

'May we sit down?' Jerry asked.

'You may not!' Randy roared back at him and thumped the blotting pad in front of his brief case. 'Now, listen, both of you, I heard every word you uttered. I even heard what Lily had to say to you, Stover. I'm warning *you*. Your appointment hasn't come through yet.' He thumped a light tattoo with his fingers on the side of the brief case, turned and surveyed his neatly piled rows of Informations and spun back to Jerry. 'Get out!'

Outside, Jerry wiped his face with his top handkerchief, folded it slowly and replaced it, propping up the ends delicately. He did it for the benefit of the eyes glued to him, expecting, as he was aware, some sign of the aftermath. Lily was elated. The Deputy Clerk was wan with excitement. Jerry stared at him and thought: You look Dickensian, and you *are* Dickensian. Lily began to hum a *mento*. She stopped as she saw Van come out of Randy's office. His manner was remarkably easy. He held his head high. Jerry noticed his entrance and realised that he, too, was playing to his waiting audience.

That afternoon at the Niagara, while Van and Jerry were discussing Randy with Silba, Berto walked in, sighed and flung himself in a chair behind their table. Jerry, whose temper hadn't been even throughout the discussion, spun round and suggested, 'Give it up, Berto.'

Berto shook his head. 'What do I put in its place? Cross-country running?'

'More pussy?' Silba said, in a tone which suggested that he was being genuinely helpful.

'That's always with us, man,' Berto said despondently.

'I've got an idea,' Jerry said cautiously. 'What about giving it a rest for Lent?'

'Pussy?' Berto asked. 'You joking?'

'The rum,' Jerry said.

'All of us?' Van asked.

'Everybody dry as *rass*,' Berto mused.

'Not a drop for the duration,' Jerry said.

'Bad news from the Vatican,' Berto added casually.

'Good timing,' Silba said. 'Lent begins two days after pay day. Lola mightn't like the idea. I can't see her putting anything extra into the poor box because of it.'

Berto guffawed and shook his head.

Jerry was serious. 'What about it?'

'Seems all right for the birds,' Berto said. Then he thought about it and said, 'Fine, if we're in it together.'

'What about the girls?' Silba asked.

'What about Paula, you mean?' Jerry flung back at him spitefully.

Silba cracked his knuckles and ignored him.

Mason walked in. 'Why the gloom?' he asked.

'Plans for the Big Thirst,' Berto said, pointing to the others. Jerry explained.

'Good way to use Lent,' Mason said, 'but you can count me out.'

'When do we start?' Berto asked, causing them all to turn and look at him incredulously.

'The day after pay day,' Jerry suggested.

'All right,' Silba agreed. Jerry was surprised, but he understood Silba's reason for joining in : he wanted to prove to him that Paula wasn't completely in charge of his behaviour and that he was still capable of making his own decisions.

'Fine by me, Jerry,' Berto said.

'And me,' Van said.

Mason looked at the four of them. Something's funny here, he thought. There's bound to be a link somewhere. He slapped the table. 'Jerry, Silba, Berto, Van!' He checked them off, his voice becoming less controlled and rasping. 'It's just occurred to me; you four are the only R.C.s in the group.'

'Does it matter?' Jerry asked.

'A bloody Cathedral trick,' Mason said.

'Character building!' Berto shouted, leaping to his feet and upsetting his drink. 'Finer morals, better nation!'

Nobody said anything. At that point, Sally, Paula and Jenny walked in. Jerry counted the party. Mabel, Wyn and Albert were the ones absent. Mabel had become a Termite only by attraction, always welcome, a part of the group when she was present.

The position's the same, Jerry observed. Jenny and Mason were still keeping up the pretence of being inseparable. Paula had forgotten Albert and had successfully transferred her affections to Silba. Berto was still precariously poised between Mabel and Jenny.

'Have you heard?' Mason called across the counter to the girls.

Jerry explained again. The girls sneered. The others took it in good part but Jerry lost his temper. He handed Lola a five-shilling note and told her to take three shillings towards the bill. She gave him his change and he left without saying goodbye. He walked slowly up King Street. He felt confused, dejected and ashamed of his display of bad temper. He wondered where he'd go. Home? Carmen? The pictures? Another bar? Back to the Niagara?

Someone shouted to him from the other side of the street. It was Albert. Jerry walked over to him and stood in the gutter.

'Where?' Albert asked.

'Dunno.'

'Seen the others?'

'Just left them.'

'What's wrong?'

'Bored.'

'Come back with me?'

'Right.' He couldn't understand why he had agreed so readily. He tried to explain it to himself as he walked back to the Niagara. He shuddered as he listened to himself deluding himself, lying, hoping.

Albert was talking at full blast all the time. He seemed in a good mood. Jerry told him about his plan for Lent. He mentioned what the others had said. Albert listened carefully, formed his own opinion quickly and waited for Jerry to stop talking.

'Foolishness,' he said quietly, as if offering him the proved advice of an older man. 'If you don't pitch a bitch, what's the alternative?'

They talked at each other, lost their temper, flattered each other and lied. When they got to the Niagara, Mabel and Wyn were there; the others were well away, talking loudly, arguing wildly, showing off. They were all over the place, sprawled across the tops of tables, standing on chairs which had been pulled towards the centre of the bar, sitting on the counter and moving about behind it. The impromptu session lasted until twelve o'clock when Lola closed the bar. The Termites moved upstairs. Lola followed with her credit book and fountain lead pencil; Vie with a shut-pan of ice and three quarts of rum. At about two o'clock, the lights went out. Lola went in search of a box of spare fuses which she had last seen on a ledge behind the stock-room door. The box was there but the fuses had disappeared. She rummaged around for a few minutes and then hurried back upstairs to the party. Jerry crept up behind her, grabbed the shoulder straps of her dress and pulled them down.

'Everybody's undressing,' he whispered.

The others had paired off in the dark: Jenny with Mason, Paula with Silba, Mabel with Berto, Vie with Albert, and Sally with Van. Wyn had passed out on the sofa in the middle of the room.

Everything was quiet. The last sound was the dull thud of Lola's credit book as it dropped to the bottom of the stairs.

Chapter Eleven

Two weeks, and pay day again, and exactly two days before the Big Thirst. The Termites had taken their accustomed positions round the 8. Lola had collected her wine cards and the old ritual was being played out as usual. Jerry was worried. Berto slapped the side of his camera and said something ironical. The top half of the 8 guffawed in unison. Jerry was distracted. He looked at Berto and he immediately thought of Jenny. He looked across at Jenny and he remembered 'upstairs' and Mason. He wondered what Mason ever felt about Dallas. Mason caught Jerry's eye and winked. Berto was still holding the floor with a long and involved *Springboard* anecdote. As soon as Mason winked, Jerry thought about 'upstairs' again.

Crashing through Berto's story, Van asked, 'What do we toast this time?' He saw Lola and Vie approaching with the new bottles and cracked ice.

'Suicidal ritual,' Jerry muttered. 'Why do we do it, anyway?' He stood and uttered a smooth, hypocritical toast. The Termites cheered.

The 8 continued until eleven o'clock, and Berto suggested

a move up the Lane to see Mabel. They all agreed to go with him.

The Writers' Nook was packed. Jerry shoved his hands in his pockets and looked round him. Ritual again? he thought. He suddenly felt he had to get away from the bar, from the Termites, from the suffocating drunkenness of the Writers' Nook. He backed his way out from the mass of drinkers and went downstairs.

Water Lane was deserted, peaceful. He crossed the street and rested his forehead against a concrete column. It was cool and reassuring. He patted it once and then a second time, and the rough surface left small traces of dust and slight markings on the palms of his hands. He held the column at arms' length and swung his body round it. When he stopped circling it, he examined his hands and licked the bruises which spread as far as his wrists and lower forearms. He spat on a particularly long gash on his right wrist and then he walked away from the column. He turned and saluted it.

He decided that he had had enough of the pay day binge.

Chapter Twelve

Two weeks of Lent had passed and Jerry hadn't once had a drink. He divided his time after work between staying at home and seeing Carmen in the afternoons. Mrs Stover, Les and Thelma were completely baffled by the Big Thirst. Miriam was openly resentful.

Jerry and Carmen had been going regularly to Kinkead's restaurant on King Street for lunch. It was a long way from Half Way Tree but he didn't mind. On their third visit they ran into Mabel and Berto, and Jerry was forced to introduce them to Carmen. The news went round quickly. Everybody was curious. The Termites decided to arrange a trap. Sally telephoned Berto and Silba and asked them to try to get Jerry and Carmen to meet them at Kinkead's on the following Monday at one o'clock under any pretext they thought likely to impress him. Berto volunteered and Silba left it up to him.

Jerry and Carmen walked into Kinkead's at about ten minutes to one on Monday afternoon, and there, waiting to welcome them, were all the Termites, Lola and Mabel. Vie would have been there but she had to look after the bar during Lola's absence.

Jerry realised the position and steeled himself to face up to the encounter. Lola was the first to speak. 'What 'bout introducin' us to the nice chil' then?' she said bluntly.

He introduced Carmen around, and, within ten minutes, they had all repaired to the Niagara for lunch-time drinks. Jerry, Berto, Silba and Van drank coconut water, while the others had cold beers. Jerry sensed that they all liked Carmen and he was waiting for Paula to suggest making her an honorary Termite. She didn't and he was grateful. Instead, she invited him to go with her to the Dung'll to help her get a special interview for the *Springboard*. She mentioned rather helpfully for Carmen's benefit that Berto was also going with her to take a few pictures of the place. Jerry agreed in order to avoid the possibility of any further demonstrations in front of Carmen, and it was arranged that they should meet at five o'clock.

Before Jerry and Carmen left the Niagara, Carmen took him aside and said, 'Are they real?' She pointed discreetly round the room.

'Real enough,' he said. He frowned.

She noticed his censure, and added nicely, 'First time I've been in a bar.'

He smiled.

Paula and Berto were waiting for him outside the Niagara. They walked up Temple Lane, into Tower Street and up to Barry Street. They turned left and headed towards the maze of back streets and lanes which would provide them with a short cut into the Dung'll.

'Why the mission, Paula?' Jerry asked.

'Rastafarian types.'

'Just like that?'

'Simple.'

They walked through tight clusters of bystanders who

looked at them furtively. Berto took a few pictures along the way. He seemed utterly detached. Jerry was annoyed because Berto looked and behaved so much like the professional he really was and which Jerry himself wasn't and perhaps wanted to be. When they got to the entrance of the Dung'll, they stopped, and Paula lit a cigarette. Her hands shook only slightly, but she was very nervous and apprehensive. She suddenly remembered the rumours of violence, the intense squalor and the abject poverty described by her fellow journalists, as the natural condition of life on the Dung'll. She also became painfully aware of her white skin. For the first time since she had been in the Island, she saw the essential difference between herself and her companions, Berto and Jerry; she glanced at their faces and quickly looked down at her hand, and she felt a faint shudder pass through her; but just as sharply, she realised that she was protected in their company.

'What sort of questions, Paula?' Jerry asked, assuming a business-like tone which didn't quite conceal his uncertainty about the venture.

'Strictly human interest,' she said. 'The sort American journalists ask when they're fishing for a fat Pulitzer. Maybe?'

Jerry wasn't impressed. Her 'maybe' relieved his mounting tenseness, and it helped her own subtle doubts. Berto was completely unaffected.

'Why's the *Springboard* doing it?' he asked.

'It's the right time.'

'You hope?' He smiled and pushed her towards the entrance.

They entered the Dung'll, walking one behind the other, with Paula in front, Jerry behind her, and Berto at the back. Paula dropped to the rear of the single file and Jerry led the way. Berto stopped and started and ran to catch them up as he selected his pictures of the place.

The Dung'll had been Kingston's area dump for many years. Only the very poor and destitute lived on it. They huddled in improvised huts, put together from old motor-car scrap parts, disused zinc sheeting, compressed cardboard and anything that might come their way which nobody wanted outside the Dung'll. Many of the people who lived there had become infamous for their *ganja* smoking, their petty crimes, and their more serious acts of violence among themselves and against others living in the West End of the city or passing through. The most notorious of the dwellers were the religious groups of bearded men who called themselves Rastafarians and who, it was believed by the police and others, not only smoked *ganja* but also trafficked in it. The Dung'll was vast, hilly, damp and sordid; everything on it was enveloped in a grey, oppressive silence.

A young boy approached the intruders from nowhere, it seemed. He may have been about twelve or thirteen, but his face was pinched and dusty, and his ashen look made him seem much older. 'Wha' you want?' he asked.

'We'd like to see your parents, your father, maybe?' Berto suggested tentatively, hoping that his camera would be of some interest, and that Paula would come to his assistance with something that sounded more convincing, more urgent, more reasonably attractive to the boy.

'Wha' you want 'im for?' The boy crossed his legs and looked up defiantly at Berto.

'We'd like to talk to him,' Jerry began, and then paused.

'Pappy not 'ere now, an' as a matter o' fac', we don' know if 'im goin' come back today at all,' the boy announced brazenly, backing away from them.

'And your Mother?' Paula asked.

'She not 'ere either,' he mumbled and stood still. 'Wha' you want wid them?'

'Take a few pictures an' talk little bit, you know,' Berto said uncertainly, and using dialect to put the boy at his ease.

'Is there anybody else around?' Jerry asked, covering up Berto's patronising slip.

'Only Bashra,' the boy said, pointing behind him in the

direction of an ancient country bus, half buried in a mound of earth, sprinkled with ramgoat roses.

'Will you take us to him?' Paula asked.

'If you want,' the boy replied doubtfully, lowering his eyes and scuffing a tiny mound of damp dirt.

Berto took a quick picture of the boy and a long shot of Bashra's hut.

'Ready?' Jerry asked.

The boy ran in front of them. When he got to the door of the hut, he knocked twice and walked away afterwards. The door creaked open and a tall bearded man appeared out of the darkness of the interior. He was about six feet, middle-aged, and black. He walked towards his three visitors and squatted before them, his back resting against a cluster of ramgoat roses.

'All we got here is plenty dirt,' he said, apparently talking to Paula, who was nearest him, but in effect, addressing the Dung'll itself, and those beyond in the West End. 'Everywhere you look, you see earth coming to get you. The hut's half under, as it is.' He paused. 'You all want to talk with me, I suppose?' His voice was controlled and impressive.

'We're from the *Springboard* and we'd like to ask you about life on the Dung'll,' Paula tried to explain, but she was cut short by the man's sudden broad gesture.

His large hand waved away her request, indeed, waved away the very presence of the Dung'll momentarily. 'I know all that already, Miss. Just ask what you want, and write down what *I* say about the filth and suffering, and not what *you* want me to say.' He smiled and invited them to squat down beside him. 'Ready now?'

Carmen had prepared an *ackee* and salt fish supper for Jerry. After he had eaten, they locked themselves in the spare bedroom at the back of the house and flung the windows open and sprawled across the bed.

'How was it?' she asked.

'Interesting and depressing as hell.'

'How like hell, Jerry?'

'Like the uselessness of a government and a society in which people, like Bashra, are virtually encouraged to delude themselves and make a mockery of their lives, of sanity and decency and order.' He held her hand. 'Where they're encouraged to kill themselves either by violence or by malnutrition or by *ganja* smoking on a dung hill in the centre of the city or in a mountain recess or wherever they're forced to hide out.'

'Never knew you thought about those things, Jerry.' She cradled his head in her arms. He closed his eyes and his mind wandered and formed urgent images of his own changed society. His eyelids felt heavy and every nerve in his body was taut, as the Utopian innovations flashed past. Other images arose. They included glimpses of Bashra, the Dung'll, W. C. Kirby, Dr C. W. Rybik, Prudence, Les, his mother, Randy and the Civil Service. They raced through his brain.

Carmen had undressed and was taking off his shirt and trousers. Dimly he felt her warm hands passing over his body and her breath on his skin, but his attention remained fixed on the images, as they danced before his eyes. He wilfully changed their faces, attitudes, ambitions, fortunes. He provided them with his own just approximations of their rewards and punishments, and their destinies, as he wanted to. He introduced other figures, other objects, other details of landscape. It was his world now. He ruled.

Suddenly, he was conscious of a great longing, and he thrust himself into Carmen. Distantly, he heard her moan and call his name, and he drifted away from her, and from himself.

Chapter Thirteen

It was Sunday morning and only two weeks to go before the
end of the Big Thirst. Jerry and his mother were walking
through the front garden. He was pretending to appreciate the
blaze of red roses on his right, but, in fact, he was rehearsing
his usual evasion of any possible confrontation. She was sensing his defensive calm and smiling inwardly. They came to
the end of the long grass path and turned back together.

'We've talked very little to each other these last few weeks,'
she began.

'We get along,' he said, bending to touch a large thorn on
a rose stem.

They both checked off the opening sentences and nodded
imperceptibly at their shared knowledge of the situation, at
their innocent strategy. They thought of the years they had
spent fighting each other, rejecting each other, avoiding each
other's traps, despairing of each other, slipping away from
collisions and then finding each other again only to lose the
connection, and, perhaps, one day for good.

'Have we finally pulled free of each other?' she asked.

'Don't know, Mother.'

He fidgeted. She noticed but she hadn't the inclination to use it against him. It's so easy to dislodge him, she thought. She questioned her right to continue. She doubted herself.

'Do you want to hear what I have to say?'

'Don't mind.'

They sat on two smooth broad stones in the rockery round the Bombay mango tree. He leant forward and clasped his knees. It was almost a gesture of supplication.

'You're your own worst enemy,' she said. 'You cheat yourself and others. You even make up excuses for those who mean you no good at all.' She paused and shook her crumpled pink embroidered handkerchief. 'And now the Dabdood girl.'

'How'd you find out?' he asked.

'People talk.'

He was very surprised. He wanted to run away from her, out to the front gate, into the street, anywhere. He willed himself to remain where he was, closing his eyes tightly. He felt her words weighing in on him, repeating and drumming endlessly, until they were scarcely recognisable as conventional sounds, mocking him, defying him, lessening whatever little power of retaliation he had left in his will. He opened his eyes and his mother was not beside him. He looked round and was just in time to see her going through the sitting-room door, her head bent and her shoulders deeply curved. Her stoop seemed exaggerated. She appeared to have aged suddenly. He felt ashamed. He decided to go for a walk up the Constant Spring Road. As soon as he got outside he saw a bus approaching and he ran to the stop. He wasn't sure where he wanted to go, and then he remembered Bashra.

He had no difficulty in entering the stretch of improvised huts which formed an avenue leading to Bashra's hut. A small gathering of men with beards bowed as he passed them, but that was all.

He knocked on Bashra's door and Bashra came out to him

almost immediately. 'I heard it was you alone. What 'bout you' friends?' he said.

'Heard?' Jerry asked. 'How?'

'I have ears and eyes all 'bout, you know. You didn't expect me to hear because I was out of sight?'

'I see,' Jerry said self-consciously. 'In fact, I don't see.' He laughed.

'What you come for this time?'

'I don't know.'

'You jus' simple come, then? A visit like?'

'That.'

'What's on you' mind? You want to tell me anything 'bout you'self? You' catching worries?'

'How d'you know?'

'It showing like a mountain top on a moonlight night. A man is a looking glass for those who can read it, 'specially if those who looking into it have worries of their own too.' He surveyed the expanse of the Dung'll yard and shook his head slowly from side to side. 'All this dirt. Jus' waiting to grab us one day.' He paused. 'You want to stay out here or you prefer to come inside?'

'Doesn't matter,' Jerry said trustingly, not really caring.

Bashra opened the door of his hut. The interior hadn't the slightest appearance of the original bus it had been. The rows of seats had been removed; only two remained. One was being used as a bed and the other as a sofa, with a crocus bag thrown over it. A kerosene lantern stood in a corner. Hanging from the side rails were four other lanterns. In another corner, heaped in three piles, was an assortment of old newspapers, magazines and books. There was a shrine at the far end just about where the driver's seat must have been, and stacked high on it were three clay statuettes of the Saints Theresa, Anthony and Francis, a cracked vase filled with ramgoat roses, two Bibles, a rosary, two large white candles, four rum bottles half filled with whitish liquid, a framed picture of the Sacred Heart, and a black crucifix.

96

Jerry stared at the crucifix and Bashra chuckled wryly. Jerry next stared at the cracked vase, and Bashra frowned. 'No water,' he said. 'What's the use, if the clay got a crack in it.'

Jerry nodded.

'What they call you again?' Bashra asked him.

'Jerry.'

'You like the altar?'

'Never seen a black crucifix before.'

'Make it myself years ago. Paint it too.' He beckoned and pointed to the sofa. He sat beside him. 'What worrying you, youngster?'

'Things,' was all he could think of saying.

'I believe it is you worrying you.' Bashra closed his eyes. 'What you looking for then?'

'What are *you* looking for, Bashra?' Jerry said uncertainly, trying to evade the question.

'I looking for peace.'

Jerry said nothing. He waited for him to continue.

'You want a smoke?' He took out two hand-made cigarettes from his shirt pocket, handed one to Jerry and placed the other between his lips. Jerry lit his own first and then Bashra's.

'Nice,' Bashra said. 'I notice you trus' me.'

They smoked, and neither spoke nor looked at each other. The narcotic fumes were sickly sweet and oppressive. They swam before the smokers' eyes and twisted in devil shapes about their heads and formed elongated twines, spreading outwards to the shrine and beyond it. When Jerry's cigarette was finished, he stubbed it out on his shoe-heel and scattered the remains. Bashra gave him a wink of approval. Jerry folded his arms and waited. Bashra got up and walked down to the shrine. He opened one of the Bibles and began reading to himself. After a few minutes he lit the two large white candles and returned to Jerry. He sat beside him. 'You feel up to a secon' *spliff*?' he asked cautiously.

They smoked in silence. Jerry looked at the shrine and secretly expected something supernatural to happen; Bashra looked at him and speculated. When they were half-way through the third cigarette each, Bashra said, 'We reaching the plains of Abraham now. When we reach proper, I going give a signal for you to start talking from you' heart. The signal will be the word "Go!". And what happens is this: you talk as if you getting rid of all you' worries and I will do the same thing. You go firs' and then I follow and you again and then me. You must remember that we not talking to each other at all. We jus' talking from the heart straight into the ears up yonder.'

The candles flickered intermittently and flushed the interior of the hut with scattered mosaics of shadow. Bashra cupped his cigarette in both hands and pulled on it, inhaling with exaggerated sucking noises. Jerry did the same. The mosaics had ceased to attract him. He was gradually sensing his own presence, the bulk of his thighs, the space he was occupying in the hut, the whole weight of his body. An energy, which he had never known before, made him aware of all this; it seemed concealed in the pit of his stomach. It stirred and leapt out in spurts. It dictated to his will. It guided his limbs. He found it easy to regard himself from the inside. He stood and discovered that his surroundings were different; he also discovered that he was someone else. He felt that he had no weight, no ballast to keep him fixed to the floor, no centre, no hold over himself.

'Go!' Bashra whispered hoarsely.

Quickly, as if he had been waiting for the signal all his life, as if he were about to plunge into an eternal release from himself, he lifted his head and called out towards the shrine, 'I must.' He paused. 'No culture. No tradition in doing things.'

Bashra waited and listened. Then he walked down to the shrine. 'My time, now,' he called out without turning round to face Jerry. 'Africa is home for me and all my people.'

After their session, they talked casually to each other for about ten minutes. Then they both agreed that it was time to leave each other. Jerry placed a five-shilling note on the open

Bible, thanked Bashra and left. When he got outside, he felt dazed and tired.

'Keep walking, son,' Bashra warned him. 'Straight in front. Head up, dignify-like. Make me see you soon.'

Jerry walked towards the entrance of the Dung'll. He threw his shoulders well back and he deliberately lengthened his stride, as soon as he started up the street. He felt confident and serene.

Monday morning. His thirst was remarkable. He drank eight glasses of iced water within an hour. Lily and Van were suspicious. Lily imagined the usual hectic weekend. Van believed that Jerry had broken the Big Thirst, but he wasn't sure. He had stood quite close to him and there hadn't been a trace of rum on his breath, and there was nothing peculiarly overt in his behaviour to make Van feel that he was stale drunk.

Of course, both Van and Lily were outside Jerry's world. Everything in the office seemed to be conforming to a pattern, as far as he could make out; he was convinced of a specific convenient arrangement of sound, light and shadow, time and motion. Space was entirely blocked into small observable areas. He checked Van's footsteps and his trips to and from his desk; he recorded his gestures and his bouts of coughing; he was even able to estimate his moments of preoccupation and his bursts of lighthearted banter. He found it relaxing to calculate the time that Van spent in walking round the office and the time he spent at his desk. His silent counting came easily and accurately. He also kept an account of the times Lily answered the telephone and of the people called to it. All this while doing his own work.

After Lily had admitted the public, Jerry noticed a slight change in his detachment. His calm deepened considerably. As it became more intense, he felt as if he was being prepared for a less compact area of observation and calculation. He found himself drawing away all the time, going farther out of himself, standing back in order to admit a completely different

99

set of sounds, a greater range of light and shadow, swifter elements of motion, faster rates of time, wider and deeper sensations of space. He closed his eyes.

'Wha' wrong, Jerry?' a voice asked. 'You giddy or wha'?'

Jerry opened his eyes. The face in front of him seemed very large, magnified, almost as broad as one of the doors directly behind it. The face assumed normal proportions gradually and there was a liquid subsidence inside his body which sent tiny draining noises driving through his head.

'You hearin' me, Jerry?' the voice asked again.

'It's you, P.D.,' Jerry said. 'What's happening?' He felt normal now; he had escaped for the first time from his stupor. All that remained was a nagging sensation of having been dragged from a cold, dark room into a warm, sunlit veranda. His nervous energy returned, and with it, his anxieties, his tenseness, and all the features of his own personality together with the normal atmosphere of the place and the problems of office routine.

P.D. was an excellent distraction. Jerry accepted it enthusiastically. 'Let's get in the corner,' he whispered. His having to whisper was enough to make him certain that he had returned to his natural world of checks and balances, evasion and fear.

Van saw what was happening and left his desk to attend to the counter. He waved to P.D., and Jerry winked back gratefully at him. Van nodded stoically. Jerry and P.D. talked for about five minutes and arranged to meet after work. Jerry had also dissuaded P.D. from taking two Dallas women to Court for Assault. After he left, Jerry joined Van and thanked him for taking over.

'I thought, for a moment, that you'd gone back on your Lent deal,' Van told him.

'Not a hope,' Jerry said.

Van returned to his desk.

'Stover!' Randy boomed from the inside office.

Van got up and walked back to the counter. 'I think I'd

better take over for you again,' he said in a projected whisper, loud enough for Lily to have heard at the back of the room and for her to have wondered whether Randy had heard too.

She looked concerned.

'That's right, Farson,' Randy called out. 'You hold the fort. Come along, Stover. Haven't all morning.'

Jerry winked at Van and walked into Randy's office. Lily shifted in her chair and faced Randy's door.

She heard Randy say, 'You never learn.'

The door clicked shut and the voices were muffled.

'What's it this time?' Jerry asked bluntly.

'Your little *tête-à-tête*.' He paused for time to savour the elegance of his opening. He stared at Jerry for the slightest trace of the effect it had had on him. He saw none. He continued with increased effort. 'Why do you bother, Stover? Why don't you give it up?'

Jerry said nothing. He tried, but he was unable to utter a single word in his own defence. He examined his hands. He hated doing so; in fact, he only did that in conversation when he felt a dry sucking silence at the back of his throat, a throttling of his wished words, a recurring childhood anxiety of losing his voice, or having lost it, which he had never succeeded in suppressing.

'You resent authority, obviously.'

Jerry smiled.

'Something funny, maybe?'

Jerry laughed and folded his arms defiantly.

Randy chose to ignore the challenge. '*You* have had it far too easy, all your generation, your so-called privileged friends, all of you. You've had all the obstacles removed. No guts, Stover. That's the result. No sense of responsibility. No grit. No stick-to-it-tiveness. You'll begin to rot inside. You'll lose your moral centre. You'll lose the fight and you and your pals will be trampled in the mad rush for the dung hill. That's what your kind of education has done for you, Stover.'

Jerry looked at his hands when he heard the words, dung

hill. He thought of Bashra and the Dung'll immediately. He looked up at Randy and slipped his hands under his lower thighs and sat firmly on them, hoping to impose a solid control over his nerves which had begun to tingle; there was a coming shaft of pain at the base of his neck.

Randy was unruffled and determined to conduct his offensive with concealed cunning. He was confident, too, of his untapped reserve of surprises. 'You've had the breaks, Stover,' he said, spreading his arms wide. 'You've had the approved education.'

'There have always been scholarships, Mr Lee,' Jerry said, smiling affably and sensing a feeling of compassion creeping up on him, a corrective sympathy, a kind of restraint which made him ashamed of his impudence and disrespect.

'I know that. There were many scholarships going, but I didn't sit any of them. I wasn't expected to, so I didn't. My place was in my father's shop. I had a job waiting for me behind a salt fish counter. There was a job all right, and I was told to work for it, to earn the right to have it later on; practice makes perfect.'

The telephone rang. He ignored it. It stopped. The Deputy Clerk had taken up the extension on his desk, knowing that Randy would have shouted to him to do so.

'In those years I learned to accept discipline, to be attentive to duty, to serve, to regard other people's wants, other people's feelings, to forget self completely. After a few years of that I started to study on my own, in secret, without my parents knowing a thing about it. Had I been caught at it, it would've seemed to them like a form of betrayal, treachery, in fact. After all, I was there to carry on whenever my father saw fit to hand over to me.'

The Deputy Clerk opened the door and showed his face, like a smiling disc, and said, 'For you.'

'Deal with it, man,' Randy said, snapping at him and forgetting him instantly. 'Naturally, I kept going, hoping they wouldn't suspect anything, and not wanting to hurt them or cause them any anxiety. I passed exam after exam, and here I am today. And under my own steam, Stover. Not far, mind you, but far enough from the smell of salt fish and pickled herrings.'

He held up his hands, pretended to smell them, made a face and chuckled.

'For years I used to do just that, when no one was looking, Stover. Good old private habit.'

He laughed.

'I could've been an R.M. long ago, if I had wanted to. There's really nothing to it. Reading for the Bar would've been the easiest thing for someone like me. Still is, as a matter of fact. But I decided I had had enough of hauling myself up the ladder. It became something I was ashamed of. It was undignified. I loathed it. At my age all late starters are a bit selfconscious, sad; the Service is full of them.'

He got up and patted Jerry's shoulder. He smiled. He walked round the office and sat down again.

'I've never resented the easy success of my contemporaries. Good luck to them.'

Jerry relaxed. He crossed his legs and dangled his arms at his sides. Randy noticed the change in his manner and pointed to him suddenly.

'I have a sharp eye for people, Stover. I can spot failures and misfits. I know when a man isn't cut out for the Service, as we know it, here, and now.'

He shuffled an imaginary pack of cards, dropped them on his desk and stood up.

'You see, I know the deck. I know every card, every single trick. And what's more, I can sympathise with the failure and the misfit. The world's packed with people in the wrong jobs.'

He folded his arms, sat down, slid back into the swivel chair and paused intentionally. Jerry wondered what was coming next. Randy saw his expectancy and prolonged the pause.

'I know the whole story, your story, Jerry.'

Hearing Randy call him, by his Christian name, unnerved

Jerry, but he showed no emotion; he behaved as if nothing had registered, as if the success of their meeting depended solely on his acceptance of the extraordinary, as if showing reaction of any sort would betray Randy's trust in him.

'Well,' Randy said, making it sound unconnected to anything he had just said.

Jerry waited for whatever would happen, surprising or not, illuminating or embarrassing; he urged himself to admit that it didn't matter to him. Innocence had run headlong into experience, scored by years and years of frustration and deep personal suffering.

Randy sat forward in his chair and placed his elbows on the edge of his desk. 'I'm never sure about conflicts these days. Years ago, yes. The conflicts were clear cut then. The clash between an older man and a young boy would've seemed right and proper. The values were simple, direct. Compromise was absent. No need for it. The soft generation hadn't yet arrived. Then, the older man had a mass of mistakes behind him, and the boy, a whole lifetime of them in front of him.' He paused. 'I'm not at all sure I'm doing the right thing. Not at all.' He hesitated. 'Results count, or so they say, even in the Service.' He chuckled. 'I feel it my duty to add just one more thing.' He examined his hands and fanned his fingers in a gesture of self-doubt, as if reflecting on his own authority, and assessing it for Jerry's benefit. He opened the top left-hand drawer of his desk and took out a small writing pad. 'Here you are, Jerry. Why don't you do it?'

Jerry didn't reply. He looked at Randy and he began to see him in a light he had failed to notice before. He had always recognised him as a failure, a very ordinary one; he knew about his years of subservience, of hoping and fretting, of self-denial and self-imposed discipline; he thought he knew, too, how he had had to defer imagination and revolt, how he had had to accept the Service gratefully, with both hands, permanently.

'I'll do it,' was all he said, and he took the writing pad and tore off the top sheet. He went back to his desk and wrote a short note. When he was finished, he took it in to Randy and placed it before him.

'A man in my job is seldom ever thanked, you know,' Randy told him, nodding and reading the note. 'Seldom.'

Jerry went back to the counter and stood beside Van. Lily was alert and thinking of going over to them.

'You look dead easy,' Van said. 'What's up?'

'I've let go, boy,' he said, tears filling his eyes. 'I've resigned.'

Chapter Fourteen

Jerry, Van and P.D. arrived at the Niagara at about half past five. All the Termites were there, except Albert, who was working late. Sally immediately demanded a binge in honour of P.D.'s visit. She had no opposition, not even from Berto, Silba, Van and Jerry. Mason assured everybody that his station wagon was at the disposal of the guest of honour and his friends. He also made it clear that he had no money.

'Credit,' Silba remarked.

'As always,' Mason said.

'Our Western way of slavery,' Paula added.

'A gross exaggeration,' Wyn said, 'but we're among fellow debtors.'

'You defender of the West, you,' Paula said.

'You've been talking about going to England again, I hear, Wyn,' Berto asked.

'I haven't,' Wyn told him, looking both ways to see the reaction of the others.

'Two Wyns around, eh?' Sally said, rubbing her nose.

'One's quite enough, darling,' Paula said.

'Anything you say,' Wyn replied, 'just as long as we can scrape up some credit for the binge.'

P.D. looked round slowly, approving what he saw, what he heard, and silently hoping to hear much more. He had missed them and had not stopped talking about their Dallas visit.

Wyn wanted to tell them all to go home and forget the whole thing, but he knew that P.D. had to be entertained; the others had to show off, and he had to tag along because he was expected to do so. He wondered how Berto had heard about his plan to return to England. He knew he had not told him anything. He knew, too, that he would never make up his mind about going, but it was something to hold on to, while allowing himself to be dragged around by the Termites.

'Well, then, let's begin at the Nook,' Van suggested.

'The old first stop hasn't killed us yet,' Jenny said, winking at Mason. Mason winked back.

'The Nook's all right,' Wyn interrupted.

'Piety, again, Wyn?' Jenny asked.

'Something bothering you, Wyn, my love?' Sally added mockingly.

'No.' Wyn thought about his approaching depression, his feeling of going nowhere, of giving up and trying less and less to come to terms with himself. And then he imagined that there must be something else to look forward to, something less ridiculously meaningless. But he told himself that it wouldn't be worth it: everything was much too much like everything else.

Jerry realised that it was time for him to make a move. He knew that they wouldn't expect him to drink, but, at the same time, he wasn't feeling up to going along on a Monday night binge, drinking tonic water and cream soda, and being bored, bar after bar. He took P.D. aside and explained his position. P.D. was amazed at the idea of Jerry's actually being faithful to the Big Thirst, and that too, in its own innocent way, caused him to regard the four abstaining Termites as drinkers of genius. 'Jerry, you' great can't done, man. All four o' you great to do a t'ing like wha' you' doin'. I don't exac'ly see why you' doin' it, but it still seem like a sort o' magic, man.'

Jerry shrugged and said, 'A rest, P.D. That's all.'

Jerry and Berto wrenched themselves away from the Niagara and took a Constant Spring bus. Berto got off two stops below Cross Roads in front of the *Springboard* offices and promised Jerry to get a copy of the typescript of Bashra's interview for him. They mock-saluted each other and winked.

When the bus stopped at the Cross Roads market, Jerry felt a sudden urge to see Carmen.

'What's wrong, Jerry?' she asked

'Nothing.'

'Your heart's racing like anything.'

'Is it?'

'Want me tonight? I do.'

'Me too,' he said mechanically. He wished immediately afterwards that he hadn't said it.

She pushed him away gently, looking into his eyes, pleading with him, begging, hoping he'd tell her what was wrong.

'I've done a silly thing,' he said suddenly. 'I've resigned.'

'Why?'

'I was told to.'

'But why?'

'Because the person who told me to feels that I won't make it.'

'Is he right?'

'I suppose so.'

'What'll you do?'

'Don't know.' He summoned enough courage to go on to tell her about his admiration for Randy, and how wrong he had been about him all along. He tried not to sound adulatory, but his enthusiasm was so obvious that she realised, for the first time since they had met each other, that he had found someone whom he could respect. She thought his objective attitude to the whole affair curiously contradictory, but she quickly forced herself not to comment or to make him suspicious. She sat passively and listened to him talking about Randy's background and early youth and comparing it with his own, and she nodded her agreement with his conclusion that Randy, indeed, was, by far, the finer person.

'Coming inside?' she interrupted him.

He smiled.

'We'll have to be quiet,' she warned, whispering and pointing towards the front of the house.

'Right.'

They tiptoed through the sitting-room and into her bedroom, holding hands and hunching their shoulders, silently hoping that Mrs Dabdood was asleep and wouldn't hear them and call out.

They undressed quietly.

Chapter Fifteen

It was Wednesday, pay day, and Jerry's last day at the Half Way Tree Courts. It was also the day before Carmen's departure for America, and five days before the end of the Big Thirst.

As he sat at his desk for the last time he thought of the prolonged passion of his love-making with Carmen on Monday night and of the coming Thursday's upheaval in their friendship. He wondered if he would be able to remain faithful to her during her absence.

Lily passed by his desk and touched his arm. 'So you leavin' today?' she said. 'You mus' make me see you now an' then when you find the time.'

' 'Course I will,' he told her. 'And, Lily, I'll miss you.'

'Me too.' She smiled and looked towards Randy's door. 'We got to survive.'

Jerry laughed.

Later on he shook Randy's hand and said goodbye formally. Randy grinned and said, 'You might make it, in spite of yourself. Good luck.'

After work, Jerry and Van took a bus to Parade. They walked down King Street to the Niagara, and on the way, they bought two water coconuts and drank them beside the vendor's cart in the street. Neither Jerry nor Van had done so for a very long time. They held the large hard fruits in their hands and timed their upward swings simultaneously. Each time they drank, the liquid overflowed and ran down their chins and sprinkled their ties.

'A proper blessing,' was Van's remark when he saw what had happened.

At the Niagara the others were in their places round the 8. Jerry knew instinctively that there was something strange about the feeling in the room. The 8 had received Van and himself coolly, as soon as they entered the room with the usual breezy abandon of the selfconscious latecomers; they had been met with a series of long cool stares and limp salutes all round the 8.

Jerry and Van sat down. Berto filled Jerry's glass with tonic water. Mason filled Van's with cream soda. Nobody spoke.

'All right,' Jerry said. 'What's the crime?'

'You didn't tell us,' Sally said, leaning forward across the bottom half of the 8.

'So, I didn't.'

'Why didn't you?' Paula asked.

'I knew you'd find out sooner or later.'

He left at about eight o'clock and went home. He greeted his mother affectionately, and then he was suddenly reminded that he had not told her about his resignation. The hug he had given her seemed a vulgar betrayal. He was in time for dinner and he decided he would think about it while eating.

Les was quiet. So was Thelma. After dinner Mrs Stover went out to the front veranda. Jerry joined her. She shifted her chair round to face his. They stared at each other.

'You've been drifting, Jerry,' she said. Knowing that calculated surprise usually worked effectively when dealing seriously with him, she went on to say, 'Either that or you must have been deliberately ignoring me when I asked you about your resigning from the Courts?'

'You asked me about that?'

'No. I'm asking you about it now,' she said effortlessly, folding her arms and crossing her legs, showing him that she was prepared to wait for his answer.

'What am I to say, Mother?'

'Mr Lee 'phoned me this afternoon.' She took off her glasses and swung them. She dropped them in her lap and closed her eyes. 'You might have told me yourself.'

He flung his arms in a wide V over his head, slipped his body slowly down to the front of the chair, his legs spread out before him, and said, 'Any advice?'

'Do you really need it?'

He was accustomed to her penetrating cunning but on this occasion her question completely disarmed him. He felt ashamed of his immaturity and his cowardice.

She got up and walked towards her bedroom. As she was about to close the door, she turned and looked over her shoulder. He sensed her presence, her stare, a lingering, silent accusation, and he hoped she wouldn't call out to him. She understood. She smiled, shook her head and closed the door.

As soon as he heard the faint, abrupt click of the lock, he breathed a sigh of escape. Alone on the veranda, he felt secure, bolstered, as if he had been whisked away from his familiar situation and had found himself in a small room, surrounded by strange people, milling around and talking openly and favourably about him.

At about six-thirty on Thursday morning Jerry awoke to find Miriam standing over him. She was half frowning and half smiling down at him. He yawned, rubbed his eyes and stared blankly at her. He thought that he had seen his mother in front of him, waiting to strike him. He defensively placed his right hand before his face and waited for the first blow of the encounter. Miriam chuckled quietly. He recognised her. He said nothing, but he frowned deeply and slashed her with his eyes. She smiled. He got up and walked over to the window and looked out.

'Who you t'ink I was?' she asked.

He was angry. He didn't reply. She had made him make a fool of himself, and what was worse, he knew she had intended him to do so. He turned round and faced her. She thought he was about to hit her. She moved back and watched him closely.

'What're you up to?' he asked, glaring at her and daring her to evade him.

She shrugged and pouted, as if trying to tell him that his question was irrelevant, very nearly insulting. He sprawled across the bed and crossed his hands behind his head. 'Well?' he reminded her.

'Like since you won't come, I decide to come to you,' she said simply, affectionately, sitting on the edge of the bed. She laughed quietly, and so did he. She looked intently at the broad expanse of his naked body, spread irregularly over the white sheet. His legs and arms were widely spaced and his body was on a slant across the centre line of the bed. She admired the smooth black skin of his thighs, the narrowness of his muscular waist, the protruding veins along his forearms and calves.

'You' lyin' all which way,' she said. 'You look like somebody jus' finish haulin' an' pullin' you an' drop you, lef' you, same so.'

They laughed again.

The second round of shared laughter was the signal she was hoping for. She slipped off her night dress. He moved towards the wall, perfunctorily providing her with the space, he knew, she would only too willingly take for granted. She was silent, co-operative, grateful. She had proved herself, it seemed to him. She had got what she had come for. Only once had it occurred to her that she did not properly belong in his bed; only once, just after they had begun to caress each other, had she doubted herself. It was, in a split second, when she had gazed up at him and had noticed the blackness of his skin, the tense spread of his chest, the strained tendons of his neck, the bulging small veins in his shoulder muscles, that she had wanted to say to him, 'We the same black people together, Missa Jerry. We really the said same, only you's different when we get up an' go outside. You' different only 'cause o' you' mother.' But instead, she had put the whole ridiculous torment out of her mind and had returned to their make-shift world of boisterous passion and settled for an easy satisfaction.

Jerry knew that breakfast would be an ordeal, and in his self-consciously child-like way, he had been rehearsing for it. His leisurely bath had helped him to assume a mask of innocence, a pretence of ease and composed familiarity with which he would greet his mother, his brother and Thelma. They were there and that was a fact, an inevitability he wanted to be kept separate from his concealed guilt and his growing suspicions. He hadn't been to see his mother before breakfast, as he had promised himself and it was worrying him. It was his first small defeat of the day. But he thought he could easily put things right afterwards, when Les and Thelma would be out of the way.

Conversation was minimal. Les talked cosily about his preparations for young Hartley's lesson. Mrs Stover talked about the garden. And Jerry listened dutifully. There was a clatter of cutlery in the kitchen and he looked up from his plate and glimpsed Miriam bending to pick up the silver she had dropped. A generous portion of her upper thighs was exposed. He stared at it devotedly. He imagined his hands moving over it and steadily going higher. As soon as she was out of sight, he felt compelled to check to see whether his mother had noticed his interest in the noise. But her eyes were closed, and when he looked at her empty plate, he realised that she was saying her closing grace before leaving the table. He was relieved. He couldn't be accused. He had escaped until later, perhaps. Mrs Stover formally excused herself from the table. A few moments afterwards Jerry left by the side door and walked through the sitting-room, out to the front veranda. He heard his mother moving about in her room. He was determined to be sincere. He would be direct and explicit. He would be humble. He would express himself simply, honestly, and he would be calm and courteous. Firmly resolute about the quality of his conduct, he walked towards her bedroom door while rehearsing his opening sentences. Just as he gripped the door knob, he heard his mother crying softly and mumbling to herself. He withdrew his hand, listened long enough to be sure that she was crying, and tiptoed away to the other side of the veranda. He did not know what to do. Somehow he was quite certain that his mother's condition was due to his stupid behaviour of the night before. He sat down on the arm of the chair nearest his own bedroom door and placed his feet on the seat of the one next to it. He closed his eyes and bowed his head. He remained like that for some time. Then he got up and went back to his mother's door. He stood in front of it and waited. She had stopped crying, and the silence made him feel less depressed and a little less insecure. He turned the door knob gradually. The door was locked.

The drive out to the airport was long and refreshing. The salty sea breeze blew through the speeding taxi at welcome intervals, bringing with it the tang of washed-up seaweed and rotting driftwood. Jerry thought about his boyhood seaside escapades, his visits to Port Royal, his first dive from the thirty-foot platform at Bournmouth, his harpooning of the large deep-sea jelly fish and his collecting of choice specimens of sea eggs and conch shells.

Carmen was thinking about him and America. She was glad that she had not gone without meeting him, without having had the chance of falling in love with him, without experiencing his love for her.

Mrs Dabdood was thinking vaguely of what she would start doing with her time now that Carmen was going away. Her new freedom seemed exciting, until she remembered that she had no one to share it with her.

When they reached the airport, Jerry left to see about Carmen's luggage. After he had arranged everything, he went to the Liner-Diner bar and joined Carmen and her mother. They chatted nervously, inconsequentially, but all the time with an undertone of anxiety and sadness. Carmen slipped away to find out about the exact time of her flight and to check in with the desk attendant. Jerry found her at the curio counter. She was writing a note. He crept up behind her and kissed the back of her neck. She spun round, surprised, quickly tucked the note into her handbag and touched his face.

'Writing to me?' he asked, a teasing edge of arrogance in his voice.

'I can tell you, now, if I'm brave enough,' she said, biting her lower lip and lowering her eyes.

Jerry wondered what to expect. He frowned.

'I'm pregnant, Jerry.'

He did not how to reply; he merely allowed himself to be prodded along through the shifting clusters of people at the curio counter, all the way along the service windows, and out to the gravel path, leading to the Liner-Diner bar. Carmen had known that it would be difficult for him; it was she who had led the way from the counter, after making the declaration to him. She knew it would work successfully that way.

'How much time have you got?' he asked her, as they were mounting the steps to the bar.

'About five minutes before we all go out to the plane,' she said resignedly. She paused, turned fully towards him and whispered, 'Everything'll be all right.'

'Why didn't you tell me before?'

'I tried to, but I couldn't.' She kissed his cheek and pressed smooth the furrows on his forehead. He returned her kiss, and they both turned towards the bar. She hurriedly kissed her mother and ran across the gravel path and into the airport building.

It was a little after midnight when Jerry got home. He had been wandering around Kingston all day, and had seen a late film. He found Miriam waiting for him in his room. He turned off the ceiling light, switched on the reading lamp and sat on the downy rug in front of his bed. He grasped his knees with his clenched fists and rocked slowly and looked up at her.

'You' lookin' real mash' up,' she said. 'Poor t'ing.'

He thought he recognised a trace of irony in what she said, but he tried to show how unimpressed he was. 'What's wrong, Miriam?' he asked her calmly, wishing urgently that she would make her explanation short. He was tired.

'It's wha' *you* cause to wrong,' she confided cryptically.

'What?'

'I breedin' for you.'

He wanted to scream with laughter. He promised he would, if only hours afterwards. He looked at her stomach. He giggled.

'Wha' you t'ink I should do 'bout it?'

He imagined a pumpkin on a pedestal standing on two slender wooden legs; he held the large vegetable up to his face and banged his head on it; he heard a dull thud. He giggled again. She seemed desperately flat-stomached.

She went on to say, 'I know you's a Roman Cat'lic, an' I know that them sort o' people don't like when you t'row 'way pickney before them born, even though they don't seem to mind when you t'row them 'way after they born an' grow up.'

He risked a smile.

'Do 'way with it is wha' I say,' she said resolutely, with more than a touch of defiance, which was intended to impress Jerry.

'Would you rather do it that way?'

'You an' you' family wouldn't want it the right way, an' you know so you'self. Them wouldn't want no bastard from somebody like me, maybe from somebody else. I not talkin' religion or anyt'ing to do with Roman Cat'lic preachin'. I talkin' 'bout you' own class o' people. Constant Spring Road is a different t'ing from Kin'ston or the country.'

'Do it your way, Miriam.' He braced himself against the flood of self-accusation he suddenly felt. 'It's the Constant Spring way, too. What about money?'

'I could use some, yes.'

'When do you want to go?' he asked.

'In the morning' firs' t'ing before sun hot an' Miss T'elma wake up busy.'

Chapter Sixteen

The next day was Good Friday. The Stovers met for breakfast at eight o'clock precisely. Thelma had already reported Miriam's disappearance and Mrs Stover had had her say, a very brief one; so had Thelma who had insisted that they both check all the kitchenware, house cupboards, and, indeed, all the rooms in the house. But Mrs Stover had told her not to bother. Naturally, her confidence in Miriam's honesty deeply offended Thelma; it was a challenge she resented, and she was still sulking when Les and Jerry came to the table.

'Storm clouds?' Les asked.

'Upset about Miriam's disappearance, I think,' his mother told him, trying to be matter of fact about it.

Jerry had heard his brother's question and had listened very carefully to his mother's reply. 'You say she's disappeared, Mother?' he asked casually.

'Yes, Jerry.'

'Just like that, eh?'

'Yes.'

'Bit of a surprise.'

'Indeed.'

'She seemed reasonably happy,' Les said.

'Fed up, I suppose,' Jerry suggested.

'She might've given us notice,' Mrs Stover said, looking straight at him.

'She might have at that,' he agreed.

They said no more. Thelma had returned. Mrs Stover said her closing grace and went to her bedroom. Les and Jerry relaxed. Thelma became confiding.

'She knows somet'ing, y'know,' she told Les.

'What makes you say that?' he asked.

'Why d'you think so?' Jerry said, speaking almost at the same time as his brother.

'She hidin' a few fac's,' Thelma insisted.

'Like what?' Jerry asked her bluntly.

'Not too sure, but she got a nose for mystery, 'special when it come to young people an' such like. She's a teacher, y'know.' She went back to the kitchen and began humming *Abide with me*. She closed the door, making sure to get her accustomed squelching noise out of the lock.

Jerry waited for it and when it came, he shook his head in acknowledgement. Les chuckled and looked up at Jerry to see what he thought of Thelma's speech. He saw nothing he could take as a clue, so he decided to probe. 'You don't suppose the old lady's got something up her sleeve?' he asked hopefully.

'Couldn't say.' Jerry knew he was evenly matched and was delighted. He could afford to string along with his brother's self-regarding trick of delicacy and concern; he could afford, also, to assume an air of friendliness, and he did so gladly.

'She seemed bent on impressing you with the Miriam business,' Les said. 'I wonder why?'

'You know what Mother's like, where I'm concerned.'

'True. But something's being deliberately played down, way down, in fact.' Les frowned.

After a few more minutes of forced friendly conversation

about nothing in particular, they left the table and went to their rooms.

Jerry dressed for the Good Friday service. He had chosen his dark grey Sunbridge tropical suit which he knew his mother would approve for the occasion, a cream-coloured shantung silk shirt, a dark grey silk tie, and his only pair of black leather shoes; he was certain that his choice would impress her and possibly suggest his willingness to co-operate with her demanding family discipline; he had hoped, too, that she would be persuaded to forget Miriam's disappearance, but he knew only too well that he would have to work much harder to attain that. When he was ready, he went out to the front veranda to wait for his mother and his brother, but they were there already. Thelma was a little way off, leaning on the upright of a veranda chair and silently admiring them. When she saw Jerry she smiled and nodded her unsolicited approval of his appropriate attire. She liked to see Mrs Stover and her two sons together, dressed and about to go off as a group. She had once confided to Mrs Stover and to Les, 'Please me ol' heart no end to see you t'ree together when you all dress to· forty-nine an'on you' way to church. Get goose flesh all over when I look an' see you all walkin' off like you was me own flesh an' blood.' Les had said nothing, and his mother had only smiled.

They waved goodbye to her and went down the marl path to the front gate. Les and Mrs Stover walked together and Jerry was in front of them. When he got to the gate, he opened it wide and stood behind it while they passed through. They thanked him with a perfunctory nod and he pretended not to notice. They hadn't long to wait before a bus came rattling up to the stop.

When they got to Holy Trinity Cathedral, instead of waiting around outside as so many of the others were doing, talking in hushed voices, gesturing politely and striking poses of pre-devotional piety, Mrs Stover headed straight for the main door, Les and Jerry following close behind her. They genuflected one after the other and sat down in their family position on the left of the centre aisle, not far from the altar rail. Jerry sat next to the aisle, his mother beside him and Les beside her.

Les and his mother knelt to say the traditional private prayer but Jerry did not. He sat and stared at the high altar and the attendant statues of Our Lady and Saint Joseph which stood on either side of it, and at Saint Theresa a few feet off to the right of the pulpit. They were all covered in purple cloth, and so were the two side altars. After a while he concentrated his stare on the Cross which was uncovered and he thought how elegant and beautiful it looked, and how simple and haunting a tragic reminder.

The service had begun and he felt inclined to follow it closely in his missal. His mother looked at him once when she thought he would be too engrossed to notice her and twice much later on, and she was pleased by his compliance, gratified at his easy observance of the ceremony; perhaps she had not expected it; perhaps she had made up her mind that he was going to be stubborn and sneering. She reasoned with herself, but she was uncertain what she had imagined his behaviour would have been. She dismissed the query from her mind and resumed her undivided attention to the details of the ceremony.

Later, Jerry was in a kneeling position while the others were standing and singing, and this did not convince her of his wholehearted participation; yet it was enough to make her know that there was nothing for her to worry about. But he wasn't praying, as she had imagined; he was trying hard to decide whether to stay or leave. He raised his head and looked around very slowly. On the right of the centre aisle were Berto and Silba; they saw him and winked. He wondered if Van was somewhere near by, but he turned back to face the high altar. Suddenly the nearness of everything closed in on him. The uniformity of the gathering came as a nagging reminder of his own incalculable spiritual block. The altar, the covered statues, the two priests and their acolytes, the volume of the singing, everything seemed oppressive and futile. He sensed a tenseness within himself, and he loathed the mockery of his presence in the cathedral. He bent his head in an attitude of prayer and questioned his belief in the objects and ritual around him, in the idea that lay behind the Three Hours' service. He raised his head and the gathering was still singing. He got up, crossed himself and tiptoed down the centre aisle without once looking back. He went along North Street and headed towards the West End of Kingston, not knowing where he was going and not caring. He heard someone shout his name and he turned but could not see the person. He stopped and waited. Paula and Jenny came round the corner of a side street and then Mason appeared walking fairly briskly behind them. They wanted to know what he was doing, where he was coming from, where he was going. He was glad to see them and told them so, making sure not to tell them that he was coming from the Three Hours' service, which, in any case, they wouldn't have believed. They seemed suddenly quite a distance from him, as though they were never his closest friends; even their faces seemed strange, from some other section of the society. He told them that he was going to see Bashra on the Dung'll. Mason and Jenny showed little surprise; Paula showed none. She merely asked what for. He told her he thought he would visit him to see how he was getting on; he also mentioned that he intended buying a large bun and cheese along the way and taking that and a couple of cream sodas for him. Then he said he would be back in the Niagara on Tuesday, and Paula clapped.

'Heard about P.D.?' Mason asked.

'Yes and no.' Jerry was being cautious.

'Who would've thought our Vie was so cool?' Paula added, watching his face for some extra reaction.

'Aren't you sorry for Albert, losing her to P.D.?' Jerry asked.

'He'll learn,' she said.

'So'll P.D.'s wife,' Jerry countered feebly, aimlessly.

'What's so profound about that?' she asked.

'Nothing,' he told her frankly, backing down and hoping to draw her out.

'Something's up.' She was brief.

'Like what?' Jerry chuckled.

'The family noose maybe?' Jenny smiled.

'A very safe bet, my dear,' Paula suggested smugly, winking at Jenny.

Jerry shook his head emphatically. 'Nothing like that.'

'Tuesday, then?' Paula said.

Even the reminder seemed alien, her uttering it, the name of the bar, the appointment itself. He listened to his mind echoing the reminder, and it persisted in its strangeness. He brightened up and began backing away from them. They said goodbye and walked off towards Church Street. Mason turned and made a V sign. Jerry waved and turned the other way. When he got to the Dung'll it was deserted. Not even the mongrel puppies greeted him. He went straight up to Bashra's hut and knocked. Bashra came out smiling. 'What sort o' bad breeze blow you round here, now?'

Jerry handed him the food parcel. 'See how you're getting on,' he said, looking away and moving backwards.

'Gettin' on well enough, nuh,' Bashra said, holding the parcel close to his chest and patting it.

They sat on a mound of ramgoat roses and looked at each other. Bashra knew something was wrong, but he felt it would be better to wait until Jerry said so; he would give him enough time to make up his mind. Jerry plucked a couple of roses and rubbed them slowly between his hands. Bashra shifted slightly.

'Want a smoke?' he asked.

'All right.'

Bashra fumbled in his shirt pocket and brought out two

124

cigarettes rolled in thin brown paper. 'Want a light?' He threw him a box of matches.

They smoked, each staring at the other, each waiting on the other's sign of liberation, the other's initial response to the concealed invitation to confess his anxiety or his guilt or his dissatisfaction, openly.

Jerry felt it was time to ask his question. 'When's the Revolution, Bashra?'

Bashra laughed. 'You'll know, son.'

'Who'll be in charge?'

'You'll know that, too, for sure.' He shook his head and chuckled hoarsely. 'You' anxious to find a way out for you'-self? Make it you' own cause, maybe?'

Jerry stared at him blankly and said nothing, though he did give both questions some thought, especially the last. He saw himself completely identified with the coming struggle, possibly as a member of the leadership caucus.

'You' not really one o' us, son,' Bashra said. 'You's a frien' o' mine an' that not enough to make you want to fight on our side. We dedicated to the life we got. The life is religious an' rough. We don't expec' no help an' we don't ask for none.'

Jerry tried to smile but Bashra saw through his pretence at once. 'How many of you?' Jerry was still smiling self-consciously.

Bashra did not answer right away.

'How many?' Jerry asked again.

'Plenty t'ousan'.'

'And how much is plenty?' Jerry was serious.

'How much is plenty?' Bashra asked himself, knitting his brows and pursing his lips as if estimating the importance of the total membershp of the brotherhood for the first time. 'I t'ink that plenty would be near to disaster, Jerry. Come we leave it at that, nuh.' He walked with him to the entrance of the Dung'll and waved goodbye. Jerry started off up the street and Bashra called out to him. 'Straight home an' leave the worryin' to people who born natural to it.'

Jerry turned and waved.

Bashra was disconsolate. He felt he had told Jerry much too much; besides, Bashra knew that his own evasiveness was inept; his silences were far too telling. He realised that he would have to discourage Jerry's visits to the Dung'll, both for his own peace of mind, and for Jerry's well being.

On Tuesday, lunch time, Jerry remembered that the Big Thirst was over and that the Termites would be celebrating at the Niagara later in the afternoon. He had a pine-scented bath, dressed himself rather carelessly in a badly crushed faun tropical suit and a cream mesh sports shirt, tying an old tie round his waist, and left the house without telling anyone he was going out. There was a letter for him in the box behind the front gate. He opened it on his way up to the bus stop. It was a very short note from Prudence Kirby. It read rather primly:

Saturday

Dear Jerry

I'd like you to attend an emergency meeting in the lecture hall at the Institute on Tuesday at 1.30 p.m. NEXUS is being host to a visiting literary editor from America, a Miss Caroline Selkirk, who has ideas of starting a little review, presumably in competition with our own. She has tentatively chosen for its name The Kingston Magazine.

Anyway, we'll see, won't we? In any case, we must appear interested, and above all, hospitable and helpful.

For goodness' sake, try not to be late.

Sincerely,
Prudence Kirby

P.S.
Incidentally, Miss Selkirk's a real live Bostonian, earnest as ever, with Vassar inevitably chucked in for good measure.

Because of an accident involving two army lorries and four parked taxis, the bus was held up at Cross Roads for a long time. Jerry got out to look at the extent of the damage done to the taxis and afterwards went into the J. Wray & Nephew bar below his favourite illuminated sign.

'First since Lent,' he told the barmaid.

She puckered her lips, inclined her head and shrugged.

He arrived at the Institute with five minutes to spare. Prudence was waiting for him at the top of the stairs leading to the lecture hall. As he got up to her, she stepped back cautiously.

'You've been drinking.'

He bowed extra-theatrically. 'Two big gills of white rum.' And reported solemnly. 'J. Wray & Nephew. Cross Roads.'

'It doesn't really matter where. You reek of it.' She led him towards the lecture hall and sat him down, far from the entrance and near the back of the hall. She flapped her hands clean, as she walked away.

The other members of the NEXUS executive were dotted about the room, every one of them hunched over an approved book. Distinctive narrow book-marks sprouted discreetly from all the books.

'How did you know I'd be able to come?' Jerry asked, raising his voice slightly and bobbing up and down in his seat.

Prudence spun round. 'You can't possibly be *that* drunk already,' she whispered venomously.

'Watch me,' he warned her.

She stood over him. 'You've resigned your job,' she hissed, triumph and menace in her smile.

'How did you know?' His voice automatically dropped down to the level of her whisper.

She smiled affectionately. Ironically, he thought.

'When did you hear?'

'The day you resigned.'

Jerry quickly thought about the Deputy Clerk, Randy himself, Van; he wondered, speculated, and then he gave up, just as quickly, realising that it wasn't important.

Prudence was serious, intent, on the verge of hissing again. 'This Selkirk woman has to be handled delicately but firmly.'

'Why?'

'You wouldn't want NEXUS killed over-night.' She leered at him. 'Or would you?'

'Our thing's not all that regular.' He was trying his best to sound kindly, even reasonable. 'A couple of numbers in how many years?'

'NEXUS appears.'

'It's practically dead, Prudence.'

'You're going to be difficult.' She left him and stood by the entrance. She huffed and puffed genteelly.

Caroline Selkirk arrived ten minutes late. She was blonde, tall, handsome, simply dressed in salmon gingham, about thirty, and much younger looking.

Jerry stood and stared at her. She smiled wistfully and moistened her lips.

He walked towards her, rubbed his hands, lowered his eyes and said, on approaching, 'A second literary review wouldn't be a bad thing.' He sensed that his beginning was shaky. Prudence glared. He rubbed his hands again. 'What would be disastrous is if it failed early and carried the other review, the older one, with it.'

Caroline Selkirk was intrigued and looked it, ready for debate, assured of her Bostonian aplomb; she moistened her lips a second time. Prudence was anxious but restrained. The others were appreciatively tense, their books dangling in their left hand, a finger stuck in the pages.

'I wouldn't mind a second review,' Jerry continued, 'a monthly, for instance, that came out every month.'

Prudence stroked her cheek, rested her hand over her left breast, and then smoothed the material of her dress along her thighs.

Jerry added to his statement. There was the merest intimation of a spray of dissenting sighs from the executive members.

Caroline Selkirk was now sitting on the platform. She leant forward; her sense of intrigue had been further provoked.

'Our thing has never quite made it,' Jerry went on. 'Two, three numbers.' He paused and coughed. 'A second review might lead the way, stimulate more writers.'

Prudence stood. 'We can't depend on quality only. Selling ads is the lever, the life's blood of any review that hasn't got big backing.' She had made her point. The executive shook itself in agreement. Prudence smiled towards it and nodded discreetly.

'I'll say something about that, if I may,' Caroline Selkirk said with excellent timing, her hands clasped loosely in front of her linen handbag. '*We* shan't need advertisements. *The Kingston Magazine* will have all the backing it needs.' She inclined her head slightly towards Jerry. She fondled her hands delicately, musingly. 'Please continue.'

Jerry chuckled inwardly and was about to give his opinion of the policy and aims he would like to see incorporated in the new review, when Prudence stood haughtily and waved him down. 'I don't think we'd better drag things out any farther,' she advised.

Jerry shrugged. 'Up to you, Prudence.' He sat down.

Caroline Selkirk moistened her lips a third time, and waited to see what Prudence had in mind.

She spoke with crisp, controlled authority. 'If you think you'll be able to make a go of it, Miss Selkirk, I can assure you of the blessing of NEXUS, not only from its editorial board, but also from its contributors.' She flicked her fingers and then clenched her fists tightly. 'When do you intend making a start?'

'Sometime in late Fall maybe. Not for another six months at least.'

'Will you edit it here, or from America?'

'In Kingston, of course.'

Prudence sat down, mustered a breezy élan, hurriedly converted it into enthusiasm and asked, 'Any questions from the floor?'

Jerry sat back and admired Caroline Selkirk's thighs. He raced his eyes up and down them. He ran over them slowly. He selected small areas for close examination.

A jumble of heated perorations and earnest contradictions were coming from the floor, speaker after speaker robustly denouncing Jerry's stupidity and trying as courteously as possible to dissuade Caroline Selkirk from taking him seriously. She was attentive and dully smiling.

When the blast was over, Prudence led her from the platform towards a group of contributors who stood and waited to be introduced. The others hung around at a polite distance. As soon as she could, without giving offence, Caroline Selkirk slipped away from the group and walked over to Jerry who was sitting on his own. He introduced himself. They sat and stared at each other. Caroline Selkirk sighed. 'I've got you into trouble. I am sorry.'

'Nothing to be sorry about.'

They both looked instinctively towards Prudence and the others.

'Why do they take themselves so seriously?'

'They have to.'

'Is this the first time you've spoken against them?'

'First time I've spoken out.'

She opened her handbag and took out a packet of Old Gold. Jerry slyly indicated the No Smoking sign on the wall behind their row of seats.

'Outside?' she suggested.

They started off together, inching their way at first, pretending they had no intention of going anywhere in particular, stopping now and then and looking around casually, and then walking to the top of the stairs and leaning on the wooden railing. Jerry wondered at her easy compliance.

'Why a literary review?' he asked.

'Why literature?' she said. 'Why adventure? Why anything at all?'

'Didn't you expect opposition?'

'Caroline.' She tore open the packet of Old Gold and tapped two cigarettes up through the top. She took one for herself and offered him the other. 'What was your question, Jerry?'

'Did you think it would be easy?'

'If you know it can be done, why do it?'

He was enjoying the seemingly rooted intimacy. He lit her cigarette, then his own. He looked at her lightly freckled arms, the attractive architecture of her thighs and hips and waistline.

'What's the catch? Isn't that the next question, Jerry?' she asked smoothly, toying with her cigarette aimlessly and secretly hoping she had asked the right question.

'I think so,' he said.

'Boston,' she said. 'It's given me a lot and I've tried to give a lot back to Boston, but Boston isn't the accepting kind; it doesn't exactly want what I've got to give. So I look around after Vassar, and Boston still doesn't think my contribution important enough. So, then, I decided I'd like to try the West Indies. I doubt myself a little bit. Then I come across a copy of NEXUS and everything clicks into place, like handcuffs.' She inhaled deeply and exhaled and watched the progress of the smoke. 'I fondly believe I know something about the public service responsibility of literature and I want to be able to serve literature herself in some way. I've chosen to be a literary editor, a sort of midwife, but Mrs Kirby doesn't like competition.'

Jerry glanced over his shoulder. Prudence was approaching. He flicked his cigarette carelessly, turned to Caroline and asked, 'When're you coming back?'

'I leave tomorrow morning and I shan't be back for at least five months, I guess. It'll take a month after I return to Kingston to settle in and meet a few people and so on, before I get going on the first number. Why d'you ask?'

'Just asked.'

Prudence came up and took Caroline's arm. 'One or two others I'd like you to meet,' she said. 'By the way, Jerry, a note for you.' She released Caroline's arm, opened her notebook, detached one of the leaves, folded it neatly and handed it to him. She paused. 'Goodbye, Jerry.'

She and Caroline turned, like conspiratorial editorial colleagues, launched into small talk, and went back to the lecture hall. Jerry leant against the banister and watched them. He opened the note and read it.

I want you to know how much it offends our relationship to have to ask you to consider yourself no longer a member of the executive, or the editorial board, or indeed a contributor to NEXUS.

After your treachery at the meeting this afternoon (and I'm sure all the members present would agree), we must deprive you of the freedom and co-operative planning of our group.

A letter of resignation from you would help to make things much easier for me and for all concerned.

Sincerely,
Prudence

It was long after three-thirty. The Niagara was practically empty. There were only two truck drivers standing near the half swing-door at the Water Lane entrance. The Termites had not yet arrived. Lola was upstairs. Vie was sitting behind the bar; generous portions of her thighs were innocently exposed, and the stout stems of her breasts, heaped in two bunches, were forcing their way through the low V neck of her cotton blouse. Jerry leant over the counter and stared at her.

'You' not tired o' it by now, nuh?' she asked, frowning and hastily adjusting her skirt and blouse. She stood. 'One o' these days when you' catchin' a free look off some woman or other, it goin' to jump out an' bite you on you' sof' parts.'

'As long as I don't get tetanus,' he whispered.

'What you' whisperin' for?'

'Mustn't let the whole world know, Vie. Think of all the women waiting to take a bite.'

'Count this one out.'

'I have.'

She cupped her breasts, inadequately, and glared at him. 'What you mean?'

'Albert and P.D.'

She groaned waspishly, sprang at him, throwing herself half across the counter, and struck out at his face with a clawed fist. He stepped back and jeered.

'You' goin' get a back han' one day when you' not lookin', Jerry, an' I goin' to be the one responsible.'

'A cold Red Stripe in the meantime?' He winked.

She bent over the Coca Cola tank to get his lager and her skirt rose suddenly, revealing the dimpled plumpness of the back of her knees and part of her naseberry-coloured thighs. I'll have you, you sweet eastern salad, you! he promised himself.

She poured his lager and slammed it down on the counter before him. 'You' blockin' up again then?' she asked.

'Lent's over.' He walked into the back room, rested his glass on the arm of a chair, arranged the 8, fixed the appropriate number of chairs, and sat down in his place. A tingle of expectancy. Then he remembered the letter of resignation he had to write. He drained his glass. He went across Temple Lane to Times Store through the back way and into the stationery department.

'You made a goat fool of yourself over Carmen, didn't you?' Pet Cole, the librarian at the Institute, said, standing beside him and waiting to be served.

'Gossip.' He walked to the other side of the counter, leaving her staring at him, stupefied and hurt.

She tried again. 'Carmen's gone, I hear,' she said exultantly.

'She has.' He frowned. 'Broadcaster.'

'Black people,' she exclaimed in exasperation.

He heard her and bowed low. She pouted and turned to face the salesgirl who had come up to her sighing impatiently.

Jerry bought a cheap packet of three envelopes and an extra thin writing pad. He swung sharp left and went straight across to the drug department, into the restaurant and out to King Street. He leant against a parked car, took out Prudence's note, read it, thought for a while, and then wrote:

Tuesday

The Editor,
NEXUS

Dear Mrs Kirby,

I resign.

Sincerely,
Jerry Stover

He complimented himself on doing it in two words. When he got to the G.P.O. on King Street, he ran into a couple of junior civil servants who congratulated him on his resignation from the Service. He grinned and walked on. There was a fairly long queue at the first stamp window he came to, so he went higher up and stood at the back of another with only four people waiting. The fourth person was Pet Cole. He stood behind her and gazed at her exquisitely *straightened* hair.

'What d'you do when it rains?' he asked, whispering in her ear.

She spun round and snarled, 'You again. What's that you asked me?' Her fury was intense. Her wide-spread nose dilated and her pursed lips trembled.

'Your hair,' Jerry explained.

'What about it?'

'When it rains, what happens?'

'What happens *what*?'

'The straightening stuff.'

'Mind your own blasted business.'

'Rain's no respecter of bad hair.'

'Fool!'

'A waste of straightening.'

'Nasty *negah*!

'True.' He admitted mock-penitently.

The stamp clerk had to shout at Pet Cole, twice. The second time indignantly.

Jerry shoved his hands in his pockets and angled his neck awkwardly and stared at Pet Cole's hair. 'Hope it doesn't rain, for your sake.' He smiled.

She left the stamp window. He posted his letter and walked slowly back to King Street. He turned down Temple Lane and headed for the Niagara. When he got to the entrance, he changed his mind and continued walking, turning left along Water Lane. As soon as he had crossed over Duke Street, he realised that he was trying to avoid the Termites and their celebration party to mark the end of the Big Thirst. He asked himself why, but the answers were self-indulgent and confused. Then, as if deciding that escape was futile, he made an about-turn, chuckled at the military rhythm of the swing and headed back to the Niagara.

As he rushed through the Temple Lane swing-door and into the back room, the Termites rose in silence and raised their glasses. He checked his speed and walked slowly round the top half of the 8 and stood at attention behind his chair. The silence continued. Jerry felt distinctly alone, a soldier singled out on parade. His arms ached and his legs were locked to vibration point. It seemed a very long silence indeed, a minute or little more than that. He circled the 8 with his eyes. Then there came a concerted outburst of shouting, cheering and raucous laughter. They all sat down.

They drank steadily until eleven o'clock. At about ten minutes past, after paying up and shouting a medley of farewells to Lola and the usual recklessly improvised taunts at Vie, they set out for the Writers' Nook to see what the night had in store for them. Jerry and Mason led the way up the Lane.

Later on at the Nook, Jerry suddenly felt sick, after downing a steel bottom of Black Seal and Red Stripe beer in one go. He staggered to one of the front windows and leant out, enough to hide himself from the others in the room, and vomited. He muttered certain incantations, self-assuring utterances, straightened up, fixed his countenance in a contemplative grimace, marched out of the room, down the stairs one at a time, and out to the Lane. When he got to the pavement, he slipped and fell. A man, passing along Duke Street, came over and helped him up. Jerry stared at him intently. Nothing registered, though he tried hard to recognise him. The man had long matted hair and a full beard.

Chapter Seventeen

On Tuesday afternoon, a week later, Jerry woke up, blinked, narrowed his eyes incredulously and realised that he was in Bashra's hut on the Dung'll. Bashra was staring down at him disconsolately. 'You' been wanderin', Jerry, man,' he said anxiously. 'You' been comin' an' goin' for a whole seven days now, an' like how we on the Dung'll not too frien'ly with the aut'orities, we jus' been tryin' little home remedy an' hopin' for the bes' without a doctor. You understan'?'

Jerry nodded. The image of Bashra's face slid in and out of focus. He clenched his fists and concentrated but the quality of his vision came and went in spasms.

'Anyway,' Bashra was saying, 'you' much improve' now than when Marcus firs' bring you in an' we start to work on you. Mos' you need is plenty res' an' such like for a few more days, an' then you can make a move an' go home.' He held Jerry's head and shoulders and raised him gently up to a sitting position, but Jerry had dropped off to sleep again. Bashra patted his cheek lightly, left the hut and sat outside on the mound of ramgoat roses.

The Dung'll was oppressively quiet; the scattered noises of traffic and street vendors which swept in from the West End lost their intensity somewhere near the entrance, engulfed, it seemed, by the irregular terracing of the huts and lean-to shacks and the heaps of festering garbage.

Jerry was snoring lightly when Bashra and Marcus walked into the hut and stood over him. They were carrying a large aluminium bath pan filled with boiling sea water and a mixture of leaves and branches swirling in it. They placed it in the centre of the hut and walked backwards out of the hut, leaving the door open. Two old women approached, nodded respectfully to Bashra and knelt at the entrance of the hut. Bashra then led them in prayer for the sick visitor, and Marcus chanted a hymn of praise, slowly, feeling his way melodically and beating time with his feet and making downward movements with his hands, his palms turned upwards and his fingers curled like claws.

'Right! We done now.' Bashra brought the devotion to an abrupt end. 'In you go, an' raise him up easy like, an' give the sick a las' bath. Try don't wake him up, all you do.'

'If him never wake the other six times when we bathe him is now him goin' wake up?' the older woman said defensively, and chirped her teeth.

'Jus' take it slow an' easy all the same,' Bashra said with a conciliatory grin.

'Peace an' love.' Marcus agreed.

After his last bush bath, Jerry woke again and felt his strength returning faintly. Bashra tiptoed down to the shrine, dipped his khaki handkerchief into a bowl of water resting between two candles, returned to Jerry's side and wiped his face, neck and hands. Jerry looked up, thanking him silently.

'What 'bout you' parents?' Bashra asked.

Jerry closed his eyes. Bashra watched the movements of his lids and knew that he was wincing.

'You mus' be causin' them plenty worries,' he said, folding his arms and shaking his head.

'Not going back, either,' Jerry announced.

'Where you' stayin' then?'

'Right here, with you.'

'On the Dung'll?' Bashra could hardly hide his astonishment. 'How you' goin' earn? You only 'ave twenty-two bob lef' after you' Tuesday spree.'

'Don't intend to earn, Bashra.'

'So?' Bashra was baffled.

'Teach. Here on the Dung'll.'

'Teach what, son? Mos' o' us can't read or write a t'ing. What sort o' teachin' you goin' do?'

'From scratch.'

'For true?' Bashra was excited.

'Yes.'

Bashra was elated. 'You won't 'ave to worry 'bout food an' shelter,' he promised. 'You'll always get that an' more besides, if even we 'ave to steal it somewhere. But what 'bout you' family? What sort o' excuse you' goin' give them 'bout the sudden teachin' business an' the Dung'll? How you' goin explain t'ings to them an' to you' drinkin' frien's?'

'Write them, I suppose.'

'You' feelin' strong enough to do that now? Marcus won't mind doin' the deliverin'. Jus' tell him where you' people live.' He rummaged around for a piece of clean brown paper which he handed to Jerry together with a stub of lead pencil.

Jerry wrote:

Dearest Mother,

I'm all right. Sorry about staying away and not getting in touch with you before now. I know you must've been wondering. Sorry again. Try to forgive me.

Incidentally, I've decided to live on the Dung'll and do a bit of teaching, reading, writing and elementary arithmetic. I'm not sure about primers, exercise books, chalk, pencils; I imagine we'll be able to steal them at night from some store on King Street, or better still, embarrass the Education

Department by sending in a requisition.

By the way, Rastafarians aren't vermin, as some people would have us believe; they're not all ganja addicts, thieves, rapists and murderers. They've been left alone too long, without hope, except, of course, for their faith in Ethiopia and a child-like yearning after Africa as their Promised Land.

Don't let on to Les and Thelma, unless you really have to; they mightn't understand. I could've taken a job in Mo. Bay or somewhere else in the country; it's up to you. I know you understand.

Love,
Jerry

P.S.

The bearer of this letter is Marcus, the deputy leader on the Dung'll, I believe; I'm not certain. He's a good man. Give him any letters which may have come for me during my absence.

I'll write often. I'm sure Marcus won't mind acting as our postman for the time being.

Any news about the old man?

That night at about ten o'clock while waiting for Marcus to return, Jerry and Bashra sat in front of the shrine and discussed their plans for the moral and educational reforms on the Dung'll and indeed for the Rastafarian Brethren throughout the Island. Bashra warned him rather emphatically that he had no intention of admitting any and every representative of the many churches from the outside world. 'Gettin' sick an' tired o' missionary zeal, Jerry, boy,' he said. 'I feel they should turn some o' the zeal 'pon themselves an' give we a break.'

He demanded that what he had built up by way of private Dung'll worship ought to be allowed to remain operative. Jerry disagreed. Bashra insisted on his right to preserve the unique personality of the Brethren within the society; he felt that morally the Brethren had a lot to offer. Rastafarians were suffering for a good reason, for the rest of mankind;

they were morally on the path to self-knowledge, peace and love. They were the children of poverty who would, one day, be the ideal builders of a balanced world, a world of compassion, freedom, dignity and everlasting tranquillity. Jerry shook his head but did not declare his doubt. Bashra noticed his caution and hoped that Jerry would be honest enough to debate the question. After another categorical statement of enthusiastic idealism from Bashra, he did so. He told Bashra that he was expecting too much; he warned him against overstatement and confused thinking.

'Every blasted action o' mankind is political, Jerry, son,' he told him. 'I know that. Religion used to be politics in the old days. Rasta not so foolish, you know. We know what we doin'.'

They talked on. They talked about how the Dung'll dwellers had always been ignored, except by the politicians when it suited them, and by the police who took pride in hunting them down at the slightest sign of suspicion and sometimes even without that much. Bashra explained the high incidence of crime: the growing and selling of *ganja,* and the petty theft and occasional violence that resulted from it. 'We got to 'ave a master plan, Jerry,' he implored. 'We got to 'ave somebody trustin' and big to talk up for us. I wouldn't mind livin' in this country, if I could satisfy the Brethren that the Island is the sort o' place we can all share an' share alike in, but it don't go so at all. Progress an' good livin' is for the others, an' only poverty, scorn an' disgrace is for we.'

Marcus walked in tired and angry. 'I get a bus go, but couldn't get one comin' back,' he explained, while handing Jerry his mother's parcel. 'The blasted conductor wouldn't let me get on the bus, because I dirty an' Rasta.' He shook his head and chuckled. 'Nice lady you' mother, Jerry, nice lady can't done, man.'

Jerry opened the parcel, took out his mother's letter, and one from Carmen. He tore open his mother's envelope carefully, while Bashra and Marcus watched him anxiously. The letter was written on a sheet of his own writing paper. He read it to himself.

Jerry,

I sincerely hope you know what you're doing. Am I to believe that your new life has been inspired by Christian action? If so, you haven't the discipline to make a success of it.

Aren't you assuming the Government's responsibility, single-handedly? I suppose I'll be accused of preaching, but you're very confused. Anyway, try not to get sucked into the mess; you'll find it only too inviting.

Why not appeal to the Methodists or the Catholics? Father Gladstone ought to be immediately responsive.

I don't know what to suggest about the textbooks and writing materials; embarrassing the Education Department might just be the thing to do (I've long wanted to do that myself); on the other hand, burglary is stupid.

I'll try to help wherever possible. Don't expect me to join you down there. I have neither the time nor the inclination.

Remember to write to the Kingston and Saint Andrew Corporation, and to the Central Housing Authority about conditions as you find them. Try to be intelligent about things. Think soberly, seriously.

Mother

P.S.

Oh, by the way, martyrs are damned silly people. There must be a way of bringing about reforms without having to die for them.

I'll tell Les and Thelma you're working for the Americans in Sandy Gully, as good a place as any, don't you think?

No news from Cuba.

Enclosed is an interesting cutting.

Jerry took up the cutting. 'Want to hear this?' he asked Bashra and Marcus. 'Something about the Brethren. From an English newspaper.'

They nodded and smiled.
He read slowly.

'*The Rastafarian sects are not a companionable lot. They smoke and sell ganja, a narcotic, object to personal hygiene, and, while most Islanders aspire to get better housing, they choose to live in mountain recesses, hovels, and on dung hills in and around Kingston.*

'*Rastafarians are regarded in their country as harmless lunatics. They take their name from that of the Ethiopian royal family, believing that their ancestors came from Ethiopia (Island Negroes are of West African descent). They wear beards in honour of Emperor Haile Selassie, who has probably never heard of them.*

'*Rastafarians form a lunatic fringe of the Garveyites, followers of the Negro Marcus Garvey, who early this century started a "Back to Africa" movement. He formed a shipping company in America, the Black Star Line, and actually took aboard one shipload of would-be repatriates. The vessel sank.*

'*Rastafarian leaders have recently been collecting money to send more of their Brethren back to Africa. It's hard to understand why they are what they are.*'

Jerry thought that the explanation could easily be found if Kirby and Rybik were put on trial, along with the other privileged members of the society. He waited to hear what the others had to say.

'Plenty trut' in mos' o' the write-up,' Bashra said thoughtfully.

'An' plenty *rass*, too,' Marcus said humorously. 'Ton loads o' *rass hole*.'

'Foreign jornalists,' Jerry suggested.

'No, Jerry,' Marcus objected. 'Foreign is a word that can cloud issue something terrible. Mos' journalists get on the same way the world over, accordin' to the laws o' the job. This one write like him plenty t'ousan's o' miles away from the happenin', an' so him is too.'

'True word,' Bashra said. 'Foreign journalists mus' be people firs' an' then journalists secon'. As a man, that journalist, who write that piece o' slanderous *rass*, is a trouble-maker with the wrong set o' fac's. But that don't mean to say that him's a bad journalist, jus' a bad man. Don't mind him.'

Chapter Eighteen

Partly in order to make up his mind and partly because it helped to distract his attention from the filth and poverty and futility round him, Jerry read and re-read Carmen's letter between his long and exhausting teaching periods during the days that followed, right up to the end of the week. On Saturday morning he felt he was ready to answer it. He spread the letter beside a blank sheet of writing paper and read it through once more.

Dear Jerry,

What little I've seen of American life and Americans suits me. I don't go into Julliard until September, so I'm looking around frantically

Everything's under marvellous control. Why don't you start thinking about coming up to New York?

My regards to Pet Cole. Naturally I'm not even sure she will get my message. I'll drop her a line later on.

Write and tell me what you think of a trip to New York.

Love,
Carmen

Jerry folded the letter and slipped it back into the envelope. It had proved once again to be too cloying for his taste; it seemed at once intense and determinedly relaxed, more assured than his relationship with Carmen as he understood and felt it. The Dung'll had begun to exert its influence on his personal way of looking at life. He walked outside and stood in front of the hut.

So far, he had fourteen members in his class: ten women, two children and Bashra and Marcus. The other men, twenty-six of them, had not yet been won over; however, he was grateful for the fourteen. He also felt that whatever they picked up from him would somehow trickle down to the twenty-six absent ones. Before long he knew he would be facing the problem of full attendance. He had set his class to work on the Alphabet, copying the first five letters in their common and capital forms, and now he was returning to see how they had made out on their own. The results were heartening. He realised with some surprise that he was going far too leisurely and cautiously with his scheme of work. The more able members of his class realised it too. He praised them lavishly on what they had achieved and introduced a new set of letters down to O. They copied them out painstakingly.

That night, Jerry and Bashra wrote their first letters to the Kingston and Saint Andrew Corporation and to the Central Housing Authority describing the conditions on the Dung'll and complaining about the accustomed neglect and apathy. After they had written the two letters and had drafted three more to the Island Welfare Limited, the Rybik Industrial Trades' Union, and to Father Gladstone, the problem of envelopes and stamps arose.

'Marcus boun' to help with that,' Bashra assured Jerry. 'If he can raise a heap o' slate an' chalk an' big blackboard, you really t'ink a few envelopes an' stamps goin' present any major worl'-shakin' problem? No, man.'

Jerry also wrote a short note to Mason. He wanted Mason to come to see him on the Dung'll.

Mason turned up at the entrance a fortnight after Jerry had sent his note to him in care of Lola at the Niagara. He looked thinner, more lined, and less self-assured than Jerry had ever seen him before; he had always had periods of physical ups and downs, particularly between binges, but this had been the first time that he had appeared so markedly changed.

'You took a long time, Mason,' Jerry said, hugging him in the style of the Brethren and slapping him hard on his back.

'You should complain,' Mason teased. 'What about your disappearing act, Brother Man?'

'Tired of the usual,' Jerry said easily, staring at the lines in Mason's face. 'Anyway, you look beat yourself.'

'Go on,' Mason said, puffing out his cheeks and making a funny face at Jerry.

'It'll need more than that,' Jerry told him. 'Look, d'you want to help out?'

'How?'

'The need's obvious. Look around you. You can smell it.'

'Point taken. O.K.'

'That means a lot to me, Mason,' Jerry said, hardly bothering to conceal how very grateful he felt. 'It's also going to mean a great deal of hard work for you.'

Mason shrugged. They talked desultorily about the Termites. 'How's Jenny?' Jerry asked.

'Gone off with her latest man.'

Jerry looked away and thought of something to say quickly to change the topic of conversation, but he was confused and only too aware of Mason's uneasiness.

'On one of her round-country trips for Thanan's,' Mason explained. 'Went after them, but all I got out of it was a bloody great row and a damn' good punch-up.'

'Who's the man?'

'Neddy Leazar. Used to be in Thanan's retail department.

Specially endowed. Lashings of cock and can't wait for his women to talk about it. Does it himself.'

Jerry smiled as Marcus walked up to them. Marcus nodded and gave him the Peace an' Love salute, a raised right hand, palm open and inclined backwards.

'So what's the plan, then?' Jerry asked Mason.

'Join you for the time being, I suppose.'

Book Three

Mason
Neddy Leazar
Dr C. W. Rybik
Mrs Stover's letter
Prudence Kirby's last letter
W. C. Kirby
The November March

Such curiosa as tease humanistic
Unpolitical palates.

W. H. Auden   *Makers of History*

Chapter Nineteen

It was, now, September and three months of hard work and wishful thinking since Mason had joined Jerry on the Dung'll. They had written many letters, notes and messages to all the prominent people and welfare organisations, but very few of them had been acknowledged. It was apparent to Jerry and Mason that nobody took the Rastafarians seriously.

Miriam had not written. Jerry was still wondering about her. He had no idea of how to get in touch with her. He knew that he would have to wait. Perhaps, after one of Marcus's return trips from Constant Spring, he would hand him a letter which would explain everything.

A certain amount of reclamation work had been done on the Dung'll, but there was much more to be done. Bashra, Marcus, Jerry and Mason had managed to clear away nearly all the garbage from the living area. The main heap in the centre had been left alone because of the enormous hole under it and because Bashra and Marcus had explained that many of the brethren and indeed they themselves had, from time to time, evaded police raids by crawling under the top layer of the garbage and hiding in the available warrens down in the hole; Bashra and Marcus called it their Manhole. The area was now generally improved, cleaner, and providing ample space for Jerry's and Mason's open-air classes.

Mason had become accustomed to his new life; its harsh discipline and continuous work had changed his attitude and behaviour radically. There were times, however, when his thoughts included Jenny and he felt sorry for himself, but he was surprised to see how easy it was for him to shrug off her memory.

Jerry and Mason squatted round a packing crate in a disused shack and Bashra thanked them for their day's teaching. They told him not to, but Marcus mentioned that it was his and Bashra's duty to do so and that they should learn to accept their thanks gracefully. He added, 'An' what 'bout a nice, easy smoke for a change?'

'Is that why you sent for us?' Jerry asked.

'The las' o' the crop, the very las', Jerry, hones' to Gawd,' Bashra said.

'Information or apology?' Mason asked, toying with the box of matches on the crate and intentionally avoiding Bashra's stare.

'Both, son,' Bashra declared. 'A little o' each an' you can't go wrong don't care how hard you try.' He paused. 'A good day's work mus' make a man deservin' a smoke any way you look at it.'

'Will it solve anything?' Jerry asked.

'What?' Bashra guffawed. 'A smoke? The weed never solve' a Jesus t'ing, son. It only make life bear up off you' back for a spell.'

'A spell at a time could add up to a lifetime,' Mason suggested.

'A lifetime is not'ing without a straight back an' a head high in the wind,' Marcus said, gesticulating freely to show how proud he was of his pronouncement.

And Bashra said, 'That true, an' besides, we got to dodge all this dirt an' nastiness 'cause it jus' waitin' to cover we up one time. Look how it spread out roun' we waitin' to close in.' He guffawed again.

Jerry and Mason realised that Bashra and Marcus had been smoking secretly long before they had sent for them, perhaps since very early in the morning. Jerry was certain that Marcus's easy rhetoric was proof of the fact, and Bashra's relaxed attitude, too. Mason could not help wondering at the new sense of responsibility motivating Jerry's thoughts and actions, and indeed, his own. But then he remembered that *ganja* meant a heavy fine or a term of imprisonment or both. Self-preservation? Responsible action? What does it matter? he told himself. One's as good as the other.

Nobody spoke until Bashra had handed out the rolled cigarettes. As they smoked they talked about the Dung'll, their own apathetic Brethren and the decadent world outside. Mason interrupted with stories about England. Jerry slipped in the little he knew about the Civil Service, a full account of Dallas and P.D., omitting, considerably, the more intimate incidents which concerned Mason and Jenny, and Sally and himself, and at Bashra's request, a sketchy biography of the Termites.

They managed to keep one another entertained as they continued smoking. After his third cigarette, Mason chuckled to himself as he watched Jerry's wholehearted participation.

'What 'bout a sort o' recitation session?' Bashra asked when he noticed Jerry and Mason showing signs of drowsiness. 'If you talk a few verses you' bound to las' longer under the weed.'

But Jerry and Mason had had more than they were able to hold. The session of recitations would not be enough to bolster them against the creeping sensation of sluggishness from the narcosis of the weed, and Bashra knew it but he had to pretend that everything was going casually, smoothly: their intimate company and their stories meant a great deal to him; their presence meant entertainment and also a kind of tutorial supplement to his daily lessons.

'The shack's stuffy,' Mason said in his defence. 'We're bound to be drowsy.'

Jerry nodded.

'Cho! You boys can't take it at all.' Bashra winked at Marcus.

'Talk you' talk, man,' Marcus urged. 'When a man drunk he mus' open up an' talk big an' deliver soul to ease himself.'

Jerry braced himself against the packing crate and said, 'Let's make up something, anything. Like a play.'

Bashra rubbed his hands. Marcus crossed his legs. Their invitation had been accepted. It was their way of saying thanks to their two young sympathisers from the outside world who had come to the Dung'll to share their lives; it was their way of giving them back something that mattered, a release from anxiety, a confessional that would purge them and make them whole.

Chapter Twenty

While Jerry and Mason were sleeping off their late afternoon *ganja* session, Neddy Leazar was leaving the monthly sales conference at Thanan's department store. During the meeting he had been thinking about Mason's disappearance. He had met him only once briefly and their encounter had ended in a fight. He felt guilty, as he reflected on the incident; he became anxious and irritable, and of course, he quickly reminded himself, in order to ease his own burden, that Jenny's being in the same office had everything to do with his becoming involved with her; in fact, she had encouraged the affair, arranged it. He shuddered from his cowardice. He straightened his tie, ran his fingers through his hair and walked through the goods' entrance round to King Street. When he got to the front of the store, he hesitated, looked down the street towards Victoria Pier and then up towards the Kingston Parish Church clock. Seven o'clock. He made a hurried mental note to do something about the sales conferences which were becoming progressively later throughout the year. Walking down King Street he thought of all the possible places Jenny had mentioned Mason may have gone to: the family house in Mandeville, the old college friends in Saint Elizabeth, his uncle's estate near Drax Hall, his aunt in Montego Bay, acquaintances in Falmouth. Later on, along Temple Lane, he wondered when Mason would return to Kingston and what he would do about Jenny and himself when he did.

The Niagara was packed. Neddy Leazar bounced and jostled his way through the standing drinkers and scattered tables round him in an attempt to reach the corner in which he had glimpsed Sally and Van huddled together.

'Just us two, Neddy,' Sally greeted him.

'Still no news about Mason?' he asked her.

'Sudden concern,' Van said. 'Conscience?'

'Just asked,' Neddy explained, as he sat on the arm of Sally's chair. 'Where's Jenny?'

'Taking a last look at Berto's exhibition, I think,' Sally said, and drained her glass.

'Berto's respectable now, isn't he?' Neddy said. 'The Institute and culture.'

'The Institute and culture,' Van repeated.

'What's wrong with you, King Kong?' Neddy asked.

'You, body snatcher,' Van told him.

'Nerves,' Sally suggested.

'Shredded,' Neddy said abruptly, lit a cigarette and exhaled in Sally's hair.

She drove her elbow into his stomach and said, 'Bad as it is, I don't think it needs fumigating.' She then shifted her position in the chair. 'We weren't all Brylcreem Syrian babies, you know.'

'What's that got to do with it?' he said. 'Am I interrupting something?'

'Not me,' Van said.

'Why the tension then?'

'Don't feel any,' Sally said, smiling and rubbing her elbow and looking at his stomach.

156

'None,' Van said.

'Cut it with an axe,' Neddy said, getting up and walking towards the bar. On the way he stepped over a shoe-shine boy who promptly bit his ankle.

'Syrian man,' the boy shouted, crouching over his customer's extended right shoe.

'Sorry,' Neddy said sincerely, 'didn't see you.'

'Nex' time I goin' bark to prove I's a dawg so you won't step on me as you like.'

'I stepped *over* you, remember?' Neddy smiled.

'*Over* an' *on* is the same t'ing for dawg,' the boy told him, 'an' me an' dawg don't like anybody shadow pass over we at all.'

Neddy ordered a quart of Black Seal and a big gill of white rum. When he got back to the corner, he rolled his trouser turn-up, pulled down his sock away from his bleeding ankle and poured the white rum into the teeth marks.

'Can't step on people and not expect the odd bite,' Sally advised.

'Little cannibal,' Neddy whispered.

'Say that and whistle,' Van said.

'And they come in all shapes and sizes, and colours,' Sally added. 'And without warning.'

Van picked up the bottle of Black Seal and kissed it. 'Sweet fire water,' he said.

'What's up with the others?' Neddy asked, ignoring all they had said. 'Berto's show too?'

'Avoiding the Syrian host,' Sally said.

Neddy pulled his sock up with great care, rolled down his turn-up and placed the glass with the rest of the white rum on the window sill behind Sally's chair.

The shoe-shine boy came up to the table and grinned. Neddy smiled cautiously. The boy stretched over Sally, reached out for the glass of white rum, peered into it curiously, quickly raised it to his lips and said, 'No 'ard feelin's, pardner, 'til the Revolution noise start up under you' arse.' He looked straight at Neddy. He swallowed, licked the corners of his mouth and shuddered.

'Tough,' Sally applauded him and he bowed to her as he backed away from the table.

'Is gone I gone 'til nex' never, nuh,' he called over the din of the raised conversations and laughter of the drinkers in the room. 'Walk good an' mind accident.' He paused. 'Syrian man.'

Neddy waved to him and began wondering about his uncertain position among the Termites. He remembered what Jenny had said on the night he first made love to her: 'It's none of their business. I know exactly what I want and I want you for the time being.' Then he recalled the incident with the shoe-shine boy and the words 'Syrian man' repeated their rhythm menacingly again and then died away as soon as he looked at the empty white rum glass in front of him. He chuckled when he recalled the boy's threat about the coming Revolution. He poured himself a large drink of Black Seal without ice or water. Sally and Van helped themselves generously immediately afterwards.

'Absent friends!' Neddy toasted.

'And enemies,' Van said.

'And our shoe-shine Revolutionary,' Sally added.

At about nine o'clock Jenny and Wyn walked in carrying four enlarged photographs from Berto's exhibition. There were no chairs available, so they both sat on the table and talked about their purchases. Jenny was particularly proud of having bought the original *Springboard* photograph of the brawl at the Jam Pot. She insisted that it was, by far, the most inspired and least journalistic piece in the exhibition. Wyn nodded doubtfully. He held up his own favourite, a profile of a market woman set against the Queen Victoria statue in King Street. He pointed out what he thought was Berto's intention of dignifying the peasant, and at the same time, implying that royalty and peasantry are inextricably linked by the very

fact that they are both willing to serve the land and are stead-
fastly loyal to their respective positions, never caring to deny
their heritage or anxious to move away from it.

Van made an obscene sign. Sally uttered a disparaging
snort. Jenny laughed in Wyn's face and told him to be careful
of the legacy of his RAF service. 'Anglophil soon becomes
Anglomaniac,' she warned facetiously, and held up her
second photograph, an unconventional treatment of a conventional subject: the delivery of the birth of a calf taken on the
slant and from ground level.

Neddy took the photograph from her and placed it on the
window sill. 'Berto can't claim respectability after that,' he
jeered.

'Neither can the poor unfortunate cow,' Sally added.

Van drank to the animal.

Wyn then showed his second photograph: a gang of stone-
breakers with their sledge hammers raised and their backs
turned to an expensive camera being focussed by a fat
American tourist in Bermuda shorts.

'Respectability reclaimed,' Neddy observed timidly.

'Political hickory,' Sally said.

'Workers' crap,' Van said. 'Berto wouldn't know a work-
ing-class problem if he went to bed with one.'

Jenny threw up her arms in the air and sagged back on the
table. Neddy eased her gently to her feet and led her outside
to the station wagon which she had parked at the corner of
Temple Lane and Harbour Street after leaving Berto's exhibition. She had left the switch key in the right-hand cubby
hole below the dashboard, and Neddy admonished her light-
heartedly.

When they reached the third house before her own, the
station wagon ran out of petrol. They got out and marched
round it and finally broke into a maudlin chant while holding
hands and quickening the pace to a hop-step-and-jump. They
soon exhausted themselves and staggered away.

After they had both had a bath, Jenny suggested that Neddy

put on Mason's academic gown which he obediently did without drying himself. Still naked, she danced round him in the bathroom, howling and clapping her hands. Frowning and narrowing his eyes, Neddy pretended to be serious and deeply concerned by her behaviour. She ran into her bedroom. He followed her. She tugged at the hem of the gown, picked up one of Mason's leather belts, handed it to him with a flourish and then lay sprawled out on the bedside rug in front of him. He held the buckle firmly, wrapped a short length of leather round his doubled fist and stared down at her. She smiled up at him.

'Why this?' he asked innocently.

'Why not,' she said simply, still smiling.

'Won't it hurt?'

'Isn't that the point?'

He raised the belt and she turned over on her stomach. The leather bit into her buttocks. She screamed. Her voice sounded like the shrill call of the kling-kling blackbird which Neddy remembered in the gully at Wolmer's, his old school. Jenny's lily white skin, however, bore no resemblance to the oily feathers of the blackbird. He smiled and dropped his hand to his side. Jenny looked up and jeered at him with her thumb touching her nose and her four fingers fanned in a child's grimace. He moved slightly backwards. She scrambled round his feet and bit his calf. He struck her playfully and leered down at her.

'For Mason, Neddy,' she cried out. 'Do it for Mason.'

He simply could not get the image of the kling-kling out of his mind. He laughed. She scratched his thigh. He struck out at her.

'For Mason,' she cried again.

And again the leather lashed into the plumpness of her buttocks, and again.

'For Mason.'

And again.

'For Mason.'

And again.

Then she spun round on her back in time to receive the full force of a blow intended for her upper thigh. She placed her hands over the burning spot, cupped it protectively and screamed.

Neddy dropped the belt and knelt at her side.

'Don't stop now, you fool,' she ordered as soon as she felt the pain wearing off.

'Doesn't make sense, Jenny,' he said, attempting to lift her.

She resisted, reached for the belt and smashed the buckle into his groin. He fell backwards, holding himself and wincing from the pressure of the darting pain.

Even then the image of the bird persisted. He inched away from her and said, 'If you were black, you'd be a loud-mouthed kling-kling. D'you know that?'

'Get out,' she said irritably, going to the door and holding it open.

'Blackbird.'

'Blackbird yourself.'

'Kling-kling.'

'Get out and tell them how horrid I am.'

'Scream again, bird brain.'

'Tell them how naive you are and how perverted I am. Go on, get out.'

'Not before I give you the beating you deserve.' He threw off the gown, coiled the belt round his fist, this time leaving the buckle dangling at the end of it, and swung it high in the air. 'You enjoyed it a while ago. Let's see how much you enjoy now.'

'You enjoyed it too but you aren't honest enough to say so,' she sneered.

He flung the belt on the bed and walked into the bathroom. When he was dressed, he went quietly along the corridor beside the bedroom, through the dining-room and out the back way. Lower down the road he stopped at the station wagon and turned off the head lamps.

Jenny had picked up Mason's gown, dusted it carefully, put it on and had gone out to the front veranda and sat down. So far as she was concerned, nothing really important had happened, nothing basically significant, unfortunate or embarrassing. Neddy had been interesting in the way that Mason had long ceased to be, and now Neddy himself had become uninteresting. The bedroom incident had been his farewell salute.

It had always been like that for her: England, during her adolescence, had been mainly the London postal areas of warmed-over tradition, trumped-up heroes, controlled chauvinism, and imported American popular entertainment; then that, in turn, shrank to the size of one small postal area of London, tired Hampstead, and after a time, that contained only one attractive experience: meeting and falling in love with Mason. Shortly after that, he broadened into the Island which narrowed within months into the Termites; Neddy had been merely a breakaway splinter attraction. And now, after her exchange of one island for another, she was alone again.

She closed her eyes and chuckled softly.

'There's still the safety of the Termites,' she told herself, placing her feet on the veranda rail and hugging her breasts through the multiple folds of the academic gown.

Chapter Twenty-one

A week later, Bashra, Jerry and Mason visited Dr C. W. Rybik at the Rybik Industrial Trades' Union headquarters. What was against them from the very outset, and they had not even given it a thought, was the fact that they had decided on their visit without having made the usual appointment with Dr Rybik's secretary. Glissada Maycroft had been his personal assistant ever since he began his political career; in fact, even before that, she had been his receptionist immediately after he had left the Government medical service at the Public Hospital and first opened his own private surgery in Duke Street. Glissada was about forty-five, a tall, frail, imposing woman who had determinedly put her peasant childhood and upbringing securely behind her, adopting a hard, professional manner which she thought suited her position in the Union.

When Bashra, Jerry and Mason climbed the large stone steps leading up to the Union's reception hall, she greeted them coldly, having first made certain that they were not entered in her duty book which she always kept tightly clutched under her left arm.

'Black people can high an' mighty when them 'ave desk job, though, eh?' Bashra whispered to Mason.

Mason smiled at the seductive generalisation and crossed his fingers. Bashra crossed his too and nodded.

Glissada stared at them stonily. 'Well,' she enquired firmly. 'What do we want, and without an appointment?'

Jerry cleared his throat nervously, stepped forward and explained that his small deputation wanted the chance to discuss the conditions on the Dung'll and in the other Rastafarian encampments inside and outside the Corporate Area of Kingston and Saint Andrew, and to ask for Dr Rybik's help in bringing the situation to the attention of the House of Representatives.

'In other words, youngster, you want advice?' she asked patronisingly.

'Yes. That too.'

'That only, you mean.'

'We're hoping for more than that actually.'

'You want to know how to go about getting better conditions for Rasta?'

'Yes.'

'Have you ever heard of the Corporation Council or the Town Clerk's office?'

'I have.'

'So, you have. Well?'

'We've written to them, but we've had no reply.'

'Did you expect a reply, youngster?'

'We did, and why not?'

She smiled and folded her arms. 'What about the Welfare people?' she asked.

'No reply either.'

'And the Church authorities, all of them? The Church Council, perhaps?'

'No.'

'No what?'

164

'We haven't tried. As a matter of fact, I didn't even know one existed.'

'I see.'

Bashra shuffled mincingly on a small area of the floor, scuffing it here and there, and muttered, 'I tell you: black people can 'ard bad, sir, 'special when them 'ave to deal with them own.'

Glissada Maycroft winced. She had overheard him again.

'Miss Maycroft,' Mason began confidently, 'if Dr Rybik isn't too busy, do you think we might see him for a few minutes?'

'The Doctor is always *too* busy, Mr Donne-Jones,' she said, smiling benignly.

'Didn't know you knew me.' Mason smiled too.

'And Mr Stover,' she bowed slightly in Jerry's direction and paused. She stared at Bashra and lowered her eyes.

'You see what I mean 'bout this woman, Mason?' Bashra muttered again. 'Black as she is, she wouldn't really know or want to know all like me so. Don't suit her career at all.'

Mason smiled nervously. He held Bashra's shoulder and winked at him affectionately.

Glissada moved back to her desk and sat down, rummaged through a pile of letters, picked up the telephone from the left-hand corner of the companion desk, sighed and dialled. 'R.I.T.U. Glissada Maycroft here,' she said easily, officially. 'About those reports for the Doctor . . .'

It was too much for Bashra. 'Fuck the reports for the *rass* doctor,' he shouted, moving in on her and leaning across to snatch the receiver from her hand, 'an' try to be civilise', you ignorant black bitch.'

She sprang out of the chair, her body shaped menacingly like a feline streak, ran to the front of the desk and grabbed his throat. 'Listen, you,' she shook him with controlled venom, 'I run this office, d'you hear? I say who's to see the Doctor and who's not to. Now.' She paused elegantly, still holding his neck like a broken stem. 'You and your pitiable deputation had better leave before I throw you out.' She pushed him away, walked to the door and held it open.

Bashra rubbed his neck and said, 'You see how her class o' people is not'ing but a bunch o' dictator an' murderer waitin' to take over control? You notice how it come easy for her to take life jus' so?'

'Out,' she said, waving her left arm briskly.

Just at that moment a tired, hoarse voice, coming from behind a wooden screen, asked, 'Having trouble, Glissada?'

Bashra, Jerry and Mason turned to face Dr Rybik who had come out of his inner office. They ignored Glissada and walked up to him. Jerry explained briefly what the deputation was about. Dr Rybik listened patiently, graciously, nodding sympathetically every now and then. He invited them inside and closed the door slowly, taking care to wink at Glissada as he did so. She smiled ingratiatingly and went back to her desk. As soon as she observed that the door was securely shut, she got up and bent to the keyhole.

Dr Rybik was offering his visitors Royal Blends from a yucca cigarette box which was placed on the current edition of *The Island Year Book*. They accepted.

'Why not get someone to raise the question in the House?' he nodded towards Mason. 'Question time might just be the spot to slip it into for a start.'

'Would a question be enough?' Mason asked. 'And put to Government by whom? One of your own members? I don't get it. Doesn't make sense.'

'What d'you have in mind?' Dr Rybik laughed.

'A campaign, if necessary.'

'Is it?'

'I would've thought so.'

'A campaign,' Dr Rybik mused. 'A campaign of what sort though?'

'The right an' proper sort,' Bashra intervened. 'A firs' class political campaign agains' conditions in all o' the slum areas 'cross the Islan', not jus' Rasta own only.'

'Yes,' Dr Rybik mused again. 'You know, of course, that the R.I.T.U. has its hands tied right now, and, apart from that, what are we to do as a Union? Our concern must be, at all times, one thing and one thing only: the economic welfare of our worker members, broadly speaking.' He paused and stared at Bashra. 'Slum clearance is another matter altogether.'

Bashra sighed impatiently. What the use o' this man education an' big time position? he wondered. He felt the gulf between himself and Dr Rybik suddenly becoming wider and utterly unbridgeable. He knew that the Island was far too intimate and highly personally mixed and conglomerate for such disparate sections to continue fixed for much longer. He looked at Dr Rybik and waited to hear what he would say next.

'You've made me think though,' Dr Rybik admitted.

'O' what?' Bashra challenged.

'Of how to use it as a stick to beat your political opponent's back, you mean?' Jerry asked pointedly.

'Naive,' Dr Rybik assured him, 'but a fairly thoughtful suggestion, coming from you.' He smiled. 'Some of us have passed the stage of playing at the thing, you know.'

'You could've fooled me.'

Bashra stubbed out his cigarette on the floor with a grunt of disgust. 'The poor class o' man an' woman is suppose' to be you' firs' concern,' he said. 'Right?'

Dr Rybik nodded.

'Then why in Jesus' name you an' you' Party don't try an' do somet'ing 'bout the Dung'll?'

'Efforts are made from time to time.'

'At election time we get plenty lip from all sides, 'nough plenty big promise an' masterful speechifyin' 'bout a better way o' life, improvement lef', right an' centre, education, 'ousin', protection from this an' that, fatter wages an' the res' o' it. An' when we elec' you, what 'appen? What really 'appen? Not a rass. Not one Jesus Chris' rass. Pure mout'.'

'You've got a fine political line yourself.'

'I can't even t'ank you for that statement, 'cause I wouldn't want to mix up with you an' the politics we got goin' here now.'

'No point waiting. Jump in with the rest of us.'

'An' mash up the majority o' we with pretty talk an' prejudice? I not in that.'

'Come and see me again, will you?' Dr Rybik looked from Bashra to Jerry to Mason, clapped his hands once lightly, got up and walked to the door.

'When?' Mason asked.

'Give me a week or two. I think we'll be able to knock some sort of plan into shape by then. As a matter of fact, I'm sure of it.'

On their way out, Glissada Maycroft rushed past them clutching her duty book and a handful of letters and looking desperately the devoted and efficient secretary. She was smiling maliciously.

When they returned to the Dung'll, they found P.D. waiting for them in Bashra's hut. 'Don't ask me no question,' he hurriedly explained. 'I see you t'ree when you was leavin' the Dung'll, an', with Marcus' help, I decide to hol' on an' surprise you.'

Jerry and Mason introduced P.D. to Bashra and Marcus. Bashra reacted coolly, though he was very impressed by P.D.'s manner. He admired his assurance, his swagger. 'But a name like Percy Dixon make you sound as if you belong to them big banana people over yonder, man,' he teased him. 'Yonder in money country.'

P.D. told him, 'It make me sound so, yes, but it don't go so, at all. Only by name, but by nature I's a country man an' without the necessaries to make the over-yonder connection. That's me.'

Jerry and Mason explained their presence on the Dung'll, and P.D. listened attentively. He approved and set about organising a Black Seal session to celebrate the crusade, as he called it. Marcus and Bashra were enthusiastic. Jerry and Mason saw that it was inevitable and gave in reluctantly.

P.D. went off at once and returned laden with three quarts, six tins of bully beef, a large paper bag of Excelsior biscuits, hard dough bread and best butter. Marcus provided the water chaser in a huge kerosene tin with an enamel dipper hanging over the side. Jerry was the only one not drinking. He was brooding over his failure at the R.I.T.U. and the deputation's child-like unpreparedness. He found himself watching Bashra's and Marcus's stealthy movements as they packed and rolled their first *ganja* cigarette. He wanted to stop them; he felt that he should object to the practised ease with which they were including it in P.D.'s innocent rum party; he wanted them to forget about the ritual of the miserable habit and its cheap imagined thrill and everything it released in their guts and confused minds.

They rolled another. Then, to Jerry's surprise, Bashra passed both cigarettes round the group. Mason and P.D. accepted them almost without thinking. Marcus expertly rolled three more. Jerry refused. Bashra and Marcus looked at each other and then at Jerry. He frowned. He got up and went back to Bashra's hut.

At first he had the urge to work on the notes for his teaching scheme, but then, after taking them out and reading the last three paragraphs he had corrected earlier, he put them aside and began a letter to his mother:

Things aren't working out as I had expected. All our attempts end in failure. Good intentions aren't enough, unless we're able to direct them successfully. We can't.

Bashra, Marcus, Mason and I must be representative of the muddled thinking in the society. Is it our youth or the Island's? Or is it our own distorted idea of freedom? We don't seem to know how to use it self-interestedly, intelligently, how to live up to it, how to make it a part of our lives, a part of our wellbeing. Did we get it too late, too easily? Or is it that we become free only after we've fought hard for the privilege of being so? Isn't the business of being emancipated something we should've forgotten by now?

Just a thought: when will we learn to take our petty sense of freedom for granted and start to think about the larger freedom of a properly planned society? Will we ever be able to contribute, in some way, to the bigger scheme of things outside ourselves, to the really important, universal issues?

Am I asking too much? Forgive the tone of adolescent insistence and write soon. Love to Les and Thelma, and to you.

He put the letter on his cot and wondered what he was pretending to be in search of, why he had written the letter, what he really knew about people, their problems, aspirations, achievements, failures? He asked himself if he was prepared and whether he knew enough about himself. He grinned and looked down on the letter. He snatched it up, folded it erratically, unfolded it and then tore it up. He was relieved. He had long felt the need to write the letter. It had occurred to him while walking down the stone steps of the R.I.T.U. headquarters and again on his way back to the Dung'll, but what he had written had been so intense and effusive with pretended concern that he knew he would embarrass his mother and give her the wrong impression of his failure on the Dung'll. Instead, he wrote:

Just a note to let you know we're still trying to find our way. Mason and I hardly seem to know how to go about it. Our recent visit to Dr Rybik at the R.I.T.U. ended miserably. We intend to call on W. C. Kirby as soon as we're able to muster enough courage. Bashra and Marcus are as hopeful and co-operative as ever.

Love to Les and Thelma.

Cuba?

Write soon.

He went to the door and looked across at the others in the area. Marcus caught his eye and waved. Jerry made a thumb-up sign with one hand and shook the letter with the other. Marcus understood. He drained his glass, hurriedly stuffed a hard dough bread sandwich of bully beef into his mouth and staggered over to Jerry. 'Thought you were too far gone to get the signal?' Jerry teased him.

'T'ought you was vex' up,' Marcus told him frankly, his mouth still full of food. 'We not doin' any lessons today, an' after Rybik, we might as well celebrate 'way the worries.' He bolted the last mouthful. 'A little somet'ing for you' ol' lady?' he asked, taking the letter from him.

Jerry nodded. 'What if P.D. hadn't come?' he asked, playfully jabbing at Marcus's ribs.

'No P.D., no merry merry,' Marcus said.

Chapter Twenty-two

It was about eight o'clock in the evening when Marcus returned from Constant Spring. Bashra and Mason were sprawled out in the centre of the area where they had fallen asleep during their midday rum and *ganja* party; P.D. had long since gone in search of the other Termites at the Niagara; and Jerry was waiting in Marcus's woman's hut while she sewed a crocus-bag patch over a hole in the back of his khaki shirt.

'Been lookin' all 'bout for you, Jerry,' Marcus said, handing him Mrs Stover's enormous food parcel and a packet of letters. 'You' ol' lady sen' to tell you that she can't understan' why you' martyrin' you'self down 'ere when you would be better off at home where you would get proper feedin' an' such like.'

Jerry tried to imagine his mother's attitude to Marcus, her fixed expression of unconcern, her easy charm and authority; then her whole personality came alive for him, and he imagined how Marcus must have coped with it. He smiled wryly.

'You should see the gran' feas' she give me to eat,' Marcus

was saying, 'while I was waitin' for her to finish the letter. She's a real good woman, Jerry, a proper lady, man. If only all black people could stan' so, what a sweet place this fuck' up Islan' would be.'

Jerry wondered about that.

'Peace an' love,' Marcus continued. 'That's what I tell you' ol' lady, Jerry. I tell her, "Peace an' love, Missis Stover." ' He belched and tapped his chest while at the same time winking and smiling apologetically. 'An' you know what she say to me right after I tell her that?'

'Go on, nuh, Marcus,' his woman urged, knowing how he liked to prolong his better stories. 'Don't ask no lawyer questions, jus' tell we straight an' short what Jerry mother say, without the trimmin's.'

'Well, when I tell her that,' he went on deliberately slowly, 'she look' at me nice an' give me a broad smile an' say, "That's a beautiful thought. Do you all really believe in it?" So, I tell her yes we all say the ol' peace an' love an' believe in it too. An' then she say sad like, "Perhaps we may yet learn from the Dung'll. Who knows?" An' she sigh' a big sigh an' look out towards Constant Spring Road as if she was expectin' to see somet'ing 'appen.'

Jerry thanked him for going to see his mother and for bringing back the food parcel and his letters, and went back to Bashra's hut. He unloaded the contents of the parcel on the floor and cleared a corner spot on the shrine. He placed the largest item, a tin of Danish ham, at the back, and piled four packets of brown sugar against it. Then he stacked nine tins of condensed milk in threes in front of them and on top he rested six large tins of sardines in oil, three bottles of honey, a bag of country chocolate and a small sack of flour. He leant a carrier bag of loose ackees, shelled broad beans, red peas, black-eye peas, a slab of cod fish, five brown paper bags of white rice and two dozen eggs expertly crated in a raffia box stuffed tightly with sawdust and cotton wool, at the base of the shrine. He looked at the display and thought of Randy, and he chuckled.

He opened his mother's letter. A five-pound note fell out of it and fluttered to the floor. He picked it up and blew on it for luck. He flattened the folds of the letter and read:

Jerry,

What a pathetic lot you people are. Even do-gooders have to work to a plan if they're to succeed. You are a do-gooder, now, whether you like it or not.

Can't the Rastafarian Brethren look after themselves? They always have. They've managed to stay alive in their abject poverty and peculiarly aloof world for a very long time.

Why should you be deluding yourself so wilfullly? Theirs is a very slight cause. Well, isn't it slight? What would you call a group of people who're living thousands of miles away from Africa, and who're not themselves Africans, constantly hoping and pining for a Utopian kingdom of their own in Africa? Visionaries, I suppose? Well, I don't.

After your deputation to Mr Kirby, which I'm sure will fail, do you think you might consider coming back home? You and I need much more help than your precious Brethren. Living on the Dung'll isn't necessarily the only way to be of assistance to those on it or to the others who're caught up in similar circumstances elsewhere. The surest way to fight for your cause is to acquire a good sound sense of politics together with a flair for welfare publicity and an acumen for impressing the conscience of the Government and the middle classes. All the sentimentality and wishful thinking will get your cause nowhere.

He stopped reading and ran out of the hut. He skirted around the centre of the area and hurried down to the entrance. He had been alone in the hut, and yet he had sought the openness of the entrance in order to feel more securely alone. The interior of the hut had locked in the vibrations of his mother's painful censure and had begun to depress him considerably. He disliked the active cowardice of hurrying down to the entrance. His temporary escape also nagged at him and did not lessen his depression, as he had hoped. He was just about prepared to take comfort from the fact that there was no one around to distract him, when he realised that the traffic and the people in the street were doing that for him. He resented the outside assistance. It was daunting. It was too easy. He preferred to resist the gloom on his own. Indeed, it was his first experience of honestly loathing escape and external help. He went back to Bashra's hut and continued reading his mother's letter:

Don't misunderstand me; your teaching won't be wasted; your, I mean yours and Rasta's, shared comradeship, your shared hardships, your co-operative effort to bring about reforms, and so on, will emerge, ultimately, as a very positive feature in all your natures. Nothing's so character-building as an apprenticeship spent serving others unselfishly, without reward and at great personal discomfort and risk.

I think you really ought to be laying the foundation for a specific apprenticeship; the basis, I am certain, ought to be partly academic and partly humanistic: an intense course of study in some chosen subject, and then, living to the full, intelligently, and with an awareness of the problems of humanity and with an appreciation of the elegance of the highest achievements of others. After that, and only after that, will you be able to attempt the sort of political and social reformative action which you're now merely playing at.

He flung himself on the cot. He liked performing small melodramatic gestures in private; he even laughed at them, immediately after he had yielded to their rhythm and ritual, however seriously intended at the moment, however self-releasing. Somehow, he did not mind that sort of self-debunking; he flattered himself that he was able to recognise its importance for his own balance and personality. The letter, though only a few pages of lightweight notepaper, felt as heavy as a book in his hand. His wrist ached. He let the pages slip and fall to the floor. A fleeting image of Miriam crossed his mind's-eye. It was followed by one of Carmen. He searched but he could find no likely connection between the images and his present state of mind. He hesitated. The images persisted. Soon, they were displaced by the rustling sounds of the loose pages on the floor, as they were disturbed by a slight breeze blowing through the door of the hut. He gathered the pages and arranged them in the correct sequence. He consoled himself that his unpreparedness would not last much longer; it could be put right by obvious measures, by accelerated experience and even by working through others who were more equipped and aware than he might ever become; if guile was absolutely necessary to gain his end, he believed that he would be inclined to think about using it.

He sat cross-legged on the cot, dismissed his former self-doubt and began the last paragraphs of the letter :

Is there really any scope for experience and personal development on the Dung'll? Variety, dissimilarity, vigorous constructive criticism, conflict, enterprise seem totally absent. The Dung'll is so artificial, if you think honestly about it; there are only two backgrounds: yours and theirs.

Your father's back on his feet and his various ventures continue to surprise; this is my impression from his last letter.

Les asks the odd unnerving question and I'm fast becoming an inspired liar, thanks to you and the Brethren.

Mother

P.S.
Try to accept the parcel and the other thing gracefully.

Still holding the letter, he went down to the shrine and sat in front of it. He looked at his neatly stacked display of food and thought about his position on the Dung'll. Everything he

176

had brought to it had come from a section of the society he knew to be hopelessly imperfect and from which he had long been escaping. He reconsidered the meaning and form of the Brethren's society with its anachronistic tribal echoes and he wondered how much of the mock substance the Brethren would allow him to destroy. He admitted that he had not consciously tried to uproot any of it, except for his attempt, which seemed successful, to frustrate the idea of the exodus to Africa and to which he had fortunately got Bashra to agree after pointing out how ridiculous an expectation it had been from the outset. He recalled what he had said then : 'Africa's got its own problems.' And Bashra, 'So, if the blessed place copin' with modern worries, it can't be paradise at all then?' Jerry had nodded and explained, 'You belong here with the rest of us, bad as things are, worse as they might become.' And Bashra's reply, 'Take a dream from a man an' *you*' got a big responsibility for life, maybe.'

Jerry was sure that his preoccupation with life on the Dung'll was mainly to ignore what was already there and try to create an attractive alternative.

He went out to the area. Bashra was alone and still asleep. Jerry gazed down at him and shook his head compassionately. He looked around for Mason. He searched behind the Manhole and tentatively jabbed a broom handle into the side on which the largest packing crates were piled. He jogged round the area and then out to the entrance. He remembered that P.D. had said that he was going to the Niagara to buy the others a drink; Mason may have remembered too, and may have been in the mood to wander off, what with the after-effects of the *ganja,* the nagging thought of Jenny, or because of boredom with the Dung'll. Jerry turned slowly and faced the huts and shacks behind him to his left. He could smell the mustiness of the interiors, the acrid fumes from the kerosene lamps, the nicotine stench from the *jackass rope,* mingling subtly, separating from one another, and then fusing again. He looked up the deserted street. A wisp of breeze tousled a heap of dry leaves in the gutter; their tiny crackling sounds came and went like whispers in a dark room. He clenched his fists and convinced himself that wherever Mason may have gone and whatever he was doing could only be his own concern; he realised this, and in spite of his doubts, he hoped that everything would be all right, that everything would remain the same as he had planned for the Brethren. Yet, he knew that if Mason never came back, there would always be Bashra and Marcus, the plan, or whatever there was left of it. He was disconsolate. He shoved his hands into his pockets and walked back to the area. He lifted Bashra, gently cradled his thin body and stood and listened to his irregular breathing. Then he carried him into the hut, lowered him on to the cot and drew the calico covering up to his chin. He sat beside him and stared at his matted hair. The oil lamp directly above burned steadily and spilled little wavering blades of light across his face. Jerry leant forward and held his hands up to the lamp and shaded it temporarily, but Bashra's face was still exposed to a sliver of light that filtered through Jerry's fingers. Jerry got up and moved his hands around the hot glass shade, touching it now and then and smarting at the pain it caused him. He took up the oil lamp carefully and carried it down to the shrine and placed it a few inches away from the display of food. He sat down at the foot of the shrine and wrote a short note to his mother thanking her for the parcel and the money. When he was finished, he left the hut and went in search of Marcus. On the way, he began thinking of Mason again.

He and Mason had always had a tacit understanding of each other's problems; they had also shared an unspoken loyalty and affection for each other. Jenny had realised this perhaps more than anyone else and she approved of it; she liked the idea as only a woman could, one who had summed up her man and his best friend, and one, too, who was obviously certain of her position of importance in the relationship.

Jerry crossed the area and passed through the first row of

shacks. He was still thinking of Mason. He entered the second row and stumbled. He got up and brushed his trousers. His mother's letter and his reply were badly crushed. Just as he was about to start off down the row, he heard Mason's voice, and a woman's. Mason was laughing softly and entreating her to be quiet.

Jerry smiled and walked away. Just as he was going, he heard the woman say, 'But Lawd King, wha' a way the *ganja* ripe' up in you' back an' make you rygin'. Is so I love the rudeness when the weed take effec', nice bad for true.'

Jerry went back to Bashra's hut, emptied his pockets and squatted on the floor in front of the piled contents. He picked up an unopened letter from Prudence Kirby, threw it up in the air and watched it flutter and plop dully on the dusty floor. He held it with exaggerated daintiness, snarled and gnashed his teeth and tore it open.

Jerry,
  This is my last letter to you. It would not have been written had it not been on someone else's behalf.
  Caroline Selkirk will arrive at the Palisadoes airport about five o'clock in the afternoon on the last day of November.
  I trust you know what to do.
                                        Sincerely,
                                        Prudence Kirby
P.S.
  It seems rather odd that Miss Selkirk should know in September exactly what hour on the last day of November her plane will arrive in the Island. I suppose we can give credit to American efficiency. It augurs well for the future editor of The Kingston Magazine. *Just a thought.*

Chapter Twenty-three

Every day after their teaching periods during the following week, Jerry and Mason met with Bashra and Marcus to discuss proposals for the welfare programme which they hoped to draft and present to W. C. Kirby at the VPP headquarters. The first proposal, *that the Rastafarian Brethren all want repatriation to Ethiopia,* passionately put forward by Bashra and Marcus as the Brethren's prime demand, was debated for two full afternoon sessions and ended in Jerry and Bashra clashing and walking out of the discussion, Jerry earnestly advocating rehabilitation and Bashra forcefully demanding repatriation. Mason, however, brought them together again, after pointing out the urgency of the other proposals, and Marcus, in his unassuming way, reminded Bashra that the majority of the Brethren would naturally welcome any proposals which would, in the meantime, help to provide regular employment, reasonably good housing and other necessary basic amenities. 'Remember, make appointment with ol' Kirby,' he said, ' 'cause we want a proper change from the las' time with Rybik. We got to get over to Kirby big one time or the same bucket without bottom goin' 'appen like what 'appen with Rybik.'

By Friday evening, Bashra was able to convene the final meeting to vote on the list of proposals. Of the eight splinter groups written to or contacted by casual visits, four sent representatives and only two were interested enough to reply saying that they could not attend. The Blood and Thunder Brethren, the most select, the most feared and violent of the groups, sent along a representative, who read the list cursorily, curtly nodded his assent and left immediately afterwards.

On Saturday morning, Bashra, Jerry and Mason got up at five-thirty, went for a swim at the end of Victoria Pier and returned to the Dung'll for a special breakfast of boiled *ackees*, bacon, fried Johnny cakes, avocado pears and country chocolate.

Bashra was particularly elated. 'You can't go wrong with a salt water start an' a proper belly-full o' real food. We' boun' to bring Kirby to 'im senses.'

They arrived at the VPP headquarters at eight-thirty. W. C. Kirby was waiting at the top of the front steps. He was holding a small memorandum pad and a fountain lead pencil in one hand and twirling a heavy pair of horn-rimmed glasses in the other.

'One man inspires familiarity, the other, awe,' Mason suggested pompously.

Jerry chucked him affectionately in the ribs with his elbow and said, 'Watch the Oxford t'ing, Mason boy. We're operating on the home front.'

Mason smiled.

Bashra said, 'This Kirby look' cool bad. Black like me, too. Could always be a brother o' mine, if I had one. Tall same way an' slender. Mus' be 'bout middle forty.'

'No matted hair and no beard,' Mason reminded him and winked slyly.

'If he' got peace an' love under the cool,' Bashra said, 'that will do for me.'

'Peace and love,' Jerry whispered, 'I doubt it.'

Kirby bowed and led them into the building, through the main vestibule and up to a mahogany double door on which the words CONFERENCE CHAMBER were neatly inscribed. Bashra admired the bright gold lettering and estimated its cost quietly to himself. The room was large and elegantly decorated. There were fourteen mahogany chairs with wine-tinted leather upholstery comfortably spaced out around a long low mahogany table, a small mahoe service cupboard and four sets of mahoe triple wall-shelves. The walls were freshly painted with ivory emulsion and the room's eight broad windows had burgundy damask curtains draped in simple good taste. The floor was oak-stained and highly polished.

'One over the baker's dozen for luck,' Kirby said, when he saw Bashra silently counting the conference chairs.

'Tha's exac'ly wha' we need to fall 'pon poor people,' Bashra said, 'more an' more baker' dozen.'

'Precisely,' Kirby said, showing them to their positions round the table. 'I agreed to meet you alone. I'm quite sure we won't need the usual secretarial fuss. Staff hardly like the idea of coming in on Saturdays if they can help it. Can't say I blame them. Hate it myself.' He sat at the head of the table. Mason was on his left; Jerry on his right; and Bashra on Jerry's right. 'I take it you're the head of the Rastafarian Brethren, Mr Bashra?'

'Jus' Bashra,' Bashra said.

Kirby twirled his glasses and smiled easily, affably, bowing slightly to him to acknowledge the correction.

'No,' Bashra went on, 'no official head, as such. All you' find is a number o' groups an' one or two self-appoint' leader an' so 'bout the Islan'.'

Kirby nodded. He pushed his glasses with a poised finger towards the memorandum pad, and then he brought the fountain lead pencil up to join the two. He seemed satisfied with the way he had assembled the trio of objects. He nodded again. 'Have you a statement of proposals,' he asked generally, looking from one face to the other and finally stopping at Bashra's. 'Recommendations? Anything written down?'

Bashra gestured towards Jerry.

'We have,' Jerry said, holding out his hand to Bashra.

Bashra handed him the list of proposals, and he gave it a quick last look before handing it to Kirby. Mason stared at the curtains. Bashra fondled his beard. Jerry folded his arms. Kirby read the list through very slowly, took his glasses off and pinched the crease on the bridge of his nose.

'Why us?' he asked.

'Why not?' Jerry asked in return.

'You know we're the Opposition, don't you?'

'We also know what to expect from the Majority party,' Mason said quickly.

'Good!' Kirby folded the list and tucked it away in the breast pocket of his jacket.

'I should like to go on the record as being absolutely opposed to repatriation,' Jerry said.

Bashra looked sharply at him. Mason placed both his elbows on the table and cradled his chin in his hands. He sighed. quietly.

'So, there's a split in your deputation, eh?' Kirby said, looking interestedly at each of them in turn. 'Why the division? Aren't you in favour of repatriation, if the Brethren want it?' He pointed his glasses at Jerry.

'Seems cowardly,' Jerry said bluntly.

'On whose part?' Kirby wanted to know.

'On the part of the Government, of course,' Jerry said decisively. 'It also works out marvellously convenient for them.'

'Does it really seem so to you?' Kirby lisped, and twirled his glasses. 'I should've thought quite the contrary.'

'If Rasta stay,' Bashra said, 'problem pop. If Rasta go 'way, problem ease. We goin' let them off light an' go.'

'I know there are certain points of argument . . .' Jerry began.

'Very definitely there are,' Kirby interrupted him. 'They're fairly reasonable and even though they sound like warmed-over clichés, they're pretty valid, you know: every Islander has the right to emigrate, even to change his nationality, if he wants to and can arrange it.' He chuckled and spread his arms in satirical self-mockery. 'The Island is overpopulated and its economy, what's left of it after the raping it's gone through, would benefit from extra emigration; and, of course, we've always emigrated in the past; we're very good at it. Panama, Cuba, America, England. Why not Africa or Ethiopia for your Rastafarian people?'

'Isn't the Government embarrassed by that sort of get-out?' Jerry insisted.

'I can't see why it should. It's for the good of the Island in the long run.'

'For the Government who can't even plan it' own tea bread, much or no way,' Bashra said. 'For the good o' the Government own skin, an' not all o' them black either.'

Kirby smiled broadly.

'An' for the few greedy capitalists them who don't want them property burn down an' them plantation mash' up,' Bashra added. 'Anyway, Rasta want to go an' we goin'.'

Jerry frowned and waited for Bashra to continue, as he showed signs of doing.

'I goin' tell you some o' the history an' ol'-time story off the record o' Rasta, as you ask' for it,' Bashra said nervously, wavering slightly between dialect and standard English, as he always did when under stress.

Jerry gripped Bashra's left thigh under the table and squeezed it. Bashra understood, paused and smiled. 'I' goin' spare you the history lesson, Missa Kirby, 'til we' ready to leave for home. Then I' goin' deliver it in me farewell speech, loud an' clear.'

'I'll send Dr Rybik a copy of your list, if I may,' Kirby said.

'T''ank you,' Bashra nodded and continued, 'very much,

t'ank you, an' I hope he' read it, 'im an' that ol' dragon Maycroft.'

Kirby rose and the others prepared to follow him out of the room. 'I suppose we act and sound very much like the Government, don't we?' he asked Mason.

'It would be a triumph to find the salient difference,' Mason said.

'My admission is a starting point,' Kirby said, shrugging listlessly.

When they were in the corridor, he took Jerry aside and said, 'Literary folk make pretty hopeless politicians, Mr Stover. Does Mrs Kirby know anything about your new interest?'

'Can't see it matters,' Jerry said.

'You've both fallen out over the Selkirk review, haven't you?'

Jerry looked away.

'I see,' Kirby said. 'Of course, even I know that the path to culture is a very hazardous one, especially with American help.'

Bashra and Mason were half way across the vestibule. Jerry looked to see how far they had got and turned back to Kirby. 'You'll try, won't you?' he asked.

'It's all very, very interesting, Stover.' He held Jerry's shoulder and started off down the vestibule. 'I imagine I'll be able to contact your group on the Dung'll?'

'Yes.'

'Well, you'll hear from my office by special messenger. See he gets back alive, will you?'

'I've got news for you,' Jerry said, smiling cordially. 'We're one society. We're all Dung'll.'

Kirby smiled too. They shook hands.

On their walk back from the VPP headquarters, Bashra, Jerry and Mason were composed, thoughtful and faintly hopeful. The streets they walked along, crossed over and bypassed, all seemed different, brighter, newly discovered. When they were about to enter West Street, Jerry suddenly ran forward, his hands flailing wildly, and shouted to a young woman who was getting on to a country bus. Bashra and Mason followed him.

'Miriam,' Jerry shouted and leapt on to the rear steps of the bus.

The woman sat at the front, directly behind the driver's seat. Jerry rushed down the narrow aisle. He tripped over the baskets and hampers which were jutting out between the passengers' feet and at the side of the seats.

'Miriam,' he said breathlessly, when he was a matter of inches away from her. He grabbed her shoulder and shook her.

The woman turned and grinned. 'Wrong one,' she said and turned round again.

Jerry held on to the back of the seat, hung his head and caught his breath. 'Sorry,' he said and began backing away.

Bashra and Mason had come more than half way down the aisle. The passengers at the top and back of the bus were quickly alerted by the shrill screams of those in the middle, some of whom had stood up round Bashra, and others who had timidly recoiled from him in their seats. In no time, the whole bus was in upheaval. A large crowd had gathered outside.

'Jesus Chris', Rasta,' some were shouting. Others, 'Beard' man them raid.'

Pressing the bulk of her huge breasts into the back of the seat in front of her, a sweating market woman tipped her chin towards the window and declared, 'I's sacrifice them want sacrifice the people 'pon the bus or wha'?'

'You're the one we want, big stock,' Mason told her, leant forward and laughed in her face. He bared his teeth and roared.

The woman sank back on her vast cushiony bottom and stared up at him. 'But wait,' she said, 'you' not a Rastaman.' She narrowed her eyes for more precise recognition. 'You' the Donne-Jones boy who 'ave the English wife a' Thanan's 'pon King Street.' She struck her knee to mark the fact. 'Is why the

Rasta clothes, an' wha' you' doin' with the other two ruffian' them?' She struggled to reach the window again. 'But, Missa Mason, I know who you is, you know. Wha' the beard an' the Dung'll uniform for?'

'All the better to eat you with,' Mason hissed.

She sank back in the seat and the upholstery squelched loudly under her weight. She was perplexed.

A piercing hysterical cry of 'Police comin'; Babylon burs'!' went up outside and the crowd surged towards the back of the bus to get a better view. Bashra, Jerry and Mason hunched their shoulders and drove themselves forward up the aisle and dashed through the side entrance.

The police, a sergeant and two special constables, fought their way to the back entrance and were met by an unexpected stampede of passengers from the top and middle of the bus. The back seats were nearly all empty.

The driver and conductor, who had been buying water coconuts from a street-corner vendor, and had been looking on at the incident with remarkably little concern, put down their two fruits and applauded the three fleeing figures.

A woman clung to Jerry's arm, as he bolted across West Street. 'I's me, Vie,' she said, before he had time to shake her off. 'The t'ree o' you better follow me. I show you which part to hide from the police.'

Jerry nodded and squeezed her arm appreciatively. Bashra and Mason understood. Mason winked gratefully. They ran Indian file along the shopping piazza. Vie led the way through a fish shop, into a disused grass yard and out to a side lane.

'You can stay an' hide, or you can go 'bout you' business straight off, if you want,' she told them.

They looked at one another and waited. Vie chuckled and shook her head. She was amused by the whole thing. Jerry introduced her to Bashra.

He said, 'Mos' t'ankful to you, young lady. Peace an' love.'
Jerry said, 'Bless you, Vie.'
Mason winked again.

'I might catch up with you all again then,' she said. Jerry held her hand and grasped it affectionately. She allowed him. 'As for you,' she continued, 'it look' like you' change you' speed from Constan' Spring to Dung'll.' She grinned. He twisted her hand, without causing her pain. 'Not my business, min' you,' she quickly added, 'but you' askin' for a 'eap o' worries, you know.' Then she did something that was quite unexpected. She hugged him round his waist. 'See you.' She crossed the lane and disappeared into the grass yard.

It was about eleven o'clock when they got back to the Dung'll. Marcus ran out to meet them. He seemed excited, jubilant. 'Big surprise, man,' he said, running towards them, his hands spread wide and his eyes smiling.

'You' foxin' the police 'pon a' early mornin' raid?' Bashra asked.

'No raid at all, man,' Marcus insisted. 'Raid not into it.'

'Found some money?' Jerry asked.

'Wha' more than pocket money?' Marcus asked rhetorically, grandly. 'Plenty good frien'. Come I show you. Quick, nuh.'

When they got into the area, the first person to greet them was Berto. He sprang from behind the driver's seat of Mason's station wagon. 'All present, except Mabes, Jenny and Albert,' he reported, standing at attention, and clasping a bottle of Black Seal and an empty glass.

Paula came up, swinging her hips exaggeratedly. Jerry could see someone hiding in a crouched position behind her. He shifted his body suddenly, but Paula swung herself in his direction to block his view. But the person darted from behind Paula and showed himself.

'So, you're the culprit, you ol' bastard, you,' Jerry said, hugging him. 'How're you, P.D.?'

'Had was to bring the others roun' to see you, man,' P.D. explained. 'They's brethren, too, you know, same like Rasta.'

Paula took Jerry aside. 'You're a cunning one,' she told

him, 'running off like that, not telling anybody and snatching Mason away.'

Berto joined them. 'Many months ago, even years,' he said, assuming a grave expression, 'we were all blood brothers and sisters. Remember? Through shit and mire. And now?' He paused, drank from his bottle and belched delicately. 'And now, what's happened to the blood brotherhood? You hide from us. You don't write. You don't send any messages. You're a West Kingston guerilla. A dedicated *rass*.'

Berto handed him the bottle. Jerry refused it. Paula snatched it, took two quick mouthfuls and wiped her lips on the back of her hand. Silba came over to them. He was swaying slightly.

'Stover, I presume?' he asked.

'Lane,' Jerry said. 'Early Saturday morning and not at office? What's your explanation?'

'Simple, my man.' Silba became expansive. 'Day after pay day, or didn't you know? Besides, we planned to ferret you and Mason out of your Dung'll warren and bring you back alive.'

Jerry was just a little offended. He frowned and said, 'So, we're rabbits, now. Where are the others?' His question was intended to cover up his shift of temper.

'Mabes faded cutely at about five o'clock this morning,' Wyn said, edging his way into the group. 'Jenny didn't turn up last night, as planned.'

'And Albert's being his usual enigmatic self,' Silba announced, saluting the group and taking a step backwards. 'Ol' Alberto regrets he's unable to Dung'll today.'

'And Van?' Jerry asked.

'I'm here,' Van reported uncertainly. He laughed without apparent good reason. 'Not exactly though.' He struggled with his information.

Jerry wanted to ask Silba about Van, but Silba was in no fit state himself, either to be questioned or to be relied upon. Instead, Jerry decided to hear the story from Paula, if there was one. 'Van's all right,' she said, when Jerry had succeeded in dragging her away from Bashra and Marcus. 'A bit fed up with the Courts, since you checked out on him.'

Sally and Mason were supervising the unloading of the rum and foodstuff from the back of the station wagon. When they were finished, Bashra was called upon to open the session.

He stood, with patriarchal poise, and thanked his young friends for their attention and their generosity. He went on to explain about the work and aspirations of the Brethren, about the deputations to Rybik and Kirby, and about the expected results.

Paula spoke next. She said she proposed to give as much personal assistance to the cause of the Brethren as she could manage. The other Termites readily agreed to do the same, and they offered to help out with Jerry's teaching scheme.

The strained formality of the speeches gave way to conversation. Bashra regretted that he was unable to find accommodation on the Dung'll for his new friends after there had been a general outcry of coming to live with him, Jerry and Mason. Later on he sprang his surprise. He called everybody round him and spoke of the possibility of a forthcoming Rastafarian demonstration, which he called the 'November march', and they all begged earnestly to be included. By two o'clock everybody, except Jerry, was speechlessly drunk.

Albert drove in to the Dung'll at about seven-thirty. He had borrowed a station wagon and loaded the two rear seats with several packets of potato chips, three long loaves of hard dough bread, a leg of jerked pork, two dozen cans of beer and two bottles of Black Seal. Being only the day after pay day at Omatt's he felt he owed it to Jerry and Mason, re-union or not; he also felt that the others expected him to impress the Brethren. He apologised for his very late arrival. He and Mason went off to compare notes on the merits of the two station wagons which were parked side by side.

P.D. joined them. His enthusiasm was robust and disarming. He refused to speak to Albert unless he shared a quadruple rum and ginger ale with him. Albert objected to the ginger ale. He poured away the drink, invoking a cryptic libation, filled the glass with Black Seal and water and drank his portion with style.

P.D. said, 'Now, you's a frien' o' mine an' a man with plenty balls.'

The ordinariness of the re-union depressed Jerry. It was as though nothing had changed within the structure of the Termites; their behaviour was the same; their development was minimal. He could find nothing to respect, nothing to be led by. Even their generosity of spirit and pocket seemed stale, rehearsed, burdensome.

Bashra sensed Jerry's discontent and said compassionately, 'Never min', son. They doin' it in them own way, 'ones', as they know how.'

At about eight o'clock, when Sally, Paula and Marcus's woman were preparing the evening meal, Bashra and Jerry withdrew to the far end of the area.

'Jus' got a message,' Bashra said, 'a while ago, as a matter o' fac'. A big meeting' o' the Blood an' T'under down Greenwich Farm way. You t'ink we should go an' maybe invite the res'?'

'Up to you,' Jerry said.

Greenwich Farm was almost two miles from the Dung'll. After everybody had eaten and Paula and Sally had seen to the clearing away of the empties, the brushing up of the area and the stacking away of the unused groceries, the entire party piled into the two station wagons and headed for the Spanish Town Road route to Greenwich Farm.

Marcus leant out of the rear window of the leading wagon and declared, 'Peace an' love.'

At that very moment, Prudence and W. C. Kirby were discussing the Rastafarian list of proposals which was spread out in front of them on the highly polished surface of their mahogany dining table.

'Not altogether naive, Prudence, I don't think,' he was saying. 'A great deal of mature thinking must have gone into the drafting of the damn' thing, and much feeling too.'

Prudence ignored the impact of the information, as he had sincerely intended, and looked away towards a tightly packed shelf of unsold copies of NEXUS. Her pretended detachment wore thin. He connected immediately.

He said, 'Ought to give old Rybik at least one sleepless night, if Glissada's foolish enough to let it happen.'

Prudence walked towards the shelf. She patted the copies and said, 'Can't possibly see why she should.'

'Come, now, Prudence,' he chided affectionately.

'Look,' she began emphatically, but coolly, 'when bright young men flare up in our dreary midst, I'll let you know. Take it from me : Jerry Stover isn't one of them.'

He picked up the first page of the proposals. 'Should I do anything?'

'Absolutely nothing.'

'I received the deputation.'

'Moses and the Promised Land. So what?'

'They're expecting some sort of come-back.'

'You should care.'

'In fact, I do.'

'Did you make any promises?'

'Can't say I did. Promised to read the list and send a copy on to Rybik. That's about all.'

'Well, then, send the silly thing on to Glissada, and, for God's sake, send it with your compliments.' She laughed girlishly and patted the copies of NEXUS again. 'Coffee?'

He nodded, carefully collected the loose leaves of the list of proposals and stood up, clutching them to his linen waistcoat.

She looked at his stooped and twisted posture, his thinning hair, the lines of fatigue under his eyes, and wondered : the dignified Opposition leader; and where does that put me? More than ever outside. Empty-handed. No bargaining power. Bait for asses like Stover and his mob. The fool even makes a mockery of NEXUS. Smashes everything.

'D'you know, dear,' Kirby said, 'the thing that bothers me is the fact that Stover and his friends quite sincerely want to do their duty by society but they don't know where their duty lies, really.'

She took his arm and said, 'It ought to be cool on the side veranda now. Don't you think?'

Later that evening, Prudence wrote in her diary, in her usual confiding style:

Must remember to tell W.C. to suggest to Rybik that he would be best advised to send a fact-finding delegation to Ethiopia and possibly to five or six other African countries which might be tempted, on the doubtful grounds of black nationalism, to extend a welcoming hand to Jerry's gang of dispossessed Rasta. After all, W.C. had better see to it that they are well out of the way. When he wins the next General, they'll be one embarrassment less.

He ought to convince Rybik of the importance and necessity to act as quickly as he can, obviously in the interest of the people and Government he now leads; that is, as soon as Glissada will allow him to.

It hardly matters whether our deeply religious brothers want a 'Back to Africa' mission or not; I think they ought to have one. I must keep at W.C. about this.

Also must remember to advise W.C. about something else, before he leaves in the morning, for that utterly ridiculous affair at Radio Port Royal. Who, in his right mind, has ever heard, or could conceive of W.C. being interviewed by a team of visiting American high school boys?

Breakfast: advise W.C. not to wear linen waistcoat as often as he does.

Much later that evening, at Greenwich Farm, Bashra, Jerry and Mason had withdrawn from the rest of the Termites and P.D. and had gone off with the chief spokesman of the Blood and Thunder Brethren to the nearest clump of coconut trees along the coast where they intended holding a private discussion about the forthcoming November march.

'Firs' o' all,' the spokesman was saying, 'we' too far 'way in the country parts; an' secon', we don't t'ink the occasion callin' for includin' our Brethren.'

'Why?' Bashra wanted to know.

'Politics.' The spokesman slapped his thighs and did a small emphatic dance.

'Domestic?' Mason asked and looked from the spokesman to Bashra and back again.

'Domestic, eh?' the spokesman tested the word. 'I like the way you put that, youngster.' He hung his head and thought for a while. Then he continued, 'I believe that domestic national, international, worl' an' the res' got no difference Politics is everywhere that people bunch up together under some plan or other.' He seemed pleased with the sudden fluency of his reply.

Jerry said, 'The November march is important, politically important.'

'See it, now,' the spokesman said, slapping his thighs again 'What a way you soun' like a big-time civil servant on the run son.' He guffawed.

'We want a concerted effort,' Mason said.

'Total impact,' Jerry agreed.

'You openin' the dictionary 'pon me. Anyway, you won' get concert an' impac', if we come in on the march. I know so.

'Why you' 'gainst we, Brother?' Bashra asked.

'You' *not* we, Bashra. You like peace an' love; we buil' with blood an' t'under. You 'ave outside people, like these two nice middle class boys an' the others, 'elpin' you out; we got *we* an *we* alone. You' extendin' the Brethren too far 'mongst the wrong element; we' militant an' tough an' tight bad.'

'All o' we can do with 'elp,' Bashra said defensively, looking from Jerry to Mason.

'You' goin' need it soon,' the spokesman said. 'You know why?' He paused. ''Cause we goin' take over from you, Bashra, an' be the big force you was. We goin' put you out to pasture an' grab all the Rasta an' organise them. Wait an' see.'

When they retired and returned to the meeting house, they were just in time to hear one of the Blood and Thunder Brethren announcing to the gathering in the yard, 'No November march for we a *rass*. Those who go can go an' stan' the consequence later.'

The spokesman looked arrogantly at Bashra, as much as to say, 'I told you so.' Bashra said, 'You' got t'ings organise' a'ready, I see.'

'We believe in impac', as you' young frien' jus' say,' the spokesman confirmed. 'If we don't take self-interes' in earnes', we goin' mash up like drop' breadfruit.'

P.D. and the other Termites joined Bashra, Jerry and Mason. Marcus remained where he was and waved; he was standing beside a *yabah* of white rum and sliced limes.

The spokesman walked away, dragging his lame left leg. He reported authoritatively to his own group on his discussion with the Dung'll Brethren. He straightened up and pounded his right fist in the palm of his left hand. The gathering in the yard muttered appreciative sighs and settled down quietly. He roared on.

Berto straddled his arms between Jerry and Mason and said, jutting his chin towards the spokesman, 'One of our great dictators or one of our *rass* idiots?'

'Both.' Jerry nodded.

Paula cuddled closely to Silba and said, 'The man's a dream.'

Silba didn't reply.

P.D. scratched nervously.

Marcus winked at Bashra. Bashra grinned openly and

turned to see what the Termites were thinking of the spokesman's performance.

Sally and Wyn were drinking and watching him attentively. So was Albert.

Van drained his mug of white rum and shuddered.

'An' now, the Creed,' the spokesman reminded the gathering. 'Time to talk hate.'

Bashra, P.D., Jerry and Mason and the Termites left after that. It was clear that they were no longer welcome at the meeting. As they were about to drive off, Bashra remembered that they were leaving Marcus behind in the yard. He went back and saw him talking to the spokesman. Both men were shouting and gesticulating. Marcus was protesting. 'But you don't know wha' you' sayin' when you say a t'ing like that, man,' he declared. 'Those is frien'ly people from Saint Andrew top. We prove them. Two o' them live with we on the Dung'll an' the others say they want to join the Brethren.'

Bashra intervened. He was about to speak when he was stopped by an arrogant waving gesture from the spokesman.

'Lis'en, you two,' he said with a note of warning in his rasping voice, 'you' goin' 'ear from we. We know wha' we know 'an' that goin' be sufficient to guide we back to Africa. Keep you' frien's to you'self. We goin' go it alone.'

Marcus raised his right hand. 'Peace an' love, Brother,' he said sympathetically.

'That same shit goin' kill you one day,' the spokesman told him.

A week later, Glissada Maycroft and Dr Rybik were the last to leave the offices of the R.I.T.U. It was Saturday afternoon and they were on their way to Rybik's country house at Above Rocks. Glissada was driving. She seemed preoccupied. Rybik looked at her and wondered how to go about finding out what was wrong. He suspected that she was resisting him, and had been during the whole week. He had tried drawing her out but she had either ignored him or had found some plausible excuse to evade his more personal questions.

She sighed ponderously and turned on the car radio and tuned it to Radio Port Royal. A visiting Candian economist was being interviewed about the future of bauxite mining in the Caribbean.

'They thrive on the so-called serious public service interviews these days, don't they?' Rybik said, looking through his side window and hoping that she would say something, in the course of the conversation, to give him an idea of what was troubling her.

'Interviews?' she said waspishly. 'So does the Opposition by the look of things.'

He smiled. She turned slightly but said nothing more.

'Only God knows what could've possessed Kirby to let himself in for that open-house interview,' he said, shaking his head and still smiling.

'Playing the sort of popular game that pleases Prudence, no doubt,' Glissada snapped back. 'You should know that.'

'Prudence, eh?' he wondered. 'D'you really think so? I'm not sure.'

'Just the sort of cultural crutch she likes.' She was defiant. 'A gang of school children. A cheap trick.'

'That's just the point, Glissada. It wasn't a trick at all. Kirby's not like that.'

'He's a damn' fool, then.'

'The programme wasn't all that bad. The boys seemed intelligent enough and frankly I couldn't see anything wrong with their questions.'

'Either prompted by the State Department or by their head master.' She switched off the radio and continued driving to Above Rocks in silence.

When they got in, Theresa, the housekeeper, came out to meet them with two large mugs of hot country chocolate. 'I' certain I did see the car from you take the firs' turnin', an' I

say to meself, "I better give them somet'ing nice an' hot." '
She welcomed them enthusiastically.

Glissada thanked her, took the steaming mug and walked
inside.

'Miss Glissada in her dumps or wha'?' she asked Rybik.

He was very fond of Theresa and regretted the slight she
had suffered. 'Sort of,' he told her. 'It's been a long drive.
She'll be all right.' He followed Glissada into the house.

'So, you don't want you' choc'late either then?'

'Yes, in a moment, T,' he called over his shoulder.

'Lawd,' she said, 'ungrateful for true. Real Kin'ston man-
ners.' She looked down on the mug of chocolate and shook her
head. 'Only Jesus know why them come up 'ere every time
them in bothers. Why them can't come when t'ings goin' right,
I don't know.' She sighed despondently.

Glissada and Rybik had dinner in silence. Neither looked at
the other. Theresa kept her distance. The evening passed
slowly.

At about eleven o'clock, Glissada could stand the tension
no longer. She was reading a back copy of the *Springboard*
which she rolled into a ball and flung across the sitting-room
floor.

Rybik got up and paced the room. He was angry.

Glissada felt that, at least, she was getting somewhere. She
knew that she could accomplish nothing until she had put
Rybik at an emotional disadvantage; he was always at a vul-
nerable pitch when he became worked up in opposition to her;
her whole stratagem depended on it. She laughed, just to put
the finishing touch to her hard-won victory.

He was still pacing the room. He was wearing his sports
shirt out of his trousers. The parted front ends flapped as he
walked and tended to accentuate his paunch.

'You soon won't be able to see when traffic comin', you
gettin' so portly,' she teased him in dialect, which, she knew
would push him conveniently near the edge of his rising rage
which was what she wanted.

He kicked the ball of newspaper across the room.

'I suppose Kirby's trying to make a jackass out of us again,' she ventured. 'And you'll allow him to, buddies as you are, on the same side and all that?'

'How?' he shouted.

'The way he usually does,' she retorted calmly. 'Usually under the guise of playing the helpful leader of the Opposition.' She smoothed the paper-ball, spreading it flat in her lap and patting it gently.

'Put that damn' thing away, Glissada, for God's sake.'

'So?' She was sure of herself now.

'So what?'

'What d'you intend doing?'

'About what?'

This was the moment she had been waiting for. 'The Dung'll frightens you. I wonder why?' She dropped the neatly folded paper on the floor beside her chair.

'You've taken a blasted week to come to that earth-shaking conclusion, have you?' He sat down and crossed his legs.

No reply.

'Well? Have you?'

'In fact, I have more cause to be scared. A very thin line divides me from the lunatic who came to see you the other day. We've got the ol' skin in common. I should be terrified of the closeness. Not you.'

'All right,' he told her, 'out with it.'

'My advice is that you do nothing about the list Kirby sent you.'

'O.K.'

'Promise?'

'Yes.'

'Right.' She sounded jubilant.

'So, what do I say to him?'

'Nothing.'

'What about the deputation?'

'Nothing.'

Chapter Twenty-four

On the day of the November march, a few minutes after eight in the morning, Burns Hector and Josiah Blake, the editor of the *Scythe*, paid an unexpected visit to the Dung'll. Bashra and Marcus were the first to see them crossing the area. Burns Hector pointed to the Manhole and spat. Josiah Blake took out his handkerchief, blew his nose and spat in the direction of the shacks to his right.

Bashra and Marcus laughed.

'Poor man no 'custom' to the sweetness o' the Dung'll life,' Marcus said.

' 'Ope it kill 'im,' Bashra said. He had recognised Josiah Blake and was secretly thrilled that he was about to enjoy an encounter with him. He turned slightly. 'Coverage comin', Jerry.'

Jerry came out of the hut and waited, taking up his position immediately in front of Bashra. Marcus shifted towards the door of the hut and admired Jerry's courage.

'You' kind o' people, Jerry,' Marcus hinted. 'Same class o' individual.'

Jerry smiled.

Marcus continued, 'Deal with 'im 'cordin'ly make I see, nuh.'

Jerry resented the intrusion of the two journalists; he felt his anger rising. He blamed Bashra for calling him before they had actually arrived at the entrance of the hut. Waiting for them to come up the path caused Jerry the kind of anxiety he had always associated with forthcoming lectures from his mother, or worse, with the long wait at school, from before lunch until after the end of the last period in the afternoon, when he would be expected to report for his punishment at the head master's study; Josiah Blake had had that effect. Jerry disliked being reminded of so juvenile an anxiety. He felt a sudden loathing for the two journalists.

'So, what's all this exile crap about, Stover?' Josiah asked, slamming his right foot contemptuously down on the mound of ramgoat roses outside Bashra's hut.

'What're you trying to prove, Jerry?' Paul asked with concealed amusement and affection. He remembered the Niagara days.

Jerry nodded at Paul and said to Josiah, 'Surely, the Dung'll isn't quite the editor's assignment? Or maybe it is?'

'Editors are journalists, Stover.'

'Running out of cub reporters and filling in snugly?' Jerry asked.

'Journalists are an inquisitive race, editors included.'

'Who told you where to find me, Josiah?'

'The smell of the place.'

'Might have led you to your own office.'

'Never you mind that, Stover.'

Bashra stepped forward and Josiah stepped back. Bashra looked down at the crushed ramgoat roses and said, 'But, don't you *Scythe* people use' to be dead 'gainst we down 'ere?'

'Press conference?' Mason said, coming up from behind the row of shacks on the right of Bashra's hut.

Josiah smiled. Then he said to Bashra, 'We're not against you, not really. We can't afford any prejudices, one way or another, or any preferences either. We print the news, for *everybody's* benefit.'

'Print changin' tune fas',' Bashra said affably. 'So, wha' you want, Missa Blake?'

'Tell us about this march of yours, or is it a Rasta State secret?' Josiah was smiling, and watchful.

'You'll see the march for yourself,' Mason said.

'You're being very helpful, Donne-Jones, thank you,' Josiah said.

'Help you on your way, perhaps?' Mason added.

'Wouldn't you and the Brethren like to make a statement to the press?' Paul asked.

'Our statement is our procession,' Bashra explained. 'Words an' twis' an' turn is you' line, Missa Hector an' Missa Blake. We got poverty, even t'ough it don't talk loud enough in this country, yet.'

'Lawd, Jesus, watch Rasta, nuh,' a woman shouted from an upstair window along West Street. She was the first of a cluster of women in the house opposite the Dung'll to see the procession leaving the area and heading slowly towards the entrance.

Except for the Blood and Thunder Brethren, there was very nearly a maximum representation of the Island's Rastafarians: most of the Kingston and Saint Andrew Brethren, those from the rural districts, and some of the others from the outlying splinter groups. Bashra expected six other groups to join in at Parade, and at five northern points, at Upper King Street, Slipe Road, Cross Roads, Half Way Tree and Hope Road. He was hoping for an estimated total of twenty thousand marchers in the procession. The six stops were intended to be check-points along the route. The procession would halt at each one so that Bashra, Jerry and Mason, in turn, could make brief inspections, welcome the new groups and remind them of the importance of the march.

At the first stop, Bashra said, eschewing dialect, 'Order and silence is what we want on this walk of ours, the whole way. We must show the public what we stand for, what we are and what we want, a peaceful and loving existence. We must show the public that we're neglected people who want a break to live like ordinary human beings. We want to remind the public that we're asking for their help in our search for a home back in Africa, since the Government and others won't ease up and give us one here.'

The procession applauded him. Jerry and Mason were noticeably proud of his speech. Yet, Jerry thought that Bashra should have spoken in dialect. He quickly forgot the matter when he saw that Bashra was getting through to the marchers and achieving an impressive immediacy.

Bashra began again. 'We want to command respect more than anything else at this time. We want our "straight back" dignity. It must never be taken away from us. Never.'

Jerry and Mason quietly congratulated him. He shrugged modestly. Marcus waved from a short distance off and gave him the Peace and Love sign. Bashra returned it.

All the groups carried banners, identification placards and protest slogans painted in green and black on gold-sprayed compressed cardboard standards. Bashra and Jerry had chosen a Sunday morning for the march, and Mason and Marcus had readily agreed with their choice; they had all realised that the traffic on the roads would be light enough to give the procession almost complete access on the long route; and, at the same time, they had speculated that the number of spectators would be greater, then, than on a working day. But, as the procession moved slowly and quietly from Upper Kingston up to Lower Saint Andrew and on to Half Way Tree, not only was there little traffic but there were also very few spectators. Only the children along the way and the yapping mongrels showed any enthusiasm. Now and then, a few motorists, cyclists and one or two pedestrians actually bothered to stop for a while, and even then they waited only to jeer and pass humiliating and obscene remarks.

When the leading groups reached the Half Way Tree clock tower, they were stopped by three squad cars and four policemen on motor cycles. The Inspector in charge warned Bashra about keeping the peace and advised him not to obstruct the traffic or the pedestrians. He also insisted that the procession should not halt along the Hope Road and in particular in front of the Governor's residence at King's House. Bashra nodded perfunctorily and led the procession round the clock tower and up Hope Road.

Jerry was thinking about King's House. He glanced at Bashra and Mason and knew that they, too, were thinking of the same thing.

'Another time, Jerry,' Bashra said. 'Not today. We'd 'ave to plan that one.'

'A petition maybe?' Mason asked.

'Could be, yes, but we don't 'ave time for a proper one now.'

Jerry listened to the exchange between Bashra and Mason, and he recalled the Brethren's motto. He remembered the spokesman's scorn at the Blood and Thunder meeting. And his disappointment in the march began to depress him. He knew that the whole plan had failed. It was the usual occurrence: being ignored by an apathetic society. He told himself that he had half expected it. Yet, he had hoped, somehow, that the march would have been impressive and would have succeeded if only because of its orderliness, calculated silence and its large numbers of the Brethren. He was also disappointed that not even one of the Termites had turned up; he reflected sadly that they *must* have remembered the promises they had made on the Dung'll. But he knew that they were not to be depended on absolutely.

The procession passed King's House and continued towards Papine, the final stage of the first half of the journey. When the marchers got there, Mason suggested that the return route ought to include the Mona Road and the University. Jerry quickly agreed. So did Bashra. But nothing happened. There was no reaction from the small groups of undergraduates who looked on passively, innocently. No reaction from the Mona villagers. None from the University staff in their houses on College Common.

Prudence and W. C. Kirby had only just sat down to their usual Sunday lunch of fricassee of chicken, rice and peas, corn on the cob and boiled plantains, when the telephone rang in the study, off the dining-room. Prudence sighed impatiently, got up and walked into the study.

'Yes, it is,' she answered abruptly. She sat on the cool leather upholstered arm of her husband's favourite wing-chair.

'You serious?' she asked.

She waited.

'How many?'

She stood.

'I see.'

She shook her head in exasperation.

'The Mona Road?'

She paused.

'The University? College Common? Yes, go on.'

She was silent for almost thirty seconds.

'All right. Thank you very much indeed. Goodbye.'

Her husband had continued eating, grateful that the call had not been for him.

When she returned, she closed her knife and fork, sat back and folded her arms defiantly. 'Somebody ought to silence that menace, and pretty quickly,' she said, more for effect than from malice.

'What's the boy wonder been up to now?' Kirby asked, diligently cleaning the wish-bone.

'*You* may well ask.'

'Defacing Bowerbank's statue in the park? Or is it Victoria's for a change? No?' His knife scraped the last fragment of meat from the bone and collided with the side of his plate.

'I wish you wouldn't do that,' she said.

They smiled at the unintended pun.

'Who called?' he picked up the wish-bone and waited.

'One of my NEXUS contributors, David Sproston.' She told him about the march. He listened, twirling the wish-bone incessantly. She repeated her story, adding personal comment to fact, until, in the end, all that remained of David Sproston's report was her own intimidating anger and her contempt for the situation in general. She asked, 'Did you know they were going to demonstrate?'

'I know all about it, dear,' he said flatly. 'Harmless enough. Besides, it's Rybik's pigeon, not mine.'

He extended the wish-bone, holding it by the stouter of its two curved bones.

'Make it a good anti-Stover one,' he said affectionately.

Glissada Maycroft, too, had been on the telephone. She had called Dr Rybik from the R.I.T.U. offices. He had been sleeping late after a large breakfast of *ackee* and salt fish, johnny cakes and coffee. When he had no duties on Sundays he always woke early, breakfasted and flopped back into bed; he had once told Glissada that that was his only bad habit, one he truly cherished and looked forward to, weekend after weekend, ever since he had returned from Edinburgh as a young general practitioner. All Glissada had done, then, was smile at him ingratiatingly and touch his arm.

'The whole filthy bunch,' she screamed over the telephone.

'Now, remember, Glissada, we knew what to expect,' he said. 'We were told in advance.'

'So what!'

'Where are they headed, d'you know?'

'God knows. Saint Andrew, I suppose.'

'Any trouble? Violence or anything?'

'Not yet. At least not as far as I know.'

'Easy, now, Glissada. What about the police? Have they intervened?'

'I don't know. What're you going to do?'

'Try to find them and have a look see.'

'Be careful.'

'I'll take a taxi.'

'Suppose the driver recognises you?'

'A chance I'll have to take, I imagine.'

'Be careful, d'you hear?'

'Bless you. I will.'

The Stover household had received no such alarming telephone calls. Mrs Stover led quite a different life from W. C. Kirby and Dr Rybik. In spite of the fact that she *was* Jerry Stover's mother, a leading Constant Spring resident and a Saint Andrew Justice of the Peace, she was no politician. She and Les had just returned from the High Mass at Holy Trinity and were having lunch on the front veranda: escoveitched fish with a combination salad. Nobody had mentioned Jerry's name recently. Of course, Mrs Stover and Thelma had been constantly thinking about him in their own secret, sentimental way, but Les encouraged himself in the belief that his brother was and always would be a fool, a restless, unreasoning, misguided, self-centred young man.

They were just about to begin their coconut ice cream dessert, when Ephraim, the gardener, came up to them. 'Jus' comin' back from 'Alf Way Tree, Mam,' he said, standing behind Mrs Stover's chair.

'Come round, Ephraim,' she suggested cautiously. 'You can't expect me to see you there, or don't you want me to?' She chuckled.

'Jus' see Missa Jerry a while ago, Mam.'

Thelma had overheard him. 'You say you' jus' seen Missa Jerry? Where?' she asked excitedly.

Ephraim grinned widely and decided to enjoy his hold over his captive audience. He liked being noticed.

'Seen Jerry, Ephraim?' Les echoed Thelma's question.

'Yes, Missa Les. In a brute o' a long line o' . . .' He broke off dramatically.

'Line of what?' Mrs Stover urged firmly.

'A long line o' Rasta, Mam.'

'Jerry? You're sure?' Les stood and frowned.

'Right up in front,' Ephraim told him.

'Wha' you really talkin' 'bout, eh, bwoy?' Thelma was excessively aggressive.

'I' talkin' 'bout wha' I' jus' see a while ago,' Ephraim slammed back.

Because of the violence of her disbelief, she lost control and said, 'You' black an' you' fool!'

Mrs Stover understood Thelma's anxiety. She merely eased her chair from the table and asked calmly, 'Did you speak to him, Ephraim?'

'No, Mam. I was too frighten' to go near 'im. You can't tell with them Rasta people at all. Them can black an' vicious bad sometimes, Mam. One time, one o' them jus' ups an' chop off a man' finger 'cause 'im didn't like the way the man refuse 'im a cigarette. An' nex' time ...'

'All right, Ephraim,' Mrs Stover interrupted. 'You didn't speak to him.'

He smiled.

'What was Jerry doing?' Les asked.

'Jus' walkin' up front, sweet an' easy like.'

'How many of them?'

'Plenty t'ousan' o' them, with plenty banner an' ol' flag an' t'ing.'

'I see,' Mrs Stover said, getting up and handing Thelma her untouched dessert and glass of water.

'But somet'ing else, too,' Ephraim hinted. He was losing his audience. It was time, he felt, to add style to his report.

'Go on,' she said, waiting on him.

'Somet'ing funny, Mam, funny can't done,' he went on slowly, 'somet'ing that I can't understan' 'bout the . . .' He stopped and shook his head.

'Ephraim,' she reminded, 'we know you're the centre of attraction; don't overdo it, please.' She held his shoulder.

Thelma chirped her teeth loudly.

Les was amused.

'Well, Mam,' Ephraim said, 'the w'ole long line o' Rasta them, all the 'ow much t'ousan' o' them, jus' wasn't makin' one single sound. You could've drop' a pin an' you would 'ear it *ping*! Not a noise was a noise. Not a Jesus soun', Mam. Jus' the long line walkin', an' so-so quiet.'

Mrs Stover released his shoulder, nodded and walked away.

The procession had got as far as Cross Roads. The return journey had attracted even less attention. There had been no incidents. Nobody had provoked the marchers, and they had conducted themselves as Bashra had instructed.

Marcus left his position and came up to Bashra. 'Look' sort o' bad like,' he whispered. 'Not a soul takin' a blind piece o' notice o' we at all. Maybe we better start singin' or so?'

'We' not singin',' Bashra said.

'We'll do it, as we planned, Marcus,' Mason said firmly. 'There's nothing so impressive as silence; besides, it's the last thing they expect from us, silence.'

'But, I sort o' believe that they . . .'

'No, Marcus.' Bashra interrupted.

'If you say so, nuh.' Marcus agreed and dropped back to his position.

Jerry was feverishly fighting off an attack of nausea. To distract himself, he began counting the passing cars. He waited but only two cyclists passed by; then another two; a little boy with an empty hand-cart; a taxi; a removal van; another two cyclists. Slowly, his nausea receded.

The taxi, in which Dr Rybik was riding, had twice passed the procession. He had the kind of undisturbed view he had hoped for. As far as he could make out, the driver suspected nothing; he had not recognised his passenger. He had been told that there was a Rastafarian march which was somewhere in the Saint Andrew area and he had found it easily. When he was told to turn back again, he had done so without question.

Finally, Dr Rybik asked him to drive past once more and

head towards Central Kingston. He did so and when he got to the procession at the top of Orange Street just as its first section was turning left across to Upper King Street, he inclined his head backwards and asked, 'Slow up again, Master?'

'Fine.' Dr Rybik grinned self-consciously. He wanted to have a last look at Bashra's face. He knew that Glissada would ask him what he had looked like in his moment of glorious protest.

Quite suddenly, he reminded himself: the essence of the whole of this damn' business is quite clearly anti-Government; I haven't replied to their silly little plea for attention, so they've decided to show me how *very* strong and silent they can be. Balls!

He now had a full view of the front line of marchers. He leant slightly forward and searched for Bashra's face.

Bashra was composed, his head thrown well back, his beard thrust out and with a half-thoughtful, half-contemptuous narrowing of his eyes and twist of his lower lip.

Dr Rybik sank back in his seat and asked the driver to take him on to the R.I.T.U. offices.

'T'ought I did reco'nise you, Doctor,' the driver said, 'but I wasn't too sure like. From the firs', I did say to meself, "Now, that face is a face I know." But you see, you pop me 'til you say R.I.T.U.' He paused. 'Look' like Rasta mean business, Doctor. Never see them so quiet. Wha' you t'ink?'

Dr Rybik laughed.

'You laughin' at me or you laughin' at Rasta, Doctor?' He was offended but cautious.

'No, neither,' he said amiably, 'at myself, really.' At that moment, he knew he would have to give him a handsome tip. He took out a pound note and folded it.

When he walked into his office, Glissada stood primly and rasped, 'Well?'

'Harmless, my dear,' he said confidently, 'completely harmless.'

Book Four

The fire burnt a great eye at the mouth of the cave.

V. S. Reid   *The Leopard*

Chapter Twenty-five

The Island autumnal heat was electric. The ramgoat roses outside Bashra's hut were struggling hopelessly against the concentrated blast of the Kingston sun. The Manhole had a constant shimmering glow surrounding it, as though it were the sizzling weather's attempt to protect the Dung'll dwellers by locking in the nauseating stench of the garbage; nevertheless, it was an attempt that failed. Often, after the Rastafarian women had hung out their washing on improvised lines of chinaman's-twine, stretching and tying the strands from the topmost crate on the Manhole straight across the area to the shacks on the other side, they would sit and watch the drying take place and pretend that the Manhole was simply not there. The ordinary domestic event had become a ritual. The women would sing revivalist hymns and work songs, and beads of sweat would cover their faces and arms, as they kept their vigil and their singing going compulsively.

It was now mid-November and more than two weeks after the march. The public had shown no interest in it. The *Scythe* had been equally silent, and neither W. C. Kirby nor Dr Rybik had replied.

Jerry and Mason had continued their teaching, using their free periods and the hot dreary nights in the area for conversation and discussion about the Termites, and about Marcus's woman who had been causing Bashra, Marcus and everyone else considerable embarrassment during the Arithmetic lessons, because she had proven her skill in doing mental calculation far faster and more precisely than anybody else in the class. Jerry and Mason also talked about Van's sudden deterioration, about Randy and the Half Way Tree Courts, about Oxford and London. The evenings were longer than usual, or so they seemed to Bashra. Once he had mentioned the fact to Jerry and Mason, and they had agreed so readily that he took immediate offence, saying that they were getting tired of their life on the Dung'll. They denied the charge and pointed out that, as soon as the Termites joined the Brethren, there would be very little time to spare or even to worry about the boredom of the long evenings or about the apathy of the outside world and Kirby and Rybik. Jerry and Mason knew that they had to give, not only Bashra and Marcus but also the Brethren, something positive and reassuring to look forward to in the days that lay shortly ahead; they felt that they owed that much to the Dung'll, especially after the terrible failure of the march. But Bashra resisted their attempts by talking once more about the desirability of repatriation and about the mystical excellence of Haile Selassie. Jerry was intensely annoyed, but Bashra ignored him and knew that they would both forget the disagreement, until it next arose.

Jerry had not sent Marcus to his mother for some time and he wondered whether he ought to or not; he feared that she would not want to see him, particularly, as he thought that she must have been told about the outcome of the march and had her own reservations and scalding advice, stored and waiting for an outlet. When he mentioned this to Marcus, he chirped his teeth contemptuously and said, 'Look, Jerry, when you' bless' enough to 'ave at leas' one person who care' 'bout you, you' lucky out o' this worl'. Don' form jackass an' forget that.'

Jerry asked him to go, and he grinned his approval.

When Marcus handed Jerry's short note to Mrs Stover, she offered him a chair on the front veranda, sat near him and stared at the rockery to her left.

'You' not readin' it?' he asked politely and with nervous hesitancy.

'How much longer is this waste of time and energy going to last?' she asked, turning to him and pleading with her deep-set, tired eyes.

He shrugged. 'I's really up to you' son, you know.'

'How would he know? He's merely using you. The longer he remains with you, the greater the damage to his will.'

Marcus smiled. He liked talking to her. He admired her school teacher's firmness, frankness and fluency. He said, 'I mean to say: i's 'im who mus' decide wha' is wha' an' when time to call the wanderin' a day.' He smiled wisely. 'You mus' know that Jerry is a 'eadstrong youngster who believe he doin' plenty good where 'im is on the Dung'll, an' when the work done an' the Government start help we to go back to Africa, well, then, that is the time for Jerry to chop an' change.'

'And I suppose he'll want to go with you?'

'Could be, but I don' t'ink so, judgin' from 'im personal feelin's 'bout the Brethren an' the Africa t'ing.'

'Why?'

' 'Cause 'im's a *re'abilitationis'*.' He was very proud of his coinage and he shifted in his chair to see how Mrs Stover had taken it.

She opened Jerry's note and read it to herself.

Then she said, 'So, your march didn't come off?'

'Not a' impac' was a' impac'.'

'What's the next move?'

'Maybe another one, but only maybe; to King's 'Ouse this time, with a petition an' a t'ree-man deputation: Bashra, Jerry an' Mason. I was listenin' them talkin' to that effec', a few days ago.'

'Is Jerry happy?' she asked suddenly.

Marcus thought long and hard. He fondly believed that she had asked him a trick question. He looked at her. Then he realised that she was utterly incapable of that sort of easy subterfuge. He shook his head and said, 'None o' we 'appy on the Dung'll. As a matter o' fac', wha' with all this big bomb madness that goin' on in the outside worl', 'appy gone.' He clasped his hands before his chest and sank his chin on his knuckles. 'No, Mam, Jerry can't 'appy no how.'

Later on, after they had had their supper, Mrs Stover and Les strolled through the damp paths of the vegetable garden and up to the disused summer house. They were not aware of it but they were being closely observed from a convenient distance by Ephraim who was calculating when to appear before them to receive the customary praise and blame for his day's gardening; but, to his astonishment, he noticed that they were talking and showing no interest whatsoever in the newly constructed terracing which he hoped would have attracted them instantly. He closed the door of the tool shed quietly and went off to the Majestic to see the latest Western double-bill.

'What did you expect?' Mrs Stover was saying. 'After Julliard, I mean? What were your hopes?'

'Oh, the usual,' Les said, throwing his arms wide and hunching his shoulders, 'forming an orchestra, composing my own work and having it performed, building up something.'

'And you've ended up teaching in the front room.' Her statement was sympathetic.

'We're only a back pocket, Mother. You either settle for it or get out.'

'What about Jerry?'

'Working things out for himself, I imagine. The hard way.'

216

'I never felt your anguish and discontent when I was young. Our expectations fitted in neatly at the bottom of the back pocket. It seemed spacious then; all our dreams fitted into it in my day. Now, suddenly, your generation's expectations are disproportionately high. You've rapidly outgrown your little Island.'

'Some island people are like that, I suppose. Their destiny, I mean.' Les turned his face away and looked at a row of stripped espaliers. He thought bitterly of the hopes he had had. Then he thought of his brother, and he felt a sudden genuine sympathy and compassion for him.

Mrs Stover continued walking in the direction of the summer house. She was crying. Her tears were for her two sons and for a generation she could only observe with pity and concern but which she felt powerless to help.

Without turning to look round at Les, she said, 'Ephraim's done a very good job with the terracing, hasn't he?'

The Parish Church clock was saying ten past three. The morning was exceptionally hot for the hour. The Termites had come to the Dung'll after a hard night. Mabel had also come along with them. Jenny, who hadn't been on the Dung'll before, was being naturally inquisitive and sneering. She took Mason aside.

'Where, for God's sake, do you people wash around here?' she asked pointedly. Her interest shifted to the Manhole before he could reply. 'What's that for?'

'It's what it is: rubbish. Crates piled up on filth, all the muck of the city.'

'Spare us the symbolism.'

They walked over to the Manhole.

'It's been ages,' she said.

'You've enjoyed it.'

'So've you.' She made a face and pointed to the Manhole. 'Live with that and you can live with the accumulated sins of the world.' She looked as though she was going to be sick.

They walked towards the entrance.

'Joining us?' He fought hard to suppress the feeling of loathing he suddenly felt for her.

'Hardly,' she said frankly. 'I've got to work. 'Course I'll help out, between times, yes, for you and Jerry. But not all day every day like you two.'

'The others don't intend living down here,' he said bluntly. 'There just wouldn't be enough space.'

'Christ, you can say *that* again.'

She was a stranger visiting for a short time. She was nothing more. Mason told himself not to expect anything more than that. But his curiosity nagged him. He tried to control it, but it urged him on. He gave in. 'What about a divorce?' he asked.

'Could be.'

Her nonchalance bit deeply into his pride. As if blindly clutching for a safe retreat, he went back to thinking of her as the stranger, the inquisitive dropper-in, the ignorant tourist; it yielded scant consolation. She had proved her ruthlessness.

'It's a nuisance,' she was saying, 'but we could talk to a solicitor, if you're up to it.'

Her cool candour was annoying and embarrassing.

'Re-union?' Jerry said, coming up to them cautiously.

'With *what*?' Mason asked coldly, after Jerry had joined them.

'Yesterday's hopes, perhaps?' Jenny suggested.

She and Jerry then started talking about the Dung'll. Mason listened to them for a while but he found himself drifting into a despairing reverie. He jerked himself out of it, rubbing his eyes and squeezing his temples.

Jenny and Jerry were still talking. They were now discussing Van. Mason, too, began wondering about him. He saw Berto and moved away. They greeted each other warmly and walked slowly away from the centre of the area. The others weren't looking their way.

'Ever thought of fighting for a larger freedom, as the big books say?' Mason asked him.

'Do we know how?' Berto challenged. 'Takes more than guts, which we haven't got, boy. We've always had things given to us, in the way we've had things taken away from us. Colonial *finks*, Brother Man.'

Mason smiled. He had forgotten Berto's capacity for lush overstatement. He said encouragingly, 'Jeremiah me, man!'

Berto guffawed and declared, 'We're the original gimme types, Mason. Hands out, palms up. Courage? Where do we find that sort of shit in a hurry? Not in these lovely English-speaking islands, Daddy-O.'

Chapter Twenty-six

Caroline Selkirk arrived at the Palisadoes Airport at five o'clock in the afternoon on the last day of November. Jerry and Mason were there to meet her. Mason's station wagon was parked near the restaurant entrance of the Liner-Diner bar; the luggage compartment at the back had been specially cleaned and lined with brown paper; it had been done on Marcus's insistence. 'You can't mash up the Brethren' reputation with a dirty conveyance, jus' so,' he had said. He had also washed the body and tyres, and polished and shined the chromium parts until they shone brilliantly. And he had sent them off to the airport with, 'Give you' 'Merican frien' a proper sparklin' welcome, me Brothers.'

Caroline's luggage was being examined. She turned round and waved to Jerry. He waved back and smiled uncertainly, wondering what was going to be the outcome of her visit. He felt responsible for her project. He knew he had influenced Prudence against her, losing her what little help she might have been given. He assumed he had to take Prudence's place. How he would do it, he had no idea, no urgency to try to find a way. He hoped the inclination would come.

'Well, here I am, as promised,' Caroline said, coming up to them with a languid, frou-frou stride, thigh-swishing as she drew nearer. 'Is Mrs Kirby here?'

'No,' Jerry said, 'and I don't think she will be.'

'Have I been blacklisted?'

'I'm afraid so, with my help.'

She shook his hand. He introduced her to Mason. The porter brought out her luggage and Mason led the way to the station wagon.

'When does the magazine appear?' Jerry asked.

'January, I hope. Early February, the latest.'

'A monthly?'

'Another hope, I believe. January's not too soon, is it?'

'Nothing's too soon, in these parts; besides, the new year's just right for a new magazine.'

'How's the financial side?' Mason asked.

'The dollar isn't resentful,' she said.

Jerry began pointing out certain landmarks. Caroline questioned him continuously. Mason drove slowly and supplied some of the answers. They drove the rest of the way into Central Kingston, sharing haphazard anecdotes and nervous bursts of laughter.

Caroline had taken a house along the Hope Road. She took them inside and showed them round. The rooms were furnished simply and comfortably. The veranda was circular and spacious.

Jerry and Mason unloaded the luggage and carried it in. Mason said he had to go. 'You literary people have problems,' he excused himself, while reversing the station wagon. 'See you later on.'

'I didn't arrange that,' Jerry said, after Mason had driven off.

'What if you had?' she asked, throwing herself carelessly into a deep veranda chair, her arms dropping over the sides listlessly and trailing along the cool tiled floor, her skirt shooting above her knees and exposing the lower portions of her thighs. 'You're so suspicious, or is it good faith?'

'Could've been collusion.' He was angry with himself for having thought so and for having said it.

'I've been alone with a man before,' she said, crossing her legs and deliberately forgetting to adjust the revealing excess of her skirt. She asked about NEXUS.

He told her that he had been ordered to resign from the editorial board.

'No longer a contributor either?' she asked.

'No.'

'Bitter about it?'

'No.'

'Relieved?'

'Yes.'

'And Mrs Kirby?'

'She's all right.'

'Still friends?'

'In our own way, yes.'

'Seen each other recently?'

'No.'

'How does she feel about me?'

'Apprehensive. Resentful, perhaps.'

'Competition for NEXUS?'

' 'Suppose so.'

'May I depend on your help?'

'We'll have to talk about that.'

He hadn't once looked at the stocking-dark undersides of her crossed legs, obviously inviting as they were intended to be. She wondered about his lack of interest. She brought her knees slowly up to her chin and folded her skirt neatly, decently. He got up and looked out across the wide sweep of the front lawn which was marked off with thick wooden stakes and lengths of white cording. She came up and stood behind him.

'Why're Americans so resented, Jerry?'

'Because they're so patently in the saddle.'

'Why're our critics so severe?'

'You attract severity.'

'That was *so* European a judgement. Did you listen to yourself?'

'Europe's no stranger in the Caribbean.'

'Why don't you want to help me, Jerry?'

Her question checked his confidence. 'I'll explain later.'

'Like that, is it?' she said, smiling and moving away from him and flopping back into the chair.

They spent the rest of the time talking about America, world antipathy to her, the uses of literature, and Island literacy. Mason returned in about an hour. He and Jerry left almost immediately.

Chapter Twenty-seven

Christmas Eve came with a riot of sustained hard drinking, brisk, insincere exchanges of the season's greetings and un-ceasing, boring chatter. Kingston looked commercially tawdry and tired. The bustle seemed pointless and vulgar; the quick, scurrying movements of the shoppers, slapdash and menacing.

On the Dung'll there was very little else to do but drink and talk. There had been more than enough to get bizarrely drunk on; the Termites had provided the Brethren with four cases of Black Seal; Lola and Vie had contributed a dozen bottles of sorrel and a crate of Red Stripe beers; P.D. had given two hams, five cartons of cigarettes and a case of white rum; and Mrs Stover's gift to Jerry had been a Christmas card with two five-pound notes tucked inside it, a large home-made plum pudding and two boxes of groceries.

At about half-past three on Christmas morning the Dung'll party went to the Niagara, compelled Lola to open the bar and took over the premises. The Termites formed the 8 and forced Jerry and Mason to sit in their positions. Mabel, Bashra Marcus and P.D. sat at a table near by and drank in accompani-ment.

Shortly after five o'clock, everybody, except Lola and Vie, left and went back to the Dung'll. On the way, Jerry thought that he saw Miriam crossing Parade. He ran to meet her and fell. The woman turned and laughed and said, 'Drink the rum 'til you tumble down, sweet bwoy.' Her laughter trailed off into a knowing giggle.

Mason went to his assistance, slipped, fell beside him and muttered aimlessly, 'Hell Passage . . . Catte Street . . . Merton Street . . . the Turl . . ' Nobody paid attention, Jenny looked his way, briefly, and swung her head drunkenly in the opposite direction.

When they got back, Marcus's woman ran out to meet them and took Bashra aside. 'We jus' get some bad news,' she said. Jerry, Mason and Marcus joined the huddle and listened. 'Little after you all leave, two outside Bret'ren come to see you to tell you that over fifty Blood an' T'under people get lick 'way by Ol' 'Arbour police. Them arres' them an' shave the 'air off them 'ead an' face an' lock them up one time *baps!*'

'Wha' for?' Bashra asked.

'For concealin' firearm' an' for possession o' *ganja.*'

'When?' Marcus asked.

'Like say some 'ours ago. Mus' be long 'fore twelve o'clock or so. From early C'ris'mus Eve.'

'Firearm', eh?' Bashra reflected. He stooped down and drew tiny concentric circles in the loose dirt at his feet. 'Them mus' be goin' back for the w'ole settlement later today?'

'Mus' be, an' them arres' a racialis' trouble-maker name' Septimus Johns a few mile' out o' Ol' 'Arbour, too,' Marcus's woman continued. 'Them fin' a w'ole 'eap o' carbine an' sten gun an' t'ings in the 'ut where 'im livin'.'

'I see,' Bashra grunted. 'Them Blood an' T'under who don' get arres' goin' take plenty vengeance when this over an' done. Plenty 'ead goin' get burs'.'

'Who's Septimus Johns?' Jerry asked.

'Call' 'imself a liberator-politican, nuh,' Bashra said. 'Usual' 'ang out roun' Ol' 'Arbour way. Not a Rasta. Jus' a jump-

225

up with a 'eap o' white-black, brown-black friggery. 'Im don't too like Rasta people either, 'cause we wouldn't let 'im join we in the ol' days.'

'Septimus like' the Blood an' T'under, all the same,' Marcus added.

'Them suit 'im purpose,' Bashra said, 'but wha' 'im don't know is that black people belong in Africa, not 'ere, an' if 'im purge the Islan' with 'im militant *rass*, 'im goin' fin' out that 'eaven don't stay so one *bumbo*.' He paused. 'With 'Merica lookin' on?'

P.D. came over, looking conspiratorial, and bouncing like a sprinter on edge. 'Me never tell all o' you this before,' he blurted, 'but me an' Mirie me wife plan a little somet'ing up a' Dallas for all o' you today. Me nearly forget wha' with the rum an' so.' The Termites cheered him. 'Don' touch not'ing down 'ere. Leave the food an' the liquor same place w'ere it is an' come. The truck park up top o' Wes' Street. Jus' pile in an' come we drive like kite.'

Everybody agreed. Marcus's woman shook her head proudly, contemptuously, and walked away.

'Let's call for Caroline,' Jerry suggested to Mason.

Mason bowed. 'We'll use the station wagon and catch up with the others afterwards,' he said.

Jerry asked Bashra and Marcus to tell the others that he would connect with them later on. Bashra nodded uncertainly and asked him about the money for petrol for the station wagon. Jerry held up one of his mother's five-pound notes and flicked it stylishly between his thumb and forefinger.

Later on, in P.D.'s truck, Bashra said to Marcus, 'Look' like Jerry' goin' back fas' to 'ow 'im was, sort o' reckless an' don' give a damn.'

'Seem' so, yes,' Marcus said a little doubtfully, 'but all the same, 'im not changin' w'ere we' concern'. Jerry' still for we an' the Dung'll.'

Bashra was upset. 'Marcus, man, I didn' say Jerry was

226

changin' 'gainst *we*. I jus' say 'im was changin' *back,* in a bad way 'gainst *'imself.'*

'Rum pressure,' Marcus observed stoically.

Christmas Day dawned with a flush of raw white and pastel blue over Dallas. A trickle of the blended light glowed, haltingly, at first, across the central coffee walks, and crept, imperceptibly, over the rest of the village. Very soon afterwards, the second glow began with a mixture of spiky fiery tints of red and yellow. Then slowly, the two rich glowing flushes fused, and birdsong and the indistinct noises of insects rose to meet them.

Caroline Selkirk was walking with Jerry and listening to him talking enthusiastically about P.D. and the villagers, whom he called the only real Islanders, along with all the others in the rural parishes.

'Impressive,' she said, confident of her right to distract him.

'What?' he asked, sensing a hint of challenge in her interruption.

'The light changing and claiming everything.' She opened her arms and hugged the sunlit landscape in a tender, telling mime.

'Yes, it is.' He was in the mood to give in and not feel chided. He was flattered by her spontaneous praise and by her gesture.

Caroline's easy command of the situation matched admirably, symbolically, her slow padded movements over the thin grass track. 'I'll always be grateful to you for this,' she was saying, while still embracing the look of the morning. 'The Island's remarkably beautiful.' She held his hand. 'Why d'you and your friends drink so much?' Even her sudden changing of the topic was not jarring.

'Christmas,' he said casually, dishonestly.

'Doesn't seem like anniversary drinking to me somehow,' she disagreed, squeezing his hand gently, as if, at once, mocking and accepting his explanation.

227

'When we get back, you ask them.' He smiled and admitted his lie.

'I most certainly will.' She laughed quietly.

They walked through the coffee walk on the left of the central groves, and sat down. He placed his head in her lap and stretched out. 'Why did you call for me?' she asked.

'Thought it a good idea.'

'And, had you been sober?'

'I'd've done the same; that is, if we were going somewhere interesting.'

'D'you want to make love to me, Jerry?'

'You're not expecting me to say no?' He hedged.

'Do you?' she insisted. She paused for his reply, then she raised his head, slid her body down and lay beside him. She kissed his lips and his neck and whispered, 'It doesn't matter.'

The others were waiting for breakfast to be served. They had all gathered together along the broad piazza at the front of the shop. Berto and Mabel wandered into the bar, while the rest remained seated on the unopened salt fish barrels and milk boxes. Everybody was drinking mesmerically and being coaxed to have more, from time to time, by P.D.

Sally was inspired to reward him for his splendid hospitality. She tore herself away from Albert, who was hugging her round her waist and uttering a maudlin stream of sweet nothings, and ran to P.D. and kissed his forehead and danced an awkward *shey-shey* round him, until she feigned exhaustion and collapsed in his arms. P.D. swept her up and pretended to throw her back to Albert. He got out of the way and dared P.D. to do so. Sally jumped free and chased Albert and cursed him for his ingratitude.

She said, 'After monopolisin' me company for so long, you refuse to catch me, when I was goin' drop like ripe mango, you dawg, you!'

'Catch you'self, sweet mango,' he teased.

They raced across the front of the shop and screamed improvised oaths at each other and howled with forced laughter. The others showed no interest.

Bashra winked at Marcus and said, 'Them beginnin' to talk an' soun' like we now.'

Marcus winked, and then he wondered what Bashra had meant.

Mirie was busy in the kitchen. She had warned P.D. not to let anyone get in her way. 'Me 'ave a 'eap o' t'ings to do, so don't put foot in 'ere 'til me call you; me wan' give them all a nice C'ris'mus mawnin' breakfus.'

Mason and Van had collided over an enamel mug of coconut water; each had wanted an extra chaser for his drink and had stumbled up to the shop counter to get one. After the shock of the collision had receded and they had found a clear area on the bar over which they could sprawl, Van said, 'You and Jenny still playing the War of the Roses?' He was hiccoughing violently and lisping.

'Have we ever ceased to play anything else, Van, ol' man?' He slapped his back and offered him the enamel mug. 'Drink the damn' thing and forget the rum.'

Van ignored him. 'Jenny needs you,' he said.

'Like an eleventh finger.'

Van bowed. 'Call her over and *pip* the life out of her, lover boy.'

'You're a louse, Van.'

'Lice are good people, firs' class people, Mason.' He staggered away.

Mason searched for Jenny. She was sitting alone at the doorway, her back to the shop and her feet dangling over the piazza. He went over to her and leant on the bulk of the folded door. 'All right?' he asked.

'Fine. You?'

'So so.'

She got up and walked to the end of the piazza. He followed her.

'How's Thanan's these days?' he asked.

'What you really mean is how's Neddy Leazar?'

'Do I?' He risked a smile.

'You never let go. Do you, Mason?'

'Seen Jerry?'

'Track Caroline and you'll find your man,' she sneered. 'By the way, what was the chanting all about?'

'Don't know what you mean.'

'Hell Passage . . . Catte Street . . . Merton . . . ?'

'Oh, that?' He grinned boyishly.

'So?' She was intent on hurting him.

'So what?' Where's the old Oxford magic now? he wondered, drunkenly. And the bitch I couldn't do without and she without me? He looked up, in time, to see her fall limply into Silba's embrace. He watched them dance erratically across the piazza and back into the shop. He moved away after they flopped over the counter, overturning the enamel mug of coconut water.

'Wish me did 'ave a wife like you,' P.D. was saying to Paula, as she wiped and blew a cinder from the corner of his right eye. 'You' got a doctor' touch.'

'Doctors heal,' she said. 'I merely corrupt, P.D.'

'Nice piece o' corruption,' he continued his compliment, 'an' a nice young gal.'

Paula thought about the ease with which she had indicted herself. She knew that she would not have done so a matter of three or four months before that moment. And, of course, P.D.'s use of the word 'young' had startled her; it was charming but it was not true of her; she felt used and old and worth very little to herself or to anyone else.

'Never ask' you before now,' he said, 'but you mus' be really like livin' 'ere with we, so far from you' born 'ome?'

'Quite honestly, P.D., I like it and I loathe it.'

'That mean' you might leave we an' go back to Englan' then?'

'Don't think so.'

'Then wha'?'

'Can't go back,' she said. 'You never return home after a long stay abroad in a country you've fallen in love with. You leave bits and pieces of yourself behind. If I went back, I'd return a shell. I know it.'

'So, you' goin' stay?' He seemed happy.

'I'll stay, yes, and see what comes of it.' She patted his cheek and linked her arm in his.

They walked over to the window which overlooked the front of the shop. They stared at the hard dirt.

'Gawd know' I' goin' pave that t'ing one day an' make it look like a proper downtown grocery front,' he said, pointing to the concrete surface of the rich brown earth.

'You do that, P.D.,' she said and pressed her body firmly against his.

Wyn passed by, fondled her bottom and smacked his lips, and she spun round and clung to him.

P.D. was delighted. He guffawed and said, 'Now me know why you can't go back a' Englan' intac'.' She agreed.

Van had wandered into the bar and had attached himself to Mabel, Berto and Wyn. Paula had slid down to the floor and was leaning against Wyn's legs.

'You lookin' beat, countryman,' Berto told Van, hugging him and bending over Mabel while doing so.

'You can't stop a coolie man from *ups* and inheriting the earth,' Wyn said. 'Columbus's own people, eh, Van?'

'Wrong coolie,' was all that Van said.

'You leave my Van alone,' Mabel said, pushing Berto and Wyn away and kissing Van's cheek.

Paula fell backwards and scrambled to her feet and limped away towards the back of the shop.

'Life,' Van said, closing his eyes.

'Nothing finer,' Berto confided. 'If you can't lick it, lie down and let it rip.'

'Now ain't that the truth?' Van said, over-emphasising his attempted American accent. 'Ain't it a bitch?'

'Never you mind, Van,' Mabel consoled him, 'we're all in it.'

'Some deeper than others,' Wyn said.

'Like me?' Van asked. He began hiccoughing violently again.

The recognition of the crack in their confused lives had come to them at last. They all recognised it in Van. They all knew it in themselves. Some of them were willing to continue as they had been, deluding themselves, contradicting their hopes; the others were frightened and panic-stricken. Both sides were without a palliative; they knew that Black Seal was never intended to be effective; both sides were without a plan for their spiritual reclamation. Jerry and Mason had claimed the Dung'll in desperation but they had not worked out a personal programme in terms of their claim; they had not willed themselves to a balanced and precise attack on their weaknesses and cruel excesses; they secretly feared a concerted voice, a possible remedy; they had no private philosophy, no binding discipline, no real faith in anything. All they had was their freedom, an emancipation that had come much too late. They had not had the time and the kind of society in which to use it intelligently, to benefit from it, to build on it. It had come, all at once, in a frightening lump. It had a tired, colonial shape. There had not been the time to divide it up, to live with it, to transmute it, to put it to work for themselves and their Island's destiny.

Mabel suddenly remembered the first time she had met Van. Burns Hector and Josiah Blake had taken her to a farewell party for a retiring magistrate at Melbourne Club. Van was a temporary clerk then. He was the tyro among the seasoned drinkers, the youngest in the group of officials; he was shy and aware of his very junior position in the Courts. Pompously and with every intention of humiliating him, Josiah had jabbed a rolled copy of the *Scythe* in his chest and asked him loudly if, one day, he, too, hoped to become a resident magistrate, and Van had shrugged modestly and said, 'Me? Don't know if I've got the brains and the staying power. Anyway, it's a long climb, and from where I am at the moment, it's crowded out with a lot of better people than me.' Mabel recalled how much she had been attracted by the honesty of his reply. For the rest of the evening she had kept reminding herself, 'He'll do it and he'll make a good magistrate.' Good God, how he's changed, she thought. And so have I. So've we all, *fantastically*.

When Jerry and Caroline returned, they saw everybody sitting in the back yard on milk boxes which were set around a long improvised table of huge crates. Mirie was serving breakfast. They were hardly noticed as they came up and sat together at the end nearest Mirie's and her daughters' quiet bustling activity.

After breakfast, the party again broke up into small groups, some going back inside to the bar, others sprawling out on the thin grass at the side of the shop. Van, Mabel, Berto and Wyn were lying side by side and talking desultorily about the dying festive season. Albert and Sally were stoning a mango tree which had no mangoes on it, and imagining their positions on the fruitless branches, and hitting them. Jenny, Paula and Silba were at the bar. Jerry, Mason and Caroline were sitting on the running-board of the haulage truck which P.D. had parked at the side of the kitchen. They were sharing a bottle of sorrel. P.D., Bashra and Marcus were walking around and chatting to some of the older villagers and their wives.

At about midday, there was a slight earth tremor. Very few of the party had felt it, because, by then, the village band had arrived and had been playing for some time.

Bashra and Marcus felt the second which had followed a few minutes after the first.

There was another tremor at about four o'clock, but everybody was too drunk to notice.

There was yet another a little after midnight. It was more severe and lasted longer. Jerry and Caroline were standing in front of the shop and talking to P.D. about Van. They did mention the prolonged duration of the tremor, but that was all. Caroline, however, was disturbed.

'Will it get worse?' she asked, looking away towards the central coffee groves, as if to make her question sound casual.

'Cho!' P.D. assured her. 'You always feel a little shakin' in these parts all year roun'. An' like 'ow this December so 'ot, you' boun' to get a few groun' shakes before the mont' out proper. Small matters. Usual 'appenin's.'

He led them inside to the bar.

The Christmas Day party broke up two hours afterwards. The band and the villagers were the first to leave. P.D. counted and packed everybody else into the back of his haulage truck and waved goodbye to Mirie. However, there remained the problem of Mason's station wagon, which Mason was obviously not in a condition to drive. Caroline looked at Mason and then at Jerry and suggested that she should drive it back to Kingston and that Jerry should accompany her and show her the way.

The two vehicles passed slowly down the narrow lane and out on to the main road. P.D.'s truck had a head start of about four hundred yards. Caroline decided that she would keep the distance constant all the way.

Chapter Twenty-eight

The morning after Boxing Day, the *Scythe* carried the following front-page report:

THIRTEEN KILLED IN DALLAS HILLS

On Boxing Day, at about halfpast two in the morning, thirteen people, returning in an open haulage truck from a Christmas Day party in Dallas Hills, were instantly killed in the most catastrophic landslip[1] in the Island's history.

The weight of fall of cliffside has been estimated at more than ten thousand tons of loose soil and stone, dislodged from an approximate height of one hundred and fifty feet.

Those killed were:

Mabel Thompson	Percy Dixon
Sally Dawes	Wyn Stone
Paula Watt	Albert Ley
Jenny Donne-Jones	Silba Lane
Mason Donne-Jones	Van Farson
Berto Sabyo	and two Dung'll
	Rastafarians.

1. The seismograph at Winchester Park, Kingston, recorded four earth tremors between midday Christmas Day and midnight.

Jerry Stover, the younger son of Mrs Lou Stover J.P. of Constant Spring Road, and Miss Caroline Selkirk, a visiting American magazine editor, who were travelling together in a station wagon at a distance of about a quarter of a mile behind the truck, were the only witnesses to the disaster. Miss Selkirk who is suffering from severe shock, has since been admitted to the University College Hospital.

Chapter Twenty-nine

During the very brief moments when Caroline was awake and waiting to be soothed back to sleep by the heavy sedative which she had been given by a watchful and concerned staff nurse, she recollected the final minutes leading up to the terrible disaster. Each time the nurse would sponge her face with a warm flannel and whisper, 'It's all over. Try to forget it now.'

But Caroline would emerge from the sedative yet again and struggle to sit up, her eyes staring wildly and her face pimpled with festoons of perspiration, and cry out, 'My God, look!' And the nurse would bathe her arms and neck and dab her forehead and cheeks and say quietly, 'It couldn't be helped. You must sleep.'

Yet, even in the warmth and protective glow of her sedated sleep, Caroline saw blurred images from the tragic event. It was then that she would toss and turn and throw off the bedclothes and wake up crying. On the fourth occasion, the nurse held her hand and said, 'Would it help, if you told me about it?'

Caroline nodded.

'Go ahead then,' the nurse said, 'and as soon as you feel the first lull coming on, stop talking and relax and try to give in, 'til next time. I'll be here.'

Caroline moistened her parched lips and began very slowly, hesitating and holding on to certain words and phrases and repeating them without seeming relevance, 'I was driving. We were well behind the truck. I thought it wise to stay well behind it. I didn't know the way back. I was following the truck, well behind, on the main road. The truck suddenly left the road and turned into a sort of country track, wide enough, but very uneven. Jerry called it a short cut, a siding, or something. I didn't worry about this. They were all drunk. The driver was drunk. Jerry said that he could take it. P.D. could take it. He was all right. I wasn't worried. I just kept on going, following well behind. I saw some hills in the distance. They were haunting and beautiful. There was a faint glow coming up behind them. It was far too early for the dawn light, but it looked that way. Jerry said that it wasn't the dawn. It was just a wash of light that would disappear soon. The Island is very beautiful. I think it is. It was lovely driving at that hour. We passed dark shapes and twists and turns and trees and sudden curves. We bumped along, not really knowing where we were going. I didn't. I think Jerry did. I suppose it was about two-fifteen in the morning. It was my second time out so early in the morning. The first time was on Christmas morning when Jerry called to take me to Dallas to the party at P.D.'s place. I had no idea of what was going to happen. None at all. I didn't. I didn't . . .' She closed her eyes and drifted off.

The nurse left her, arranged the screen round her bed so that it blocked the full glare of the brilliant morning sunlight, and went back to her desk in the open ward.

Caroline slept for the greater part of the morning and awoke just before lunch time. She was sweating. She did not cry out this time, and the nurse casually remarked on the change in her mood and behaviour. She asked her, 'Do you want to continue? Or would you rather not?'

Caroline's lips were scored with tiny, dry marks and hints of cracks. She moistened them, pondered for a short while, tried to sit up but slid down again. She said, 'Well, there we were, going along. They were singing and laughing, and the truck was swaying and swerving. P.D. must've been singing, too, and beating on the steering wheel. He was in the enclosed cabin but we could see the others at the back in the open. I wasn't worried. Jerry said that P.D. was all right. Their voices came belting back towards us. *Mento* songs, Jerry called them, I believe. The truck was all over the place. We were going through a very dark patch somewhere. I was well behind. I couldn't lose them. In any case, Jerry knew the way. A hill loomed up before us. We had reached a corner, a deep one. I turned into it. Then I heard a strange sound, like a low-pitched roar, and yet it wasn't like that at all, but it was strange, very strange. I had never heard that sound before in my life. I saw the truck ahead. It was passing very close to the side of the hill I'd seen. They were still singing. I heard the sinister sound again. It was a little louder and it actually did sound like a roar. It was coming from somewhere inside the hill or so it seemed to me. Jerry was dozing. I woke him up. He heard the sound and sat up and looked in the direction of the truck. 'It's coming from the hill,' he said. 'It isn't the truck.' The truck was immediately under the overhang of the hill. From where we were, it looked like a very high, broad shelf; the overhang, I mean. I remember saying so to Jerry. Then we heard a loose, grinding sound and I shouted, "My God, look!" The tremendous avalanche of earth was so fast that I thought I saw it, but then, I might not have. The impact sounded like a muted explosion, like a jolting thud. I looked for the truck but I didn't see it. It had disappeared. There wasn't a trace of it anywhere. It was completely buried. I felt sick. My stomach heaved. It was horrible. Horrible. Then suddenly there wasn't a sound. The whole place was a vast curtain of dust. Jerry and I got out of the wagon and ran to the spot. We could hardly see where we were going. We didn't know what to do. What could we do with our bare hands? In fact, the hill had shifted its position and emptied itself into the roadway. It was still a hill. We couldn't shift it with our bare hands. We couldn't. Jerry tried in vain. He was crying. So was I. We clawed at the earth. We didn't know where to start. It was a hill. It was there before us. We just clawed and clawed. It was too large a mass. It was too high. It was a complete hill. I tell you it was a complete hill. It had merely shifted its position. That was all. It was horrible. I was sick. I must have passed out. The next thing I knew I was here in hospital. Oh, my God, it was horrible.'

Epilogue

It was New Year's Eve. Immediately after breakfast, Jerry walked into his mother's room and sat on the edge of her bed. She was arranging a cluster of scarlet zinnias in the porcelain vase which Les had bought her with the fee from his first public lecture in America. Her hands were shaking and the rayed blooms of the zinnias were swaying and trembling as she tried to suppress her anxiety. She even went so far as to wonder whether Jerry would be offended by the colour of the zinnias or whether he might feel sensitive about her using Les's vase. Jerry noticed her effort and felt sympathetic to her deep concern. He felt a renewed respect and affection for her. She lifted the vase and carried it across the room and placed it securely on her writing-desk. She turned back.

'I don't suppose you want to talk about it?' she said.

'I'd rather not, Mother.'

She had stood outside his bedroom on the morning she had read the newspaper report, but his loud sobbing had made her turn away. This was the first time that she had mentioned anything about the disaster.

Thelma came into the room and looked around. She avoided Jerry's face and his mother's and went over to the vase and touched it. She stood back and looked at the arrangement of the zinnias and nodded her approval. She was about to leave the room, when Mrs Stover said, 'Don't go, please.'

Thelma then looked at Jerry and waited. He called her name and smiled faintly. She walked over to him and touched his arm.

His mother asked, 'Would you like to go away somewhere?'

'What for?'

'That's for you to choose, Jerry.'

Thelma looked at her and nodded, and then she patted his shoulder. He got up and went to the writing-desk. He stared down at the zinnias and admired the profusion of scarlet. He heard his mother's voice saying, ' . . . need is a break from it all.'

'I suppose I'll think of something to do,' he said. 'I'll come and talk to you about it.'

It seemed to him that there was nothing else to add, nothing else to find out. He left the room.

He had been sitting on the front veranda for some time when he suddenly felt in his pocket for Carmen's last letter which he had read twice before. As he held it, it seemed to him to be the most convincing evidence of another area in his life where failure had scored deeply. In a curiously perverse way, failure had come to mean so much in his reckoning, in his moments of self-criticism, that he was no longer afraid to encounter it or examine it closely. He knew that it meant the dilemma of unpreparedness; it was the shortsightedness of his parents' generation; it was the ignorance, waywardness and impatience of his own; it was the colonial situation; it was his arrogance, deceit and indiscipline; it was in himself, and himself totally. It had become his way of life, because he had allowed it, wished it to be so, and had lost himself in it conveniently.

His hands shook slightly as he opened the folds of the letter.

December 23rd

Dear Jerry

I can only think that you're no longer interested. I've had a long time to think things over. We're wasting each other's time.

I can't go on hoping anymore. It hurts too much. You needn't reply.

Carmen

He thought of Miriam and the suffering he had caused her. He imagined her humiliation. He recalled her planned disappearance, his part in it, and his cowardly relief. Then he reflected on her hallucinatory reappearances.

After supper, he left home and wandered down Constant Spring Road. When he got to the square at Half Way Tree, he sat hunched on the parapet facing the clock tower. His conscience began to trouble him, when he remembered that he had not attended the mass funeral. He kept on reminding himself of the fact; he even dared himself to be objectively self-critical. He tried but he failed; he argued that no one would have wanted to go, had he been in his place; the Termites and the others were not an inert mass when he knew them; they were separate, alone and real. They were a group in which each one was without the other; each was searching for a different result, a unique explanation, his own independence.

He thought of going to Randy's house; he wanted to find out what his advice would be, but he denied himself the escape. He thought of Prudence, and again he refused to give in easily. He knew he could always go back to his mother.

He walked a little way up Hope Road and back again to the clock tower. Caroline was still in the hospital. He began to think about the answer that he would give her about the magazine, and of the future course of their friendship.

It was shortly after nine o'clock when he got to the Dung'll. The first person he saw was Marcus's woman. She was sitting in the area and staring at the Manhole. He went up and touched her shoulder.

'We' been usin' up the food,' she said. 'You don' min'?' Her question seemed her only way to avoid talking about Marcus and Bashra, and he accepted it. 'All o' we usin' it up, 'cause we feel that that is the right an' fittin' t'ing to do now that C'ris'mus come an' gone.'

Again, he accepted her unnecessary explanation, and nodded. Her face was haggard and she had been crying; the tear-stains were apparent along her cheeks, at the corners of her mouth and around the curve of her chin.

'Don' suppose you' stayin' roun' 'ere any longer, Jerry?' she asked.

He shrugged doubtfully.

'Like say 'ow t'ings turn out for all o' we,' she went on, 'we feelin' that you wouldn't want to bother with the teachin' an' such like.'

He had to reply. He said, 'I don't know what to do, really. Everything's so confused and uncertain.' He didn't want to uspet her. He knew that he would never go on with his work on the Dung'll, but it was kinder not to say so.

'Me an' some o' the others decide to go back to country to live with we people up there, bes' t'ing.'

'Why?' He was sensitive to the irrelevance of his question but he had to ask it; he suspected that she wanted him to.

'Too much mix-up, Jerry, an' police an' t'ings like that. Too much gun an' killin' goin' go on, wha' with all the Blood an' T'under business an' Missa Septimus Johns.'

'Will there be many people left on the Dung'll after you've gone?'

'Plenty, man, an' more comin' in.'

He wondered what would happen to his idea of rehabilitation. Would someone with more experience take over and work at it? Would there be anyone to confront Kirby and Rybik? Who, among the Brethren, would have the political awareness, persuasiveness and courage to go against the accepted Rastafarian principle of repatriation and plan for the re-entry and rehabilitation of the thousands of members into the Island society?

He ended his self-questioning abruptly when he noticed that Marcus's woman had turned away from him. He understood what she had done. He went into Bashra's hut. Nothing had been touched, except for the Christmas stock of drink and the food parcels which had been moved to Marcus's hut. The shrine was covered in dust and the cots were unmade. There were many pieces of clothing, Bashra's and Mason's and his own, lying around. He glanced at his extra khaki shirt, a tie which he had used as a belt, a pair of white canvas shoes, his teaching notes and a pile of letters. He picked up the notes and the letters and left.

The area seemed, to him, more spacious than usual, forbidding and alien. Its strangeness was a very real presence, an impact, a reminder of the threat of failure to all who persisted in living near to it, and to those who might possibly conceive a plan for its improvement. It was unswept and cluttered haphazardly with the customary seasonal detritus. He stood in front of the Manhole and threw the notes and letters into a small opening at the side. There was no point in destroying them before he disposed of them; no one ever searched the Manhole. A spasm of nausea rose in his throat and left an acid taste in his mouth. Marcus's woman had gone back to her hut. He turned away quickly, spat and waved to three women who were leaning on a disused refrigerator which had been dumped recently in the area. The broad, white enamelled door and the storage compartment were cracked and gashed and partly dismantled, and the plastic-coated shelves were peeling and lay twisted in the side grooves.

He had been walking aimlessly about the streets of Lower Kingston for nearly three hours and had stopped outside the Niagara. He looked in at the side entrance. Lola and Vie were serving a long line of sailors at the bar. The wall clock was saying ten minutes to twelve. He turned and went along Temple Lane, passed over Harbour Street, and down to Victoria Pier. The warm sea air blew into his face, as he tilted his head backwards, welcoming the tang of raw salt, old harbour wood and cargo smells, and ceasing to care about the continuing stream of his tears. He could hear the singing and wild cheering, coming from a distance behind the Pier, of a marching group of the Blood and Thunder Brethren, as they crossed over King Street. Some were calling the name, Septimus Johns, and others were declaring, 'New Year comin'. Africa, for we; Islan', no!'

Danny Boy

James Bradner

Danny and Lily are childhood sweethearts, growing up together in Guyana. No matter that Danny is black, while Lily is Indian and their friendship frowned upon by her father. They know they are right for each other, and their love is tender and true.

But envious eyes are watching and waiting in the shadows . . . and this is one love story that does not have a happy ending.

Drumbeat 36
ISBN 0 582 78536 7

The Dragon Can't Dance

Earl Lovelace

All the year round Aldrick lives in the Calvary Hill slums of Port of Spain, waiting for the two days of Carnival, when he will parade and dance in pride and triumph in his resplendent Dragon costume. But this year is different. How can he prevent seventeen-year-old Sylvia from selling herself to rich, middle-aged Mr Guy for the sake of a Carnival costume?

Aldrick and Sylvia are just two of the colourful characters in this brilliant novel by the author of *While Gods Are Falling*.

'This novel is a landmark, not in the West Indian, but in the contemporary novel. . . . Nowhere have I seen more of the realities of a whole country disciplined into one imaginative volume.'

C. L. R. James in *Race Today Review*

'A tough, sharply written book which rewards careful reading.' *Trinidad Express*

Drumbeat 26
ISBN 0 582 64231 0